‖‖‖ ‖‖‖‖‖‖‖‖ ‖‖‖‖‖‖‖‖ ‖‖‖‖‖‖‖‖‖ ‖‖‖

✂ **W9-APU-790**

"I'VE CHANGED MY MIND."

"It's too late," Graystone claimed.

She gave a ladylike sniff. "I do not wish to have you kiss me, after all, sir."

He returned her gaze unflinchingly. "You have made a request of me, madam, and I fully intend to comply."

"Why?"

Was that the merest hint of a bemused smile on Graystone's features? "Because I want to."

She breathed in and out. "I don't understand."

"Cecile . . ." Her name came on a soft whisper.

Something inside her crumbled. "James . . ."

He took two steps forward—they weren't even big steps—and ended up standing directly in front of her. His eyes, those elusive yet somehow familiar gray eyes, pinned her to the spot where she sat. "Don't you know that I've wanted to kiss you since we first danced at your ball?"

Cecile was fairly certain she said no out loud, but she wasn't altogether sure.

James leaned toward her—the pounding of her heart was thunderous in Cecile's ears—and touched his mouth to hers.

"Suzanne Simmons makes this wicked, glittering era her own."
—Amanda Quick

You and No Other

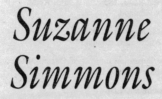

Suzanne Simmons

A TOPAZ BOOK

TOPAZ
Published by the Penguin Group
Penguin Putnam Inc., 375 Hudson Street,
New York, New York 10014, U.S.A.
Penguin Books Ltd, 27 Wrights Lane,
London W8 5TZ, England
Penguin Books Australia Ltd, Ringwood,
Victoria, Australia
Penguin Books Canada Ltd, 10 Alcorn Avenue,
Toronto, Ontario, Canada M4V 3B2
Penguin Books (N.Z.) Ltd, 182–190 Wairau Road,
Auckland 10, New Zealand

Penguin Books Ltd, Registered Offices:
Harmondsworth, Middlesex, England

First published by Topaz, an imprint of Dutton NAL,
a member of Penguin Putnam Inc.

First Printing, September, 1998
10 9 8 7 6 5 4 3 2 1

Copyright © Suzanne Simmons Guntrum, 1998
All rights reserved

  REGISTERED TRADEMARK—MARCA REGISTRADA

Printed in the United States of America

Without limiting the rights under copyright reserved above, no part of
this publication may be reproduced, stored in or introduced into a
retrieval system, or transmitted, in any form, or by any means (electronic,
mechanical, photocopying, recording, or otherwise), without the prior written
permission of both the copyright owner and the above publisher of this
book.

BOOKS ARE AVAILABLE AT QUANTITY DISCOUNTS WHEN USED TO PROMOTE
PRODUCTS OR SERVICES. FOR INFORMATION PLEASE WRITE TO PREMIUM
MARKETING DIVISION, PENGUIN PUTNAM INC., 375 HUDSON STREET, NEW
YORK, NEW YORK 10014.

If you purchased this book without a cover you should be aware that this
book is stolen property. It was reported as "unsold and destroyed"
to the publisher and neither the author nor the publisher has received
any payment for this "stripped book."

This one is for Maureen Walters:
talented woman, supportive agent, dear friend.

"Like glimpses of forgotten dreams."
—Alfred, Lord Tennyson,
The Two Voices

Prologue

*S*he was naked.

He was naked, too, for that matter.

They were in a small, ill-lit room, on a small, ill-fitted bed—was the bed swaying or was it his head again?—a single coverlet entangled around their bodies.

Her skin was pale; not the colorless kind of pale, not pallid or ashen, but as light and creamy as the milk from a goat back home.

Wherever home was . . .

She was like a piece of beautifully carved ivory, as smooth as silk and without a flaw. Her arms were long and slender. Her hands were elegant and cool, so cool, on his overheated flesh. She touched him: first his brow, then his jaw, his shoulder, his chest, and farther down his body to his thigh. He never wanted her to stop touching him. He wanted this moment to last forever.

He reached out and caressed her. She was as soft and sleek and silky as she appeared.

He kissed her. Her mouth was cool at first, bringing relief, like eating an ice on a warm summer's day. Then it heated up and became a flame that set him on fire. He was burning up, consumed by his own needs, his own desires, his need and desire for her.

She gave a little gasp and a mew of arousal. He heard his own answering groan.

He slipped a hand between her long, lovely legs, intent upon making a place for himself. He leaned over her, touching his lips to her mouth, the tip of a perfect breast, a soft, white belly.

This was all new to her, he could tell. He was a gentleman. He must make it right . . . and he would as soon as he had finished kissing her, caressing her.

Somewhere a door banged loudly.

A woman screamed.

A man let out a shout.

The sounds were coming from behind him.

He didn't wish to be disturbed. He glanced over his shoulder just as several pairs of rough hands clamped onto him.

They were torn apart.

He was yanked off the bed, separated from her, forced to stand there naked, aroused, exposed for all to see, restrained by God knew how many strong, brutal, vicious hands, his arms twisted behind his back, as she was quickly wrapped in the sheet and covered by a pair of protective, coddling, feminine arms.

Angry voices.

Angrier voices.

Someone raised a cane or a walking stick or a slab of board—and a good-sized one at that—and brought it down across his shoulders, driving him to his knees.

This time she let out a scream and reached for him.

Her concern was for him.

He saw her eyes, her beautiful eyes, brimming with tears as he was forced to stand and pull on his pants.

He was dragged down a narrow corridor.

He heard the man with the sonorous voice talking.

She was propped up beside him. He could feel her trembling, and he knew she was afraid. He wanted to comfort her, to tell her it was all going to work out in the end.

He was not permitted to speak.

Then he was poked in the back with what must surely be the tip of a sword and told to answer.

He answered.

She gave him something.

Then they were separated again. She was taken away by her friends—they didn't seem like friends to him—and he was hauled off to another place. But not before he called out to her: "I promise . . . I will find you."

A door creaked open and he was shoved inside.

Darkness.

Then there was only darkness.

Chapter One

London, 1879

*H*e *was losing his mind.*

James Gray, thirteenth Earl of Graystone, shot straight up in bed. He was naked and covered with sweat. The damp bedsheets were twisted tightly around his legs.

He couldn't breathe. He gulped for air, trying to fill oxygen-starved lungs. His heart was pounding furiously. His head was throbbing. He reached up and massaged behind his right ear. He could feel the familiar lump on his skull.

He took in a deep breath, then slowly released it. He inhaled and exhaled, again and again, until his breathing and heart rate gradually returned to normal.

James blinked several times in rapid succession and peered into the shadows beyond the dim, yellow glow cast by the bedside lamp. An all-too-familiar feeling of panic began to rise to the surface from somewhere deep within him.

Where was he?

This wasn't his bed. It wasn't his bedchamber or

his furniture. It wasn't even his house; he was quite certain of that. This place was definitely not Graystone Abbey, which meant, of course, that he was no longer in Devon.

"So where in the devil am I?" he asked in a sleep-rusty voice.

The answer came to him in a rush. He was in London. He was an honored guest, the honored guest, the only guest, at Cork House, the magnificent Mayfair mansion belonging to Miles St. Aldford, Marquess of Cork and husband to his niece, Alyssa, who had, some months before, become Lady Cork.

Yes, he remembered now. He was staying in one of London's great houses: A house situated in the most fashionable part of town, a house of imposing proportions and notable architectural design, a house filled with works of classical art and splendid furnishings.

In fact, he was sleeping in an ornately carved Byzantine-style bed that had once belonged to the Emperor Charlemagne. This particular piece of furniture had been purchased by Miles and Alyssa while they were on their wedding trip to Venice last autumn. James swore he could detect the scent of balsam and musk and exotic spices from a long ago time and place embedded in the silk and ivory bedframe.

He leaned back against the intricately carved headboard and closed his eyes for a moment.

He'd been dreaming again.

Was it a dream or a nightmare? A *cauchemar* as the French called it, an *incubo* to the Italians, *pesadelo* according to the Portuguese. James knew he spoke some French, a smattering of Italian, and absolutely no Portuguese.

Why did words in languages he *didn't* speak keep popping into his head?

It was another of the unanswered questions he had about himself, about his own past.

Working his legs free, James Gray threw back the covers, stood up and made his way across the elegantly appointed yet masculine bedroom to stand at the row of windows that overlooked the garden at the rear of Cork House.

It was several hours before dawn, and the night was drawn in charcoals. He could barely make out the imposing stone wall surrounding the garden, let alone the garden itself. But he knew from glimpses he had caught yesterday upon his arrival in London that the trees and shrubs were already greening and the first early roses would soon bloom. There was nothing to equal an English rose garden in springtime.

" 'Oh, to be in England now that April's there.' " He murmured aloud the words of the poet Robert Browning.

It had been fifteen years since James Gray had seen spring come to his native country. But he would be in England for April this year. It was a promise he'd made to himself.

When had he made that promise?

He didn't know.

James heaved a sigh of frustration and drove his fingers through the tangle of damp curls at his nape.

Browning had also written, "You will wake, and remember, and understand."

Well, he had awakened, but he didn't remember and he sure as hell didn't understand. Why did he always see the same face in his dreams? Was she real? Or was she a figment of his imagination?

The beautiful, naked woman wasn't the only image that haunted him. Night after night he relived the terror of being trapped in darkness, a darkness so thick, so black, so complete that he couldn't see his own hand before his face.

Night after night he experienced anew the horror of awakening and not knowing, at least for a few heart-stopping moments, exactly who he was, where he was, what he was about. Hence, a lamp was always left burning beside his bed.

"Christ, Graystone, put the bloody past in the past where it belongs before you drive yourself insane," James swore at himself, and then followed his outburst with a sharp, sardonic laugh.

Of course he knew who he was and where he was and what his life was about.

Didn't he?

Since late last summer when he had recovered his memory—well, most of his memory, there was still a gap of nearly a year that he couldn't recall beyond bits and pieces—he had spoken several times with the local doctor back in Devon.

"Time, Lord Graystone, it will take time," Aristotle Symthe had advised him upon the occasion of their last conversation concerning his amnesia.

James had confided to no one, not even to the good doctor, the circumstances of his nightmares and insomnia.

"How much time?"

The kindly physician had patted his arm and observed, "You are young and impatient."

James had been impatient, but he hadn't felt young. He had felt old. "How much time?" he had demanded to know.

The gentleman had shrugged his slightly stooped shoulders and had offered philosophically, "Who is to say?"

Who, indeed?

The whole business had proved to be damned awkward, especially at local social functions, which James had begun to avoid like the plague. He had been in no mood to explain to every curiosity-seeker who had inquired after his health: *I'm very well, thank you. Except, of course, I suffer from a rare form of amnesia. I think I was coshed on the head on my way back from India nearly two years ago. By the by, would you care to see the corroborating, telltale lump on my skull? Or perhaps the rather nasty scar on my shoulder?*

Anyway, it's true that I was making the journey home to England, to assume the titles and position left vacant by my elder brother's unexpected and premature death from fever, when our ship, having recently set sail from Bombay, became embroiled in a terrifying and violent storm at sea. I don't know what happened after that. I believe I was washed overboard. I can't seem to remember.

But he remembered in his dreams.

Was the young woman real? Or was she someone conjured up by his mind to preserve his sanity all those long months he had spent . . . where? Where had he spent those long months?

James's fist closed around the thin leather cord he always wore about his neck.

He had been a sorry sight when he had suddenly appeared in the West Country last June. Bone-thin and utterly destitute, he'd had no food but what he could beg from strangers or forage from the land, and no clothing beyond the few tattered rags he wore on his back. He had possessed no other belongings. He had commanded no other resources. No money. Not even a name. In fact, for several months he had referred to himself as simply The Hermit.

Nevertheless, driven by some instinct, some memory buried in his subconscious he had managed to find his way back to Graystone Abbey, back to his boyhood home.

Home.

In the past year the word had taken on a new and profound meaning for James Gray. For his first spring in England since the age of nineteen, he would have preferred to remain at his home in the country. But duty had beckoned.

Or rather, Queen Victoria had beckoned.

The letter of correspondence had been written by a lady-in-waiting, of course. It had arrived at Graystone Abbey by special courier. The message was appropriately regal, relatively succinct and crystal clear:

It would please Her Majesty the Queen to have Lord Graystone in attendance for a ball, and at any subsequent social events, welcoming Her Serene Highness, Princess Cecile of Saint-Simeon, cousin to Her Majesty and to His Royal Highness, Albert Edward, Prince of Wales, to London for the upcoming Season.

He could read between the lines as well as the next peer of the Realm. It would greatly *displease* his sovereign if he were to choose not to accept her invitation. It would also be unwise and extremely foolhardy on his part.

James Gray considered himself many things, but he was no fool. To that end, he had arrived from Devon yesterday and had taken up residence at Cork House.

James stood there, for God knew how long, staring into the black London night. Then he turned his head. The clock on the mantel told him it was three o'clock.

The rest of the world was still asleep—even the housemaids wouldn't be up and about for another hour or two, quietly shuffling through the deserted corridors, dusting the bric-a-brac, laying the fires in the morning rooms—but James was wide awake. He knew from experience that there would be no more sleep for him tonight.

He threw open a window, took a deep breath, and filled his lungs. The air was a peculiar mixture of city smells, garden scents, and the dankness of a foggy night. Restless, he began to pace back and forth between the bedroom window and the hearth.

At least in the country there had always been a way to keep the demons at bay. He would arise from his bed, pull on a pair of breeches and a shirt, his boots, and sometimes a jacket, and he would head for the stables.

The first piece of business that James Gray had conducted as Earl of Graystone—well, the very first had been to hire a butler for Graystone Abbey since the country house had lacked a proper butler for several years before his disappearance—but his second piece of official business had been to purchase a horse for himself.

He had finally found the right one. In honor of the nearly fifteen years he had spent in India, he had named the magnificent black stallion Amritsar, after the holy city of the Sikhs.

Then, on restless, sleepless nights, James Gray would ride the land that had been in the Graystone family since before the time of the Crusades, the ancient land that was now *his* land, the wind whipping through his hair and Amritsar's long, flowing black mane; man and horse becoming one as the country air cleared the cobwebs from his brain and lifted the darkness from his soul

It was not to be on this night.

Amritsar was happily ensconced in his stall back home, under the watchful eye of Ian McKennitt, the best of Graystone Abbey's stable lads, and James was stuck in the city, cooped up inside Cork House.

If only the queen had not commanded his presence

in London. If only he'd been left to his own devices and desires. If only he hadn't developed an uneasiness at being confined indoors. Nay, it was far more than unease; it was dread, perhaps even fear, and it had to do with his nightmare of being locked away in a place with no light. If only he could recover the memory of those months missing from his life. If only he could find some measure of peace.

"Hell and damnation!" James swore as he brought his fist down with a resounding thud on the edge of a nearby table.

A few moments later there was a discreet knock on the door of his bedchamber.

"Enter," he barked.

His valet, Goodenough, appeared in the doorway. "You rang, my lord?"

James scowled. "No. I did not ring."

The young man reconsidered his choice of words. "You knocked, my lord?"

He gave a grunt. "I didn't knock."

Goodenough was a pleasant-looking fellow even when he was frowning. "You . . . thumped, my lord?"

James conceded that he may have thumped, but it hadn't been his intention to summon his valet. The fact that he had come meant a misunderstanding existed between the two of them as to Goodenough's duties. It wasn't entirely unexpected, he supposed. Goodenough had entered his service only the previous month.

James cleared his throat. "At some time in the near future, Goodenough, we—that is, you and I—will need to discuss the circumstances under which I am actually summoning you and those under which I am not."

Goodenough snapped to attention. "There is no time like the present, my lord."

"Trust me, this isn't the time," James informed him.

"Your wish is my command, my lord."

Naturally, that was reassuring to know.

James noticed that his valet was dressed, as he always seemed to be, in a neat black suit, a pristine white shirt and collar, and a pair of black shoes polished to a mirror sheen. In addition, every hair on the man's head appeared to be in place. No small accomplishment on such short notice *and* at three o'clock in the morning.

Curiosity drove James to inquire, "How do you do it, Goodenough?"

"Do what, my lord?"

He made an all-encompassing gesture with his hand. "How do you manage to keep your appearance so—?"

"Immaculate?" The younger man was good enough to supply the missing word.

"Yes."

"I have made a particular study of the subject, my lord."

James rubbed his hand back and forth along his jawline. "Exactly which subject would that be?"

An explanation was immediately forthcoming. "I have studied the most efficient method of organizing my apparel so that I may dress in the shortest amount of time possible and yet still achieve perfect results."

Good Lord, the man was serious.

James held back the beginnings of a bemused smile. "I take it you're a student of the subject of efficiency, then."

There was no false modesty apparent when the other man stated, "I consider myself a student of numerous subjects."

James prompted him to continue. "Numerous subjects?"

"Beginning with human nature, itself, my lord."

That one seemed to cover a fairly large amount of ground. "And the others?"

"Since you have inquired, my lord, firearms."

"Pistols and the like?"

Goodenough nodded. "Precisely."

His newly hired manservant might prove to be a handy fellow to have around. "Anything else?"

"Tobacco."

"I didn't know you smoked, Goodenough."

"I don't smoke tobacco, my lord. I analyze it."

"Why?"

"Tobacco and its telltale residue are often found at the scene of criminal goings-on."

James was intrigued. "Do you frequently find yourself at the scene of criminal goings-on?"

"No, my lord."

"So it's strictly academic curiosity on your part."

"Exactly, my lord."

"What else do you study?"

"Poisons."

"With the same curiosity that compels you to analyze tobacco, I assume," James said.

The man nodded his head. "I consider myself something of a sleuthhound, my lord."

"Sleuthhound?"

"Detective. Armchair variety only, of course."

"Don't tell me you're one of those who rush out every week to buy the latest installment of the 'penny dreadfuls.' "

Goodenough sniffed. "Most assuredly not, my lord. Although I confess that I've read the stories of the American writer Edgar Allan Poe and our own Mister Wilkie Collins, of which my personal favorite is *The Woman in White*."

James felt a strange shiver ripple over the surface of his skin.

"Are you chilled, my lord?"

James Gray was suddenly aware that he was still standing in the middle of the bedchamber without a stitch of clothing on. He reached for his robe and, instantly, Goodenough was there to assist him.

"Not so much chilled as tired," he admitted. "I awoke some time ago and have been unable to fall asleep again."

"I've made a study of insomnia, as well, my lord."

"Have you, indeed?" Evidently there was very little Goodenough had *not* made a study of.

"I find myself fascinated by the conclusions of Wilhelm Wundt, who recently established a psychological laboratory in Germany devoted to sleep problems."

"What are Wundt's conclusions?"

Goodenough didn't mince words. "The principal cause of insomnia is either a physical or a mental problem."

James knew that.

"Wundt and his colleagues are also collecting scientific information about dreams, which they believe may contribute to certain disturbances in human sleep patterns."

James was suddenly feeling distinctly uncomfortable. He changed the subject without any further ado by announcing: "I have decided to go for a walk in the garden, Goodenough."

"Now, my lord?"

"Now."

"Would you like me to accompany you, my lord?"

"No."

"I will lay out the appropriate clothing for you."

James shook his head. "That won't be necessary. I'll see to it myself. Please return to your room and the comfort of your bed. I won't be requiring your services until morning."

"As you wish, my lord." Goodenough paused in the doorway. "I'll just fetch you the key."

"The key?"

"The garden is private, my lord, and kept locked at all times. Only the masters of Cork House and Guest House just beyond—" Goodenough indicated the stately mansion opposite, its roof visible from the window "—have a key to the gates."

"Then, by all means, fetch me the key."

James tossed his robe aside and quickly pulled on a pair of soft, well-worn breeches, a loose shirt, and a pair of his favorite riding boots. He might as well be comfortable. After all, there would be no one to see him.

He made his way downstairs some minutes later, slipped out of the rear entrance of Cork House, and followed the flagstone path that led to his destination. He thrust the key into the lock and turned it.

The wrought-iron gate swung open and James Gray entered the secluded garden.

Chapter Two

She felt as if she were suffocating.

It was the dream. It had come again tonight, unbidden, unwanted, undesired, bringing with it need and want and desire and a kind of suffocating fear that left her gasping for air.

She couldn't seem to catch her breath. She was trembling from head to toe. Her heart was pounding so violently in her breast that she thought it would surely burst. Dear God, she felt like a wild creature caught in a snare and fighting with its last breath to free itself.

Cecile sat straight up in the huge canopied bed and stared wide-eyed into the darkness.

Light.

There was no light anywhere.

She groped for one of the silver candlesticks that she knew was somewhere on the table beside the bed. Her hands were ice cold: She couldn't seem to stop them from shaking. She lost count of the number of times she tried and failed before she managed to locate a candle, strike a match, and light a taper.

At last a single small amber flame flickered in the otherwise pitch black bedchamber.

Cecile attempted to swallow and found that her throat was as dry and parched as the desert. She reached for the crystal carafe, poured herself a glass of water—regrettably she spilled half of it onto the exquisite Belgian lace doily—and raised the goblet to her lips. She drank thirstily. Then she took in a deep breath and slowly released it.

It was time to stop deceiving herself. The dream—was it a dream or a nightmare—was occurring more frequently. In fact, she'd had the identical dream every night since her arrival in London and that was nearly a week ago.

Why was she dreaming the same frightening sequence of events over and over again?

The reason seemed obvious: Just knowing how near *he* was to her here in this country, in this city, struck terror into her heart.

Tears pooled in Cecile's eyes.

Perhaps she should not have come. Perhaps the elaborate scheme she had devised in order to persuade Cousin Victoria to invite her for the season had been a mistake.

It was too late to change her mind. Besides, she'd had no choice in the matter, Cecile reminded herself. She'd had to come. For it was here in England, specifically here in London, that she would find the answers to all of her questions.

" 'Screw your courage to the sticking-place, and you'll not fail,' " Cecile whispered into the darkness.

She must not fail.

Upon her soul, she could not fail.

There was too much at stake if she should fail: her

beloved country of Saint-Simeon, the freedom of its citizens, the blessed memory of her parents, her brother Alexandre's ascension to his rightful place on the throne, even her own future.

If she did not succeed in her appointed task, she would truly be the last princess of Saint-Simeon, that ancient and breathtakingly beautiful principality nestled between the *bellesoleil* region of southern France and the Mediterranean Sea.

"Don't be a silly goose," Cecile admonished herself as she plumped the pillows at her back, "of course you'll succeed."

Wide awake, she reached for one of the books she always kept beside her bed. The small leatherbound volume of poetry fell open and, in the glow of the candlelight, she could make out the printed words on the page. They were the strangely prophetic words of the American poet Henry Wadsworth Longfellow.

She read them to herself:

Ships that pass in the night, and speak each other
in passing,
Only a signal shown and a distant voice in the darkness;
So on the ocean of life we pass and speak one another,
Only a look and a voice, then darkness again and a silence.

Cecile suddenly found herself unsettled. She snapped the book of poetry shut, thrust the bedcovers to one side, padded barefoot across the bedchamber to the window, parted the heavy brocade draperies, turned the latch and opened the window an inch or two. Then she leaned forward, rested her cheek against the window frame and breathed in deeply: The night air was slightly cool and quite damp, as London's night air was wont to be.

London—England—had proven to be very different from Saint-Simeon. Saint-Simeon was a land of sunshine and blue skies and even bluer waters. Saint-Simeon was lush, green grass and colorful stone cottages and high mountain meadows of wildflowers. Everyone knew everyone else in Saint-Simeon.

When she looked back now Cecile realized that hers had been an idyllic childhood growing up in the tiny kingdom by the sea. She had been cherished and protected by her mother and father, her older brother, and the fifteen thousand residents of her country.

Yes, she had been the most fortunate of young women, educated at her parents' insistence in mathematics, the latest advances in the sciences, philosophy, and psychology, as well as the more traditional pursuits of a well-educated female: music, poetry, and dance.

From the age of eighteen, she had been courted by the young noblemen of Europe. She could have had her pick from princes, dukes, and even a minor king or two. Indeed, until tragedy struck her family, the world had been her oyster.

It was her oyster no longer.

Cecile gave a great sigh and inhaled deeply. At least the air here at Guest House, overlooking the garden below, didn't smell of horses and unwashed bodies and raw sewage dumped in the streets as so much of London did.

Shelley had described the city very fittingly when he had written, "Hell is a city much like London."

Of one thing Cecile of Saint-Simeon was certain: Hell was right here on earth.

She wondered if the same could be true for heaven.

A knock on her bedroom door interrupted her reverie.

"Are you awake?" came the familiar voice of her dearest friend and lady-in-waiting, Ann Faraday.

For an instant, Cecile considered not answering. The time she had to herself was so very scarce and so very precious. Indeed, since the accident that had claimed the lives of her parents two years before, and, more recently, since the "Incident" of last year, her attendants, her closest advisers, her beloved brother, even dear Ann rarely left her alone.

They assumed that she continued to grieve over the loss of her mother and father. They feared that if left to her own devices she would brood, and brooding was unhealthy.

She wasn't brooding.

She was plotting her revenge.

They were two entirely different things.

"Come in, Ann," she finally called out in a voice that would carry to the door and no farther.

The door opened. Ann Faraday, her blond hair a golden cloud around her shoulders, stood there, lamp in hand, eyes big and dark and worried.

"Are you all right, Cecile?" she inquired as she closed the door to the suite behind her.

"Of course I'm all right."

"Do you know what time it is?"

Cecile shook her head. She hadn't bothered to glance at the clock. "Late? Early?"

"Three o'clock."

"Both, then."

Ann was solicitous. "Are you having trouble sleeping?"

God forgive her for yet another lie. "No."

Lady Ann Faraday had been at Cecile's side since they were both eighteen. No one knew her better.

"Cecile, are you having those . . . dreams again?" The word *nightmare* was avoided.

She loved Ann, perhaps more than anyone in the world save her brother, but she needed privacy and it was nearly impossible to obtain, especially when she suspected that Ann knew more about the "Incident" than Cecile did herself.

"I simply awoke," she said offhandedly.

It was the truth. It just wasn't all of the truth.

"What awakened you?"

Cecile shrugged her silk-clad shoulders. "Perhaps it was sleeping in a strange bed in a strange bedchamber." She added for good measure, "And London is different from Saint-Simeon."

"It's very exciting, isn't it?" Ann's eyes danced with delight. "I remember my debut in society. It was handsome young men and magnificent parties every night. Why, there were more dinners, balls, receptions, concerts, teas, and breakfasts than anyone could possibly attend. I had so many beautiful gowns that my wardrobe took up an entire room. At the fancy dress ball given in my honor I danced every single dance. It was marvelous fun."

"I'm sure it was."

Ann was immediately contrite. "I didn't mean to rattle on so, Cecile."

"I don't mind," she quickly assured her friend. "Honestly I don't." Then she raised a hand to her mouth and made a pretense of stifling a yawn. "I believe I'll return to my bed, however. I'm feeling quite sleepy now. I'll see you in the morning."

"As you wish." At Cecile's insistence they did not stand on ceremony when they were alone. "Good night, my dear."

"Good night, Ann," she murmured as she tucked herself in and pulled the covers up to her chin.

The door closed quietly.

Cecile waited five minutes.

She waited another five minutes to be certain.

Then she slipped from her bed, this time not bothering with a light. She went to the open window. She looked out on the garden she knew was somewhere below. The idea of a walk enticed her.

Cecile had always thought it utterly ridiculous that a lady could not, should not, dress herself. Posh, she would manage quite well enough on her own.

She pulled on a plain white chemise and a plain white dress. She slipped her feet into a pair of comfortable shoes and tossed her braided hair over one shoulder. On her way out the door, she decided to throw a cape around her shoulders.

Cecile made her way along the upstairs corridor of Guest House without making a sound. It was another skill that she had perfected out of necessity and desperation.

The key to the garden was kept in a large mahogany desk in the study of the gentleman who owned this grand house. Surely Julian Franklin Guest, Earl of Stanhope, would not mind if she borrowed his key or if she strolled in his garden. After all, he had been gracious enough to offer her the use of his house, his carriage, even his servants while he was away in Tuscany.

Cecile located the key and found her way to the back entrance of the house. Once outside she practically ran toward the key garden; the only sound was the swish-swish of her skirts as they brushed along the stone pathway.

She inserted the large brass key into the lock and gave it a twist. The gate opened, and Cecile escaped into the private garden where she would be alone at last.

Chapter Three

It was a ghost.

That was James Gray's first thought.

Then he realized that the creature coming toward him along the garden path was a woman dressed all in white from the tips of her satin slippers, which peeked out from under her skirts as she moved, to the top of her hooded cape.

The Woman in White.

They both came to a dead stop.

Despite the short distance separating them, James couldn't see her face. The late hour, the thick blanket of fog shrouding the garden, and the hooded cape concealed her features well.

For a moment neither spoke.

Then in cultured tones and with the slightest trace of an accent—the accent may have been French or Italian or even Viennese, James couldn't tell for certain—the lady demanded, as if it were her right to know, "Who goes there?"

"Who, may I ask, is inquiring?" he countered.

There was no immediate response. Instead, the young woman raised her head a fraction of an inch in the night air: just enough so that James could make out the jut of a determined chin beneath the folds of the fur-trimmed cloak.

"I would have you know, sir," she declared, taking few if any pains to mask her displeasure at his sudden appearance, "that this is private property."

James was equally irritated at not finding himself alone in the garden. "I am well aware of the fact, madam."

She said, a shade haughtily, "Indeed, a key is required to gain entry to the *jardin*."

Ah-ha! He had been correct in his assumption: She was French.

James thrust his hand into the pocket of his breeches and took out the key that Goodenough had fetched for him. He held it up in the dim light filtering through the fog and the trees from the gas lantern on the street corner. "*C'est ça, mademoiselle.*"

In turn, the young woman retrieved an identical key from somewhere on her person. James didn't see exactly where she'd had it stashed. "This key, sir."

James Gray blew out his breath expressively. "It would appear that we both have a legitimate right to be in the garden."

"So it would appear," she agreed reluctantly.

"I am a guest at Cork House," he volunteered with a glance back over his shoulder at the stately mansion behind him.

"I am staying at Guest House," she replied in kind.

They were at an impasse.

"Under the circumstances, I suggest that you continue to go your way, sir—" a graceful and feminine hand emerged from the folds of the white cape and indicated the direction in which he had originally been walking "—and I will go mine."

Somewhat belatedly, James Gray came to his senses. He cleared his throat and proclaimed, "As a gentleman I would be remiss if I failed to point out to you, madam, that this is no place for a lady to be in the middle of the night."

"Your concern is duly noted, sir."

As a gentleman he had no choice: She was now his responsibility. "I am afraid I must insist."

She went very still. "Insist on what?"

"Insist that you return to Guest House without delay," he said clearly and firmly.

James heard her intake of air.

"I will go where I please when I please, sir," she stated.

Although the lady spoke flawless English, she must have misunderstood him. Perhaps she was unfamiliar with the customs of polite society.

James decided he must try again. "A young woman of good breeding, such as yourself, should not be out at any hour of the night—or, for that matter, any hour of the day—unless she is accompanied by her maid or a suitable chaperon."

"My maid is asleep. I would not dream of awakening her at this hour," she said with a sniff.

"A suitable chaperon, then."

She deftly sidestepped his line of reasoning. "I want to be alone. Surely bringing along a chaperon, suitable or otherwise, would defeat that purpose."

James felt his patience begin to slip. "We do not always get what we want, madam."

"I am well aware of that, sir."

"You should not be walking in the garden unescorted."

"You are."

"That is another matter altogether," James said, kicking at a small stone on the pathway with the toe of his boot.

"Why?"

The lady was deliberately being obtuse. "Because I am a man and you are a woman."

She made an exasperated sound. "So a man may do as he pleases but a woman may not."

"Precisely." Perhaps now the creature would see reason.

"Why?"

Apparently he had expected too much in the area of sensibility from one so young *and* female. The lady was refusing to think or act rationally. Indeed, she seemed bound and determined to be difficult. It was vexing. And annoying, besides.

Well, two could play at that game. Although James would be the first to admit he was sadly out of practice. Truth to tell, he had never been very good at verbal sparring with the opposite sex.

Blast! He'd gone and lost his train of thought.

"Why *what*?" he growled.

The lady was willing—in fact, she seemed almost eager—to continue the maddening tenor of their conversation. "Why may a man do what he pleases, go where he pleases, see whom he pleases while a woman is required to follow the strictures of society?"

"Because that is the way it is. Because that is the way it has always been."

"Posh!"

He would not lose his temper. He would not resort to profane language, however strong the temptation might be to do so. He would make one last attempt to explain the situation to her in a logical and straightforward manner.

"A man may do what he pleases, go where he pleases, and see whom he pleases, madam, because he is, by nature, larger and stronger and, therefore, more capable of looking after himself."

The woman in white drew herself up to her full height—she was quite tall for a female, surprisingly so, in fact, although the top of her head scarcely reached his chin by James's estimation—and informed him, "I am nearly as tall as any number of the gentlemen of my acquaintance, sir. And I know women who are both taller in stature and stronger than the average man."

She had missed the point entirely. "It goes beyond physical size and strength, madam."

"Indeed." Her cloaked head was cocked to one side. "Pray tell, then, sir, exactly what is it?"

He had to think fast. "Well, for one thing, a man remains calm in the face of danger."

"So do many women. Surely you would agree that keeping one's composure under adverse circumstances has more to do with individual temperament than gender."

He decided to ignore that last comment. "A man

is experienced in handling pistols, swords, and the like."

"I, myself, am an expert marksman," she claimed.

James Gray felt a muscle in his face start to twitch. "Then there are the expectations and conventions of polite society."

The lady didn't budge. "Society is rarely polite if one looks beneath the surface."

James ground his teeth together.

She went on. "Somehow I do not think that you are a man overly concerned with the expectations and conventions of society, anyway. Lest why else would you be wandering about the garden at this time of the night half dressed."

Half dressed?

Hell and damnation, he was fully clothed. Furthermore, who did she think she was? The queen of Sheba?

James slowly counted to ten. "My concern for you is that of a gentleman who has been taught from birth to respect and protect the female of our species."

She would not give an inch. "Does your respect and protection, learned and nurtured over a lifetime, extend to all females or only some females?"

His hands, James suddenly noticed, were clenched into fists at his sides. "They extend to ladies certainly."

"What if a woman is not a lady? Does that change the conventions and rules of society?"

The creature had him going around in circles.

It was maddening.

It was infuriating.

It was strangely exhilarating.

Apparently she had even more that she wished to say to him. "So some females, if they are born through no fault or to no credit of their own into the lower classes, may go where they please, do as they please, and enjoy a degree of freedom usually accorded only to men, but a highborn lady, especially if she is unmarried, is virtually a prisoner in a gilded cage."

James rammed his fingers through the hair at his nape and resorted to his true feelings. He said to her in earnest, "We are all prisoners of convention to one degree or another."

"Yes. I suppose we are," she said wistfully.

It wasn't as if he didn't understand the desire for freedom or the need for solitude. He did. It was the reason he'd sent Goodenough back to bed. James had wished to be alone.

"I simply cannot allow you to walk about by yourself in the dead of the night. It isn't safe," he told her.

"I am safe enough, I assure you." There was a thoughtful pause. "Unless I am mistaken in my assumption, sir, and you are not a gentleman, after all."

Of course he was a gentleman.

There was a certain arrogance, and more than a little sardonicism in his manner, James recognized, as he said, "Put your mind at rest, madam, you are perfectly safe with me."

"Then I need not worry about walking about in the *jardin* whether this be day or night."

"An unscrupulous villain could scale the garden

wall," he proposed, knowing the likelihood of such an occurrence was remote.

"There are any number of unscrupulous villains lurking about in the finest drawing rooms of polite society," she said with absolute conviction. "If the truth be told, there is nowhere a lady feels out of harm's way."

"I repeat, madam, you are safe with me."

"Then, since you have insisted that I must not walk alone, sir, *you* may accompany me."

Bloody hell, he had been bested at his own game, James Gray realized an instant too late.

He was presumptuous.

He was impertinent.

He was arrogant and overbearing and domineering and very, very English.

And he was quite the handsomest man that Cecile had ever seen.

Even scowling, as he was at the moment, and taking into consideration the fact that his features and his masculine physique were illuminated only by the pale yellow gaslight filtering through the trees from the lantern on the street corner, the sight of the stranger took Cecile's breath away.

He was tall and dark, broad-shouldered and muscular. She had intimated that he was half-dressed. In truth, his informal attire revealed him to great advantage. Few gentlemen of her acquaintance—in fact, not a single one came to mind—would, should, could go about wearing only a pair of skintight riding breeches and a loose, free-flowing, collarless shirt open at the neck.

Indeed, the man's shirt was open nearly halfway down his impressive chest.

His hair was the hue and cast of the last chestnuts to fall to the ground in late autumn. Cecile judged its color to be so dark as to be indistinguishable from black. It was slightly wavy in texture and had a decided tendency to brush back and forth along the back of his neck when he moved his head.

While his speech and manner clearly signified that the stranger was a gentleman by birth and breeding—there could be no mistake on that account—his hair was conspicuously longer than the current fashion. Yet, it somehow suited him.

On some young gentlemen, she had noted since her departure from Saint-Simeon—the journey had taken Cecile and her entourage through the southern regions of Italy, spanned the entire length of France, and a fair portion of England as well—long hair had become an affectation; the mark of the so-called sensitive poet or long-suffering artist or the rather too-pretty dandy.

There was no suggestion, not the merest hint, of this man being anything but exactly what he was.

No, indeed. There was nothing overly sensitive, nothing pretty, nothing of the dandy, about the man standing beside her. He was who he was. And although Cecile had a feeling, call it a woman's intuition, that the stranger was a bit more complicated than she had thought him on first meeting, she found that she liked—nay, that she greatly preferred—the man as he was.

Perhaps it was just as well the hood of her cape and the dark night shielded her from the stranger's scrutiny. For he might be surprised to discover that her cheeks were pink with pleasure, that her eyes sparkled with excitement, that she occasionally wetted her lips with the tip of her tongue, that her palms were damp and her hands were trembling, that she was . . . aglow.

It was gratifying—piffle!—it was *thrilling* to talk to a man, to be with a man who didn't treat her like a princess.

Of course, the stranger didn't treat her like a princess because he didn't know she was a princess. And Her Serene Highness, Cecile of Saint-Simeon—for tonight plain Cecile Girardet—intended to keep it that way. She was determined, whatever the cost, to keep her identity a secret from this man.

And he would be her secret.

Surely even a princess was entitled to have one small secret—*une petite indiscretion*—that was hers and hers alone.

For here, in the seclusion of the key garden, there were no titles. There was no pomp and circumstance. There was no proper or improper protocol. There were no servants, no ladies-in-waiting, no advisers, and no chaperons. There was no one to tell her what she must do and what she must not do. It was freedom such as Cecile had rarely known in her twenty-three years.

The stranger muttered under his breath, gave a

stilted bow of his head, did an abrupt about-face, and fell into step beside her.

They strolled for some distance past newly planted beds of flowers, several varieties of blossoming trees that seemed weighted down with buds, even a life-size statue of Aphrodite—or was it Venus?—before the man inquired, "What brings you out into the garden at this unusual hour, madam?"

She chose to answer his question with one of her own. "What brings you out in the dead of night, sir?"

He shrugged his broad shoulders. "I found myself wide awake. Taking a walk in the garden seemed like a good idea."

Cecile was surprised by his reply. It had the ring of truth to it. "I, too, awoke and knew I had a long night of wakefulness ahead of me. I occasionally suffer from insomnia."

"As do I," he admitted.

'What form does yours take?"

"Sometimes I can't fall asleep," he revealed. "Other times, like tonight, I wake up and I can't get back to sleep."

She moved her head beneath the white mantle. "I will confess there are times when I'm roused by disturbing dreams."

"I, too, have strange and disturbing dreams," he granted.

"Mine can be quite frightening. I suppose one could correctly call them nightmares," Cecile finally murmured, her head bowed, her voice scarcely audible.

A slight breeze came up and gently rustled through

the leaves on the greening trees overhead. There was a smell of newly turned earth on the night air and the first subtle scent of spring flowers in bloom: tulips, daffodils, and hyacinths.

Off to one side of the stone path was a small gazebo. Farther on was a whimsical fountain: water spouting from the mouth of a large fish before emptying into an ornamental pool.

Cecile wondered aloud, "Do you think we humans sleep at night because we are afraid of the dark?"

The man appeared to seriously consider the matter. "Maybe for some of us it is the opposite. Maybe it is fear of the dark that keeps us awake at night."

Cecile heard herself give a small, self-conscious laugh. "I do believe, sir, that this is the most curious conversation I have ever had with a gentleman."

"It is certainly the most unusual conversation I've ever had with a lady," he stated

"Perhaps it is blessed anonymity," she said with a sigh.

"Is anonymity a blessing?"

"Oh, yes, it can be wonderful blessing. There are so many expectations that must be met, otherwise. So many duties one must perform. So many niceties one must convey. So many responsibilities one must assume." Cecile couldn't prevent another sigh from slipping through her lips. "So many things one must be."

The stranger kicked at another, and somewhat larger, stone on the pathway: There was something almost boyish, almost gleefully rebellious about the gesture. "Then for tonight we will both remain anonymous, if you like," he said to her.

"I'd like that very much."

They walked on in comfortable silence.

She added after some minutes had passed, "I haven't been in the garden during the daylight."

"Neither have I," he replied. "In fact, I caught only a glimpse of it upon my arrival in London yesterday."

Cecile paused, leaned over a flowering bush whose name she had to confess she did not know, inhaled its sweet fragrance and straightened before asking conversationally, "Do you know London well?"

"I know the city and the country scarcely at all," the man informed her. He went on to say cryptically, "I was away for many years and have only recently returned."

"I visited England once as a child. But that was a long time ago and I remember very little of the experience or of London," she said in a pensive tone.

Again, the man slowed his pace to match hers. Cecile could not help but notice that his legs were unusually long and muscular.

"We are both strangers in a strange land, then," he commented.

"A quote from the Book of Exodus," she said.

A darkly handsome head was nodded. "Sophocles also wrote much the same thing."

This time she nodded. "It was Oedipus at Colonus who said of himself that he was a 'stranger in a strange country.'"

It was peculiar to be discussing an ancient Greek

dramatist with a gentleman whose name was unknown to her, while the two of them strolled along a secluded garden path in the heart of London on a dark and rather dreary night.

And yet Cecile of Saint-Simeon realized that she felt more at peace than she had in months, perhaps more than she had in years.

It was the oddest thing.

Then, from somewhere in the distance came the lilting and plaintive sound of a fiddler playing his instrument.

"What is it?" she inquired, tilting her head to one side.

"A street musician playing for a copper or two."

"Do you know the name of the song?"

Her companion listened for several minutes. Then it seemed to come to him. "I remember now," he claimed. "It's an old Celtic tune titled 'Are Ye Sleeping, Maggie?' "

They listened to the haunting air as it seemed to express melancholy and sadness, hope and joy all at once.

As the music faded into silence Cecile said in a hushed whisper, " 'Was it a vision, or a waking dream? Fled is that music:—Do I wake or sleep?' "

The man at her side appeared taken aback. He stopped and stared down at her. "I beg your pardon, madam."

"It's a line from Keats's 'Ode to a Nightingale.' "

He said nothing.

After a while, she added: "The music was both beautiful and haunting."

His back was ramrod straight. "Yes, it was."

Perhaps it was time to turn their conversation to the subject of the garden.

Cecile commented first on a nearby folly constructed in the form and fashion of a mock ruin. The "ancient" ruins were overrun with lichens, maidenhair, pennyleaf, and mosses of various hues from olive green to emerald to a dark forest coloration.

"There are dozens of buds on this particular rosebush," she also observed, pausing to study a large rambler that cascaded over an archway. "When will the roses bloom?"

"The garden will doubtlessly be transformed within the coming fortnight," her escort estimated.

"Then I will see spring come to England, after all," she said with a kind of satisfaction. Cecile glanced up. "What is that glow, sir, on the horizon?"

"Dawn breaking through the clouds," she was told.

Cecile usually welcomed the dawn after a troublesome and sleepless night, but this time she found herself disappointed by the prospect. "It will be daylight soon."

"In another hour, perhaps less."

There was nothing to be done about it. She could not keep the sun from rising.

Cecile pulled the hood of her cape more closely around her face. "I must go, sir."

"As must I, madam," he said.

She suddenly realized that she would doubtless never see the handsome stranger again. Cecile was surprised by the sense of loss she felt.

"Good-bye." She quickly turned away and hurried toward the back entrance to Guest House.

"Not good-bye," the man whispered as he watched the retreating figure of the woman in white, "but *au revoir*."

Chapter Four

"What the bloody hell is she doing here in London?" demanded the woman stretched out beside him on the bed.

The rumpled satin sheets were pulled up only to her waist, all the better to display her bare breasts to their best advantage. Her complexion was flawless, her flesh firm, her thirty-five years belied by constant narcissism and pampering: No sunlight was ever permitted to touch her skin, lest it leave its unwelcome mark of a wrinkle here or a slight discoloration there.

Special creams and exotic concoctions—he had once overheard her maid describe one such potion as the powdered testicles of the rare Siamese tiger—were imported from the East and applied daily to every inch of her lush and remarkably well-preserved body.

Moira, Lady Pale, was a hedonist.

She loved pleasure. She loved to pleasure and to be pleasured in return, especially in bed. In truth, she was insatiable. No one knew that better than Rodolphe Girardet.

Suddenly weary of her presence—the lovely Moira had many assets, but she occasionally wore a bit thin—Rodolphe tossed aside the bedcovers and reached for his silk dressing gown.

A carnal and sensually inviting voice followed him. "Come back to bed, Rudy."

Rudy.

How he detested that nickname.

But he had purposely never made his aversion known to his latest mistress. For every time Moira referred to him by the loathsome moniker it served to remind Rodolphe Girardet just how much he despised the lady—and he employed the word *lady* very loosely—in spite of her numerous talents.

For Moira, the notorious Lady Pale, was the widow of the late and legendary Lord Osgood Pale, according to Rodolphe's sources, which were the best money could buy.

To his sources, Prince Rodolphe was known as a demanding client. There was to be no stone left unturned if he so desired; no job not performed to the best of a man's, or a woman's, abilities; and certainly no disloyalty was ever tolerated, not if one wished to quite literally keep one's skin intact. But the rewards for serving the prince well were considerable and remunerative.

The meticulously and methodically collected file on Lord and Lady Pale was at least twelve inches thick and contained every detail of the couple's lives.

It seemed that having outlived three wives already—one had proved herself to be barren, the other two had died in childbirth along with their newborn babes—Lord Pale had decided, at the age of eighty, to wed sixteen-year-old Moira Munson, daughter of an ambitious North Country gentleman farmer.

Money had exchanged hands.

The ceremony had taken place.

Scandal had ensued.

At the time there had been some in society forthright enough, at least in private, to condemn the marriage on the grounds of common decency. They asserted that *infamous* or *degenerate* or even *debauched* more aptly described the aging libertine, who was the first and only Earl of Pale. (Indeed, if Lord Pale had any offspring they had all been born on the wrong side of the blanket and, therefore, in society's eyes were of no consequence.)

Some ten years after making Moira his countess, Osgood Pale had been discovered dead in the red velvet and gold tasseled bed of a well-known London prostitute. The cause of death had not been heart failure or apoplexy or even natural causes due to the gentleman's advanced age, but arsenic poisoning.

Another scandal had ensued.

The "mopsy" involved had mysteriously disappeared. No other culprit had been named or charged with the crime.

Good riddance to bad rubbish.

In the end, the earl left behind a sizeable fortune, no legitimate heir, and a beautiful young widow: Moira.

Arsenic: In the last century it had commonly been referred to as the "inheritance powder." Not a very subtle means of dispatching a lubricious spouse, Rodolphe reflected.

So, when all things were considered, it was, perhaps, little wonder that the countess lacked a certain subtlety in her person and manner. Lord Pale had doubtlessly been a man of somewhat obvious tastes.

On the other hand, Prince Rodolphe liked to think that he was a gentleman who appreciated the subtleties and nuances of life more than most.

Sometimes one simply had to make do.

He tied the belt of his dressing gown around his own still-firm waistline and strolled across the magnificent bedroom. From the solid gold mirrors to the silk wallcoverings to the ornate Louis Quatorze furniture, it was a bedchamber fit for a king, and it had cost him a king's ransom, which, fortunately, he could well afford.

Rodolphe paused at a gilt-decorated japanned bombé bureau, opened a secret door—revealing a cache of fine liquors inside—helped himself to a glass of imported cognac, took an appreciative sip, held the brandy on his tongue for a moment, and then swallowed.

"Rudy, what the bloody hell is she doing in London?" came the repeated demand.

The Prince continued to the window where he stood gazing out on the nearly deserted boulevard for several minutes before he finally said, "I assume you mean my niece."

"Of course I mean your ruddy niece."

Prince Rodolphe's spine stiffened. He slowly turned his head and glanced back over his shoulder at the creature reclining on his bed. His voice softened in warning. "You will refer to my niece properly, Countess, or you will refer to her not at all. She is Her Serene Highness, Princess Cecile of Saint-Simeon, and don't ever forget it."

Moira wasn't a stupid or foolish woman. She knew when she had made an error in judgment. Her tone immediately became respectful. "You didn't tell me that Her Serene Highness was coming to London for the season."

In his opinion, he was under no obligation to tell his paramour anything. "I only found out myself recently," he said.

Not quite a lie; not quite the truth—like so much else about Rodolphe Girardet's life.

The woman in his bed pouted prettily: A technique that had held more appeal for the male of the species when she was eighteen or nineteen than it did now in her maturity.

Still, the countess was the most beautiful woman the prince had ever beheld; as long as one did not subscribe to the belief that beauty came from within. For she possessed that rare combination of porcelain skin, dark amber eyes, hair that was somehow naturally both silver and gold, and a perfect figure. Then, too, Moira had maintained the illusion of youth far better than most women.

She continued, as she absently stroked the satin sheet in a provocative manner, "I found out quite by accident at Lady Whitehouse's dinner party last evening. I tell you, Rudy, I felt positively the fool for not knowing."

"I seriously doubt that, my dear." He didn't bother offering her a drink. She had no appreciation for fine brandy, anyway. "I've never known you to be anyone's fool."

"Why is she here?"

He was very careful to give no indication of his inner agitation. "I assume for the reason that has been put forth publicly: Cecile wished to visit London during the season."

Moira seemed willing to accept the official explanation. "I suppose Saint-Simeon is a deadly boring place."

Rodolphe struck a pose of studied nonchalance: crystal glass steadied in the palm of one hand, the other hand half-in and half-out of the pocket of his dressing gown. "As I have mentioned to you on more than one occasion, my dear, why else do you think I eagerly went into self-imposed exile as a young man?"

"Boredom?"

"Precisely. There is nothing in Saint-Simeon but goats and goat-herders, high mountain meadows, and one monotonous little village after another." He reached up with a graceful and manicured gesture to cover a well-staged yawn. "Other than a pretty view of the Mediterranean Sea, and a collection of paintings in the palace, a suit of armor of some distinction, and perhaps a family heirloom or two, there is little of interest about the place."

"Unless you happen to be the reigning prince of Saint-Simeon," she pointed out. "Then you would be the ruler, the absolute monarch of your own country, and there are so very few absolute monarchs in this day and age."

Moira wasn't quite as clever as she liked to think. It would take far more than a thinly veiled insult from a fancy courtesan to make Rodolphe Girardet lose his temper. For he had schooled himself a long time ago to show no reaction to such comments.

His voice possessed the precise amount of inflection required—no more, no less—as he related his usual speech: "I was never intended to be the ruler of Saint-Simeon. That was a duty, a responsibility, that I always knew would befall my elder brother. Believe me, a younger son understands these things from birth."

Moira turned over onto her back, fanned her hair out along the satin-covered pillows, raised one perfectly shaped and completely bare leg in the air, pointed her toes toward the elaborately stenciled ceiling and said, "Does he?"

Rodolphe took another sip of cognac and casually shrugged his shoulders. "I quickly discovered that there were many benefits to being the second son."

The challenge was issued. "Name one."

"Freedom."

The Prince wondered if Moira had any idea that there was a pronounced wrinkle created between her lovely eyes when she frowned. "Freedom to do what?"

Rodolphe Girardet was never caught unprepared. He had played his role and recited his lines on so many occasions during the past twenty years that he had almost come to believe the story himself. "Freedom to do as I please. Freedom to travel the world. Freedom to live wherever I want to live in whatever manner I desire. Freedom to acquire wealth, power, land, this house, a chateau in France, influential friends, even mistresses, on both sides of the Channel."

Amber eyes narrowed to catlike slits. "What did the Comtesse Tournaire say when she found out that you had become the lover of an English countess?"

In truth, Thérèsa had never mentioned Moira, or, for that matter, any of his indiscretions. After all, the Comtesse was a true Frenchwoman and very wise about matters of the so-called heart.

Rodolphe chose to lie at this particular moment because it suited him to do so. "She is very jealous of you, *naturellement*. Surely you realize, cherie, that your unequaled beauty and stellar wit are as well known in France as they are here in Britain."

That pleased Moira immensely. As he had known it would. In many ways Lady Pale was utterly transparent.

She was also tenacious. "I hear that Princess Cecile is very young and very beautiful."

He finished off his cognac and set the empty glass down on the bureau. "I haven't seen my niece in many years." That wasn't entirely true, but his business was none of Moira's business unless he decided it somehow served to further his plans. "I remember her as a pretty child."

"She is no longer a child."

"I suppose you're right."

"She is a woman."

"She would be . . ." He stroked his chin thoughtfully and made a production of trying to recollect his niece's age. Actually the prince knew her current age to the year, the month, the exact day. As a matter of fact, he knew nearly everything there was to know about Cecile of Saint-Simeon. "I believe she must be seventeen or eighteen."

"I hear she is twenty-three."

It was just like the countess to ask a question to which she already knew the answer. He had often played the same game himself. It was a useful device in the right hands.

"There is a ball to be given in Princess Cecile's honor," the woman informed him.

He listened.

"Her Majesty won't be present, of course. The queen never appears at such affairs, herself. But Their Royal Highnesses, the Prince and Princess of Wales will make an appearance."

He did not speak.

"Everyone in society who is anyone will be in attendance tomorrow evening."

Rodolphe finally opened his mouth. "Then I think we should attend, as well, don't you?"

Moira slowly lowered her leg, rolled over onto her stomach and came up onto her knees in the middle of the bed. She clasped her hands together with delight. Her eyes were suddenly overly bright and a small, perfectly round circle of pink appeared in the middle of each pale cheek. "Do we have an invitation?"

Not *we.*

He.

"Of course," Rodolphe replied.

Moira gnawed on her bottom lip. "I thought you were estranged from your family."

"Not so much estranged from as separated from." He added for good measure, "My brother was always envious of the wealth and power I enjoyed."

Again, a frown appeared between her lovely eyes. "Your brother is dead, isn't he?"

"Yes. There was a terrible accident several years ago: Maximilian and his wife, Judith, were both killed." Rodolphe dropped his chin to his chest. "I don't like to talk about it."

"I'm sorry, Rudy."

"It's all right, my dear."

Moira flopped down, tucking one leg beneath her and dangling the other over the side of the mattress, and heaved an audible sigh. "I don't have anything to wear."

Rodolphe's head came up. "Wear where?"

"To the ball."

He couldn't help himself; he laughed out loud. "You have a roomful, a houseful, of expensive evening gowns."

The countess's expression was downcast. "I mean I don't have anything new."

The woman was self-centered and vain and put great store in the accoutrements of fashion. Sometimes Rodolphe wondered why he kept her. But he knew why. . . .

"You've just spent a month having an entire wardrobe made for the upcoming season," he pointed out.

"I mean new *and* spectacular."

"You are spectacular, cherie, no matter what you

are wearing." But the prince recognized that his words were of no consolation to a woman with lady Pale's penchant—in truth, it bordered on obsession—for being the center of attention. "Perhaps this is the time."

Her ears immediately perked up. "The time for what?"

He could tease her without the slightest remorse. "I was saving it for a special occasion."

"This *is* a special occasion," she was quick to respond.

"Perhaps it is."

"What were you saving?"

"A little surprise."

"A surprise?" Moira grew impatient. "Where is it, Rudy? Please tell me. Where have you hidden it?" Her voice wavered slightly. Her eyes glittered with avarice. She almost smacked her lips in anticipation. She could be a greedy little beggar.

"Let me think." He furrowed his dark brow. "Where did I put it?"

"Rudy!" she cried.

He wasn't in the mood to play games, after all. "In the bottom drawer of the bedside table."

Moira flew off the bed and was down on her naked haunches by the time he finished speaking. She jerked open the drawer and began to rummage through its contents. What she was searching for was found at the very back, by design.

She lifted out the jewel box. Her hands were shaking as she raised the lid. He heard the sharp intake of air. She finally exhaled on the word "Diamonds."

"The necklace was made for a grand duchess who can no longer afford to keep it," Rodolphe explained as she trotted over to him with the case and held the necklace up for him to place around her neck. "I thought it would suit you."

He hooked the intricate clasp, and then rested his hands on her bare shoulders for a moment, fingers extended toward the piece of jewelry: warm flesh against cold gemstones.

Moira dashed to the nearest mirror. She stood and stared at herself. Her dainty nostrils flared. "It does suit me." She turned around. "Don't you agree?"

The beautiful woman standing before him wearing only a diamond necklace—a necklace created for a grand duchess—waited for his approval. He finally gave it. "I do."

She sashayed toward him, hips swaying, breasts jiggling, tongue licking her lips. "You will have to think of a way I can thank you, Your Serene Highness."

His body reacted as he had suspected it would. He felt himself growing hard and rigid. "Yes. I will."

Calculating eyes dropped to the front of his dressing gown where the material was moving, shifting, parting, seemingly of its own volition. Knowing hands delved beneath the luxurious silk, found him, cupped him, stroked him.

Moira laughed huskily in the back of her throat. "I think you've already found a way."

"I expect you to thank me again and again, Countess," he made clear.

A fingernail scored his sensitive flesh. It was all he could do not to flinch.

"Again and again?" she repeated.

"It was a very expensive necklace."

"I'm worth every pound, franc, or ruble you paid for it," she claimed.

He urged the beautiful woman to her knees in front of him as he untied the belt of his dressing gown. He firmly placed one hand on the back of her head. He ran his thumb back and forth along her bottom lip until her mouth opened. She needed no further inducement or encouragement.

Indeed, Rodolphe Girardet reflected as Moira went to work on him, he expected her to thank him over and over again, but not in the way she obviously imagined.

The prince had his own plans for Lady Pale.

Chapter Five

He was late.

He had not wanted to come at all, of course, but Goodenough had laid out his formal black trousers, his black jacket, a black waistcoat, and a white tie and shirt, even a pair of de rigueur white gloves, and then had stood by, as any valet worth his salt would, the efficient young man had informed him, in case Lord Graystone needed any further assistance.

In the end there was nothing to be done about it. James had dressed, climbed into the waiting carriage and arrived, although an hour or two after everyone else, at the formal ball honoring Her Serene Highness, Princess Cecile of Saint-Simeon.

James stepped into the grand ballroom. It was a vast sea of faces and swirling figures attired, it appeared at first glance, in either black—gentlemen in their formal wear; or white—ladies in evening gowns, kid gloves and a preponderance of pearls.

At the far end of the ballroom was the orchestra; they were playing a waltz. There were brilliantly lit chandeliers overhead, rows of potted palms lining the walls, and French doors leading to an outside terrace. To James's right was the card room, to his left a sweeping white marble staircase leading downstairs to a sumptuous buffet.

Since he wasn't interested in playing cards—it seemed to be the last bastion of white-haired matrons with too much time on their hands and too many diamonds festooning their ample bosoms—or in dancing or in eating, for that matter, and since he hadn't recognized a single soul so far, James Gray picked an advantageous spot, planted his feet, and stood there observing the crowd.

He had not intended, of course, to eavesdrop. But it couldn't be helped.

Two young ladies entered the ballroom, paused, and hovered in his vicinity for several minutes. They were all atwitter, with silk fans fluttering and pink tongues wagging.

"Did you catch a glimpse of her?" the first young woman wanted to know.

"Yes," the second replied.

"She is quite the most beautiful creature I have ever seen," whispered her companion with an envious sigh.

There was an agreeable nod of a pretty head.

Wait.

There was more.

"Her dress is exquisite, as well."

The second young lady lowered her voice to a scarcely audible level. Indeed, James had to strain to hear what she was saying. "Mama has said that the material alone for such a gown could easily cost several hundred pounds per yard."

Silk fan froze in midair. Impressionable eyes grew round as saucers. "Truly?"

"Truly."

The first young lady was unwilling to be bested by her friend. "And I have heard that the large blue stone in her tiara is a rare gem called Cecilite. In fact, it is the only gemstone of its kind in the world and it was named in the princess's honor."

"How perfectly romantic," exclaimed her companion. "Imagine having a precious gemstone bearing one's name."

The first sniffed and expressed her personal disappointment. "I was only hoping that a rose might be christened in my honor one day, and that doesn't seem very likely."

"*A rose by any other name . . .*" James reflected as the duo moved on across the ballroom.

They were shortly replaced by a pair of gentlemen some years past their prime.

"Do you think they're real, Castle?" posed one of the sexagenarians as he leaned heavily on his companion.

"Damned if I know, Lloyd-Worth," growled the second elderly gentleman. He added as an afterthought, "But I understand the fellow has money to burn."

The first didn't bother lowering his voice. Perhaps he thought it was one of the privileges of reaching a certain age. "Girardet is rumored to be a prince of some sort, isn't he? French, I gather. Of course, titles are a shilling a dozen across the Channel. Every other

Frenchman you meet is a descendant of some noble family."

"Impoverished noble family. None of them seem to have any money," the second pointed out.

"Mark my words, this one does."

"The lady is a beauty." Castle jabbed his companion with his elbow and cackled, "Some years younger than Girardet, too. I'll bet she leads him a merry chase, if you get my drift."

"Wouldn't mind having her lead me a merry chase just once," came the snicker.

"It would be the death of you, Lloyd-Worth," predicted his fellow peer, "assuming you could meet the lady's price."

"So, you do think they're real."

"They're real all right," came the pronouncement as they began to make their way slowly around the perimeter of the ballroom.

James was tempted to follow the pair. He had to admit that his curiosity had been roused by their conversation.

"Conversation? Gossip is more like it," he muttered to himself, half-amused and half-disgusted at his own prurient interest.

"Talking to yourself these days, Graystone," came a deep, baritone voice from behind him.

James turned. The face was familiar. The voice was familiar. Even the devilish smile was somehow familiar. But he couldn't put a name with the face, the voice or the smile.

"Since it's been fifteen years, I'll give you a clue,

old chap," the handsome man offered generously. "We were together at Oxford."

James's brow furrowed into a thoughtful frown. "Oxford." That had been a lifetime ago.

"Here's another clue," the gentleman submitted with a grin. "We went shooting at my family's country house in Scotland, and you bagged twice the number of birds as anyone else in our party. It was an impressive performance."

"Silverthorn."

They gripped hands.

"Graystone." His arm was vigorously pumped. "How the devil have you been?"

"Well, and you, Silverthorn?"

"I've been well, as well."

They laughed at themselves and at each other.

The Earl of Silverthorn, eldest son and acknowledged heir of the Duke of Northcote, was tall enough to look James Gray straight in the eye: Few men were.

"You left Oxford and went out to India as I recall," he said conversationally.

James nodded. "I spent fifteen years there."

"Military?"

He shook his head. "Tea."

James Gray rarely spoke of India, and never of his endeavors there on behalf of queen and country. As far as anyone knew, outside of a handful of government officials, he had been exactly what he had appeared to be: the owner of a prosperous tea plantation.

If he had also been very good at gathering certain

kinds of information, if he had been an expert marksman and a first-class swordsman and a handy man with a knife . . . well, so much the better for him under the circumstances in which he occasionally found himself.

"It's good to have you back, old chap." The sentiment expressed seemed genuine.

"It's good to be back."

Silverthorn gazed out across the crush of dancing couples and gawking onlookers. "All of this must seem rather frivolous to a man who has experienced as much of the world as you have."

James wasn't willing to go that far in his censure. "A bit foolish, perhaps."

Silverthorn appeared to be in no hurry to end their reunion. "Where are you staying while you're in town?"

"Cork House."

"That's right. You're related now, aren't you?"

James answered in the affirmative. "My niece, Alyssa, married the marquess last summer."

Silverthorn seemed well informed. "I understand they aren't in London for the season."

His answer was relayed in a slight tongue-in-cheek manner. "Lord and Lady Cork have decided to forego that pleasure since they're awaiting the birth of their first child."

"I haven't had the good fortune of meeting Lady Cork," his old schoolmate said, "but I understand from all accounts that your niece is an extraordinary young woman."

"She is, indeed."

"Lucky devil, Cork."

"Very lucky," James agreed.

"I've never married," Silverthorn went on to confide to him as they stood side by side and stared out at the profusion of swirling colors and nonstop music.

"Neither have I," Graystone echoed. And, yet, for a moment he wasn't quite certain.

"Most of my family have trotted off to Tuscany for some reason," the earl stated. "Damned if I know why." He added after a lengthy pause: "I believe the weather was mentioned before they packed up and fled town en masse."

The Duke and Duchess of Northcote and their brood of nine children had always been regarded as unconventional by the rest of society, James recalled now. They were a big, happy, and rather boisterous family. It was one of the reasons he had always liked the Duke's eldest son.

"Weather is as good a reason as any, in my opinion, for vacating London during the unconditional frenzy of the social season," he remarked to Silverthorn.

"Why did you come, then, feeling as you do?"

"I was invited."

They both knew by whom.

"Yes, well, I see why it was impossible for you to decline the invitation."

"At least you know who the players are in this infernal game," James muttered. "So far you're the solitary person I seem to remember, and you're the only one who has recognized me."

Lord Silverthorn took half a step back and gave James a quick looking-over. "Can't imagine why. You haven't changed that much since our Oxford days, Graystone."

"Neither have you, Silverthorn."

The handsome man suddenly dropped his voice and murmured under his breath. "Prepare yourself."

"For what?"

"Count Dupre is headed directly for us."

"Count who?"

"Dupre. He's a kind of aide-de-camp and right-hand man to Her Serene Highness, Princess Cecile."

"What does it mean?"

There was no time or opportunity for his old friend to answer.

The diminutive man with the thinning hair came to a halt in front of them, snapped his heels together, gave a scant but polite bow of his head, which sent the gold-fringed epaulets on both of his shoulders swaying back and forth, tapped his silver-tipped walking stick on the ballroom floor, and proclaimed in a distinctive voice, "Lord Silverthorn. Lord Graystone. I have been asked to make your acquaintance, my lords. I am Count Dupre."

They acknowledged him one right after the other.

"Count Dupre."

"Count Dupre."

The count turned to James. "Her Serene Highness, Princess Cecile of Saint-Simeon, has requested that you, Lord Graystone, be formally introduced to her before your dance."

"Before *what* dance?" The words flew out of his mouth.

Count Dupre's expression changed from a stilted smile to a stilted frown. "I have not made a mistake, have I? You are James Gray, Earl of Graystone, are you not, my lord?"

"I am."

The stilted smile reappeared. "Then there has been no mistake. You are the gentleman who will be honored to dance the next waltz with Her Serene Highness." The count stepped to one side, tapped his cane again, and made a motion with his arm. "If you would please accompany me now, Lord Graystone."

"I'll see you later, old chap," Silverthorn said with a congenial pat on the back before they parted company.

There must be some mistake, James decided as he proceeded to walk the entire length of the grand ballroom, the princess's man at his side, the rhythmic tap, tap, tap of the count's cane seemingly beating out the cadence of his own heartbeat.

Why would he be requested to waltz with the princess?

When was the last time he had danced with a woman?

When was the last time he had taken a woman into his arms for any reason?

James silently swore at his own dimwittedness. He should have polished his social skills, particularly his dancing, he realized. After all, this was a ball.

It was too late now.

Suddenly he became aware of the sheer number of people watching their every move.

"Being followed, are we, Count?" He expanded his comment. "By several hundred pairs of eyes."

Count Dupre looked neither to the right nor to the left, but straight ahead. "I suppose we are at that, Lord Graystone."

"It can't be me," James speculated with a touch of irony in his tone. Not that he personally cared if the whole population of Britain was watching him.

"It is and it isn't."

He was beginning to get the picture. "It's the princess, of course."

"It is a great honor that is about to be bestowed upon you, my lord," came the response.

James's back stiffened. It wasn't as if he had asked for the bloody honor. It wasn't as if he had invited the young lady, princess or otherwise, to dance with him. Nevertheless, this wasn't the time or place to be a boor.

"Yes, I suppose it is," he finally acknowledged.

They were no more than ten feet from their final destination when James Gray started to get that feeling in his gut. He knew better than to ignore it. He had learned a long time ago in a faraway place that he couldn't afford not to trust his gut instincts.

The feeling came again.

He narrowed his gray eyes slightly. "May I ask who the tall dark-haired gentleman is standing beside the woman in white?" he inquired of the count.

"Prince Rodolphe, uncle to Her Serene Highness," came the discreet reply.

One thing was abundantly clear to James. The young lady speaking with Prince Rodolphe—her rigidly straight back was to them as they approached the royal enclave—either disliked the prince or feared him . . . or both.

Then James heard her speak. Surely he had heard her voice before. He closed his eyes for an instant. Yes, he had. It was the same voice he had heard in the key garden the night before last. It was the voice of the woman in white.

Count Dupre halted.

James did likewise.

She turned her head. Perfect features were outlined in profile. "Yes, Count."

"Your Serene Highness, may I present the Earl of Graystone, who is to be honored with the next waltz?"

The princess turned around.

The earth shifted beneath James Gray's feet. Impossibilities became possibilities. Possibilities became improbable, then impossible. Truth became lies. Lies became the truth. The world—his world—was suddenly turned upside down.

"Lord Graystone," she enunciated his name in perfect and nearly unaccented English.

James forced himself to go through the motions. "Your Serene Highness," he responded and bowed.

"I am looking forward to our waltz," she said graciously.

"As am I," he responded in kind.

That voice.

He knew that voice.

That face.

He knew that face.

Obviously he had finally lost his mind, James Gray decided as he stood there, staring down at Her Serene Highness, Princess Cecile of Saint-Simeon.

For hers was the face of the beautiful young woman who haunted his dreams . . .

Chapter Six

She recognized him instantly.

It took every ounce of self-control that Cecile possessed not to react or show the slightest sign of recognition. For the man standing before her was none other than the tall, dark, handsome stranger that she had walked with and talked with in the private garden that Guest House shared with Cork House.

He must not give her away. Not here. Not now. Not in front of her uncle and Count Dupre and the rest of her entourage, not to mention the crème de la crème of English society.

No one must ever learn of their meeting in the key garden, however unintentional or innocent it may have been. If anyone were to discover that she had left the house in the dead of night and slipped off by herself—her actions that evening had gone beyond imprudence as Cecile well knew; she had not needed a lecture from this man to be aware of that fact—she would never again experience a moment's peace or a moment's freedom.

She gave a small, nearly imperceptible sigh. The truth was neither she nor the House of Girardet could afford a scandal.

Another scandal.

Surely Lord Graystone—she was now acquainted with the gentleman's name, of course, and he with hers; they were anonymous no longer—would not give her secret away.

She must be certain. She must not stand idly by. She must take the proverbial bull by the horns.

Cecile took a step toward him. "I believe this is our dance, Lord Graystone."

His features were expressionless; they revealed nothing. She was both relieved and mystified. Surely the gentleman had recognized her. Was he as accomplished an actor as she liked to think she had become in the past twelve months?

Then it occurred to Cecile that during their tête-à-tête her face had been concealed by the hood of her cape and the thick fog permeating the night air. It was highly unlikely Lord Graystone could identify her as the woman he had encountered in the garden.

"I believe it is our dance, Your Serene Highness." He politely offered his arm and escorted her to the dance floor.

They said not another word to each other as the orchestra began to play and the waltz commenced.

Cecile put her head back slightly and cocked her chin at an advantageous angle. It provided her with an opportunity to study the gentleman without seeming to.

James Gray, Earl of Graystone, was even more handsome than she had perceived him to be upon the occasion of their first, and what she had assumed would be their last, meeting.

Indeed, she had never seen a man more well favored in every aspect. He *was* tall and muscular and broad shouldered. His features *were* strong and well defined and aristocratic. His hair *was* the color of chestnuts: dark brown and richly autumnal. His voice *was* deep and resonant, and the sound of it sent shivers down her spine.

There was more.

Unlike that night in the garden, Cecile could clearly see his eyes. They were intelligent, intense, and self-aware. They were large and well shaped, and they were situated upon his face in such a way as to be in perfect proportion to his other features.

Furthermore, his eyes were framed by dark brown eyebrows and even darker brown eyelashes—again so dark as to be indistinguishable from black—while the irises, themselves, were gray.

Cecile quickly observed that their color was elusive. One moment they were the gray of a London fog. The next moment they were like quicksilver. Then the next surely the cast of heather on the hill after a drenching rain.

Gray: What a common word for such an extraordinary and uncommon pair of eyes.

Although the earl wore his formal clothes without fault, Cecile found she still preferred him in the informality of his riding breeches and his loose, uncollared shirt.

She blinked several times in rapid succession. Had she been staring at James Gray? She mustn't stare at him. She must say something. According to protocol, it was up to her to initiate any conversation that might take place between them.

She cleared her throat delicately. "London seems to be having very fine weather, my lord."

"Yet it has been damp and foggy in the late evening, has it not, Your Serene Highness?"

Did he suspect?

She swallowed with some minor difficulty and allowed, "I suppose it has."

Their eyes met for an instant only. "Do you enjoy flowers, Your Serene Highness?"

The question seemed guileless enough. "As a matter of fact, I do, Lord Graystone."

He was pleasant and amiable as he made polite and impersonal conversation, yet Cecile sensed something beneath the pleasantries and the amiability.

"I imagine that Saint-Simeon has excellent climate for growing roses," he proposed.

She answered truthfully yet with great care. "Saint-Simeon enjoys the perfect climate for growing roses."

"Roses are plentiful."

"We have an abundance of roses and flower gardens in my native country."

"Do you enjoy walking in the flower gardens of Saint-Simeon?" he inquired.

What was he getting at?

If the eyes were truly the mirror of the soul, then hers must be reflecting her inner turmoil. "I try to take a daily outing for an hour or two in the palace gardens."

He tilted his head somewhat to one side. "So you are a great walker, as well."

Cecile wasn't convinced she would refer to herself as a *great* walker. Although she would go so far as to acknowledge that she had found physical exercise to be a welcome balm to a sometimes troubled mind and heart.

"I enjoy the peacefulness of a garden," she allowed.

"And the solitude?"

She paused. "Yes, and the solitude."

Her dance partner glanced over her shoulder at the huge crowds of people crammed into the ballroom. "At least you have ample chaperons on hand this evening."

Dear Lord, he knew.

The breath caught in Cecile's throat. Her heart sank to her feet. Lord Graystone had recognized her. She must be very careful and very discreet until it could no longer be denied.

"I am not certain I comprehend your meaning, my lord," she confessed.

He made his meaning perfectly clear. "You may recall that I mentioned the absence of a suitable chaperon during our unexpected meeting in the key garden, madam."

He knew.

She would—could—pretend no longer. Not with this man of all men.

Cecile deliberately dropped her voice to a confidential level. "You know."

"I know."

Her curiosity was piqued. "How?"

He waited until they had steered past several couples before revealing, "I recognized your voice."

"I see." Cecile took a fortifying breath. She could only hope and pray that James Gray was the honorable man she believed him to be. "No one must find out."

Her companion nodded his head. "It would be an unfortunate turn of events if they did."

She was frank to the point of indiscretion. "It would be a disaster if they did."

There was something in his expression and manner that reassured her even before Graystone stated unequivocally, "I would never allow that to happen."

She did not bother to hide her relief from him. "You won't tell a soul."

"I won't tell a soul."

They glided around the ballroom: it was an out-of-focus swirl of bright lights and splashes of black and white. Only James—she dared to say his name silently to herself—was in focus.

"I understand now why you claimed that anonymity was a blessing," he said.

She couldn't prevent the sigh that escaped her lips. "Blessed anonymity."

"It's ironic, of course."

"What is?"

He proceeded to explain, albeit briefly. "Nearly two years ago I was journeying home from India when I received a severe and damaging blow to the head. For a very long time I couldn't recollect where I was going or why or even who I was." She wondered if he realized that his hand was clenched into a fist at her waist. "All I wanted was to remember. Yet I could not."

Cecile grasped the situation immediately. "And I would like, if only for a few moments, to forget."

He took in and let out a deep breath before he responded. "One is as much a curse as the other."

Amazed by her own temerity, she said, "I was hoping you wouldn't find out who I am."

He was curious. "Why?"

"It changes everything."

"Everything?"

Cecile reconsidered. "Some things."

Graystone continued to probe. "What things?"

She put it simply. "The way people treat me, and the manner in which they speak to me."

A frown formed between his quicksilver eyes. There was a tautness around his mouth. "Am I treating you differently or speaking to you differently, madam?"

Cecile thought about the matter for a moment or two. "You are not, sir."

He apparently decided to continue with his customary candor. "The circumstances of our initial meeting were unconventional." Broad yet elegantly clad shoulders were raised and lowered in a semblance of a shrug. "I am unconventional. Perhaps you are as well."

"Perhaps I am," she agreed.

"You will always be first a woman to me, madam, and then a princess."

It was all Cecile Girardet had ever wanted: to be regarded as a woman. It was what she rarely—it was what she had *never*—secured from any man save this one.

She must learn more about James Gray. "Do you think you are unconventional because you were abroad for a time?"

"For a time?" The masculine mouth curved humorlessly. "I spent fifteen years in Bhárat."

Cecile suddenly realized how naive she sounded. "Fifteen years is a very long time."

The Earl of Graystone let out a slow breath. "It seemed like a lifetime."

"You must have still been a youth when you left England," she ventured.

"I was not yet twenty."

So young, Cecile reflected, to be so far from home.

Her curiosity and interest were genuine enough. "Do you speak the language?"

James Gray's expression didn't change. "I am familiar with one or two of the local northern dialects, in addition to classical Sanskrit and Hindi."

She regarded him with open amazement. "That is impressive, indeed, sir."

"In context I think not, madam. There are well over eight hundred regional dialects in India."

She blinked rapidly. "That is astounding."

"To a linguist it is mind-boggling."

"Are you a linguist, Lord Graystone?"

"I speak a few words in a number of languages, Your Serene Highness. I comprehend slightly more than I speak. But I am not a linguist."

Cecile wasn't sure she concurred, but there was no sense in debating the issue.

"Have you seen the Taj Mahal, sir?"

"I have, madam."

"Is it everything that they claim it is?"

"What do they claim?"

"That it is the most beautiful building in the world," she announced a little breathlessly.

A bemused expression made its appearance upon James Gray's darkly attractive features. "There is only one other place on earth that I consider more beautiful."

"What place is that?"

"Graystone Abbey, which, as you may have surmised, is a prejudiced viewpoint on my part."

"I think I should like to visit this Graystone Abbey of yours," she remarked.

"Perhaps you will while you are in England."

"I would also like to see the Taj Mahal, of course," Cecile added as an afterthought. "To think that Shah Jahan mourned his beloved wife so much that he had a white marble mausoleum of unequaled beauty and splendor built for her."

"She was his favorite wife, after all."

Cecile raised one eyebrow slightly. "Should I ask how many wives Shah Jahan had?"

"Somewhat fewer than the number of Indian dialects in existence, I would say."

"In that case, I prefer conventional wisdom when it comes to matrimony."

He seemed puzzled. "Conventional wisdom?"

She enjoyed the prospect of teasing him. "One wife is, or should be, enough for any man."

"One wife may even be more than enough," he said with sardonic humor.

It was some little time, and they had made another full turn around the ballroom floor, before Graystone offered, "There is another reason for my unconventionality."

He obviously wanted her to inquire as to what it was. So Cecile did. "What is that?"

"I never expected to inherit the title, the properties, or the responsibilities that went with being the Earl of Graystone. I was the younger son, and as such I was permitted to go my own way and determine my own course." He was surprisingly straightforward with her. "It was frequently an unorthodox course."

"How I envy you," she disclosed.

"In what way?"

In so many ways. "In the independence you have achieved. In the freedom you have enjoyed to travel the world as you will, when you will, where you will."

A ghost of a smile flitted across her partner's patrician features. "Now we are back to our discussion of what a man may do that a lady may not," he pointed out.

"I suppose we are," she acknowledged.

"Surely you would not wish to be a man," he speculated.

Cecile felt her face turn very warm. "I only wish to be granted the same prerogatives that a gentleman enjoys."

At least Lord Graystone was too polite to laugh at

her. "You might as well wish for the moon and the stars while you're at it, Your Serene Highness."

She knew he was right.

Their waltz was quickly drawing to a close. Cecile did not wish for her dance with the earl to be over quite so soon. She glanced toward the orchestra, caught the attention of the conductor, and made a subtle gesture with her hand. The conductor bowed respectfully and raised his baton. Without missing a beat, the musicians began to play the popular waltz again from the beginning.

If there was a raised eyebrow scattered here and there amongst those attending the ball in her honor, Cecile of Saint-Simeon did not care a whit. What was the sense in being a princess if one did not occasionally enjoy a small privilege or two as a result?

She picked up their conversation as if nothing out of the ordinary had occurred. "We have unusual discussions, sir."

"We do, indeed, madam."

She was forthright. "I rather enjoy them."

"As do I."

She followed his lead around the great ballroom, surprised that they managed so well together. He never once trounced on her toes or faltered in his movements. It was almost as if they had waltzed together their entire lives.

"You are an accomplished dancer, my lord."

Graystone put his head back and laughed unselfconsciously. It was an unexpected and joyous sound. It was a sound Cecile found was very much to her liking.

"Pray tell, sir, what is so amusing?" she inquired.

"I would expect to be complimented on almost anything else before my skill on the dance floor," he declared. "I can't even remember the last time I attended a ball or danced with a lady. It must be years and years ago. If fact, when I was informed earlier this evening by Count Dupre that I was to be honored with a waltz, I suddenly realized I should have practiced."

"I cannot imagine why," Cecile said, speaking the truth. "You are a wonderful dancer."

The gentleman's amusement was still apparent. "I don't believe it is me."

"What is it, then?"

"It is you, of course."

It was meant as a simple compliment. Simple, yet sincere. Cecile of Saint-Simeon had heard enough insincere flattery in her twenty-three years to tell the difference.

The question was: Why was her heart beating all of a sudden in double time?

James Gray liked to think that he was a man who kept his wits about him. A clear head, a cold heart, and icy Himalayan waters running through his veins instead of warm human blood: Those had often been the kind of compliments paid to him.

He'd had to learn how to maintain his composure—some called him utterly fearless, but he considered a man without fear a fool—under the most threatening and dangerous circumstances. More than once his enviable self-control had meant the difference between life and death, not only for himself, but for others.

Then why was he tempted to recklessly throw caution to the wind now?

Because he wanted answers.

Because he wanted to blurt out every question that had been plaguing him for the past year.

Because he wanted to haul this lovely young woman off the parqueted floor of the grand ballroom and into a secluded corner of the adjoining terrace and find out who the bloody hell she was and what the bloody hell was going on.

Because he wanted to pull her into his arms and kiss her until they were both breathless, mindless, heedless.

It seemed he was quite mad after all.

Nevertheless, the temptation and the thoughts persisted. They niggled at James and would not leave him be. For he was certain that hers was the face he had seen again and again in his dreams.

It couldn't be, of course.

She was Her Serene Highness, Princess Cecile of Saint-Simeon. The very proud and very beautiful Princess Cecile of Saint-Simeon with her coal-black hair and her clear blue eyes: hair the shade of the midnight sky on a starless evening and eyes like the Mediterranean Sea on a cloudless day in high summer.

Or the incredible color of the large faceted blue stone adorning the front of her tiara.

What had the gossiping young socialites whispered about the gemstone?

James remembered. It was the only one of its kind in the world. It had been named for the princess, herself. It was called Cecilite.

The music was drawing to a close. This time the princess would not dare to signal the orchestra to play the waltz again. It was remarkable that she had already done so once.

A hundred questions, a thousand questions, still plagued him, but this wasn't the time or the place to ask a single one of those questions. Instead, James stated, "Our dance is about to conclude, madam."

"Indeed, it is, sir."

"To my regret."

She looked briefly disconcerted. "And to mine."

"There is much I have not said to you."

A short, brittle pause followed. Then, "There is even more I have not spoken about to you, sir."

"We must be discreet."

"We must be very discreet." Apprehensive eyes were raised to meet his. "Perhaps a woman in white will walk in the private key garden tomorrow night."

"Perhaps I will chance to meet the lady."

"Perhaps."

James Gray lowered his voice. The words were out of his mouth before he could think better of expressing them. "I promise . . . I will find you."

Cecile of Saint-Simeon fell back half a step on the heels of her white satin slippers and stared up at him. Then she collected herself and said courteously, "Thank you for the waltz, Lord Graystone."

"It was my pleasure, Your Serene Highness."

James bowed his head politely and escorted her back to the royal enclave.

Her last words to him were, "Good-bye, sir."

And his were, "*Au revoir*, madam."

Living well was said to be the best revenge.

The adage was only partially true. He had lived, breathed, plotted, and dreamt his revenge night after night, year after year, even decade after decade. Now it was all coming to fruition, and the anticipation was sweet, indeed.

For revenge had been the one, overwhelming, driving, *secret* force in his life. And he was determined to have it whatever the cost. Indeed, he had accumulated wealth, power, and far-reaching influence all in the name of exacting his revenge.

When it was all said and done, his retaliation would be complete, absolute, and utterly without mercy. There would be no room for pity, no matter how pitiable the circumstances. There would be no appealing to his better nature; he had none. There would be no invoking his nobler side; he knew himself to be without nobility.

He took no prisoners.

Rodolphe Girardet licked his lips as he watched his niece dancing with the Earl of Graystone. His plans were going even better than he could have hoped.

First, Cecile had come to him, here in England, here in London, where he was in control.

Now it was time for her to fall in love: mind and body, heart and soul. Completely. Wholly. Hopelessly. The Earl of Graystone would do as well as the next man, and perhaps better than most.

Then, just when happiness seemed to be within her grasp, he would strike like a cobra: swiftly and deadly.

Rodolphe Girardet smiled and licked his lips again, savoring every morsel of perverse gratification.

It was all too delicious.

"What in the world can you be contemplating that makes you smile with such sheer pleasure, Your Serene Highness?" purred Lady Pale, who appeared suddenly at his elbow, diamonds glittering upon her well-displayed décolletage.

"I was thinking they make a handsome couple," Rodolphe replied as the pair concluded their waltz and James Gray proceeded to escort his niece in the direction of the royal enclosure.

Immediately attentive, Lady Pale's brilliant amber eyes followed the direction of his gaze. "I have never seen that man before." One pale porcelain-like hand fluttered to the expanse of pale porcelain skin revealed by her simple but stunning evening gown. Moira had been wise enough to wear a costume that did not attempt to compete with the spectacular necklace draped around her throat. "Who is he?"

Rodolphe instilled a suitable amount of interest into his voice. "The Earl of Graystone."

One finger paused to stroke the large center stone. "I thought the Earl of Graystone was middle-aged, married, and preferred country life to town."

"That was this gentleman's elder brother, Thomas Gray, who is now deceased. James Gray is recently back from India to claim his title and his inheritance." The prince had it on the best authority.

Moira was Moira. She was practically salivating. "James Gray is very attractive."

"And very rich," he added, knowing full well that telling her about a handsome, eligible man who also possessed a large fortune was like dangling a delectable carrot in front of a donkey.

"The Earl of Graystone has one of the oldest and most respected titles in the country," she said.

"So I have heard, as well."

"Do you believe Her Serene Highness is interested in the gentleman?" the countess inquired.

"My niece had the orchestra play their waltz a second time," Rodolphe mentioned nonchalantly.

"How intriguing."

He had expected Moira to find that tidbit intriguing. For she would enjoy nothing more than to gain the attention—in or out of bed—of the man in whom the princess had showed an interest.

It was her nature.

Depraved as it was.

"Now, Countess," Rodolphe deliberately began in a reprimanding tone that he knew she disliked, "I believe the gentleman must be considered off limits to you."

"Don't 'now Countess' me," the beautiful woman spat in rebuttal. "I may take an interest in any gentleman I wish to."

Rodolphe Girardet bit down hard on the inside of his mouth, drawing blood. He must be careful not to smile too quickly or give himself away too soon.

After all, Moira wasn't utterly a stupid cow. And he was counting on her notorious appetite for men.

In the end, her seduction of the Earl of Graystone would make his revenge all the sweeter.

Chapter Seven

I t is time we—that is, you and I—had our chat, Goodenough," James Gray declared, having summoned his valet to the study of Cork House.

It was the morning after the grand ball given in Princess Cecile's honor. Breakfast was finished, newspapers were read, invitations had been responded to, Parliament was not yet in session, and Graystone was ready to start his day.

Indeed, James found himself literally chomping at the bit to get started.

He paced back and forth before the oversize solidmahogany desk that dominated the room. There was an equally large globe beside the desk. He gave it a whirl with the flat of his hand and spotted Bhárat several times as the Indian subcontinent flew by.

"Actually the name India is of Greek origin rather than Indian," he remarked, thinking aloud.

"Indeed, my lord." Goodenough had entered the study through the side entrance off the servants' hallway and had advanced exactly three steps into the room: no more, no less.

His valet was a precise man.

And he, himself, was no longer in Bhárat, James

reflected with no small measure of regret. Which meant that he was no longer operating in familiar territory. Here in England, especially here in London, he was a stranger.

A stranger in a strange land.

He knew exactly what needed to be done. He even knew how to go about doing it. But he must be discreet. He must be circumspect. He must be careful.

He must be damned careful.

There were forces at work in this business that he could only begin to guess at. Furthermore, he had reached the conclusion sometime during the night that he could not do the job alone. (It had been an exceptionally long, restless, wakeful night, which he had decided to put to good use by examining the problem from every possible perspective.) He required assistance.

Goodenough's assistance.

James began to pace back and forth again in front of the desk, hands loosely linked behind his back, fingers intertwined, brows furrowed, eyes boring holes into the Savonnerie carpet beneath his feet.

He paused and turned.

Goodenough was still standing at attention: head held high, shoulders squared, back straight, feet together, gaze unswervingly fixed somewhere over his employer's right shoulder, chin slightly raised.

James did not wish to make this an inquisition. In fact, he desired just the opposite.

He cleared his throat and made an attempt to put his valet at ease. "How long have we known each other, Goodenough?"

"Scarcely a month, my lord."

"That long?" It wasn't long at all, of course. "You came very highly recommended. Your credentials are impeccable." As impeccable as the young man's appearance.

Goodenough's expression never altered. "Thank you, my lord."

James picked up a porcelain piece from the desk. It was one of a pair of vigorously modelled *famille verte* horses, in a recumbent but rising position, bridled for riding and positioned on an oval porcelain base, rendered, he would judge, at the turn of the last century and originating in Canton. "I believe you were previously in the household of the Duke of Deakin."

"I was, my lord." Goodenough was good enough to expand. "My uncle—my mother's elder brother—Jenkins, became valet to His Grace after Her Grace promoted the previous valet, Bunter, to his current position of butler."

James assumed it would all make sense to him sooner or later.

Goodenough went on. "The Duchess of Deakin is, if I may be so bold as to say so, my lord, the most organized person I have ever had the honor of knowing."

High praise, indeed.

James was curious. "Under the circumstances, what made you decide to leave the duke and duchess's service?"

"I believe Their Graces regarded the change as a wise career move for me, my lord."

James was somewhat taken aback. "Would you care to explain that?"

"Jenkins was named valet to His Grace less than two years ago. Bunter—"

"The valet promoted to butler?"

"Exactly so, my lord. Well, Bunter is also a relatively young man. There would be no place for me to advance to within the household for years, possibly for decades."

"I see." James Gray wasn't altogether certain that he did see, of course.

"Frankly Their Graces felt it was a waste of my talents," he recounted.

Modest fellow, Goodenough.

"May I speak freely, my lord?"

"By all means, do."

"All men may be created equal, my lord, but not all men *are* equal," Goodenough commenced.

James couldn't wait to see where his newly hired valet was going with this one. For sometime in the middle of their "chat," Goodenough had assumed control of the conversation.

He went on. "Through your association by marriage with the Marquess of Cork, the Duke and Duchess of Deakin are acquainted, naturally, with both you and your family. Several months ago they were made aware of your need for a personal servant. Someone you could trust implicitly. Someone you could rely on without fail. Special circumstances and certain conditions were mentioned. In short, my lord, your reputation preceded you. I do not think I would have left the household of Their Graces for anyone but yourself."

Graystone was stunned. And moved. It was a full minute before he managed to utter a succinct, "Thank you."

"It will be an honor to serve you, my lord, in whatever capacity you need me."

This was the opening James Gray had been waiting for, but he wasn't prepared to take the direct approach just yet. "I realize this has been a difficult first month, Goodenough. You were hardly settled in at Graystone Abbey when we were up and away to London."

The change in residence didn't seem to bother his manservant. "One must always be prepared, my lord."

James wore a pathway between the desk and a row of east-facing windows that flooded the study with morning sunlight and that overlooked a perimeter of mature lime trees situated on either side of the street. "I suppose so." He wasn't getting any closer to the subject he wished to discuss. Perhaps the time for subtlety was over. "I must be blunt, Goodenough."

"Your wish is my command, my lord."

So he had been informed by his valet before. "Are you a man of honor, sir?"

For a time the younger man regarded him with hooded eyelids. Then John Goodenough raised his chin a fraction of an inch further in the air and looked straight into James Gray's eyes with a clear, intelligent gaze of his own. They were not servant and master in that moment, but two men seeing each other, perhaps, for the first time.

"I am," he declared.

"Are you also a man of discretion?"

"I am."

"Can you keep your own counsel?"

"It is absolutely essential if a manservant wants to do well in this world, my lord."

"What do you know of me, Goodenough?"

James witnessed his valet's sudden hesitation and understandable wariness.

Stalling, the question was repeated. "What do I know of you, my lord?"

"Please speak."

Goodenough spoke. "You are thirty-five years old, Lord Graystone. You never expected to inherit the title and lands that were your elder brother's, so you left Oxford and went out to India to make your own fortune. That was nearly fifteen years ago."

"Continue."

"You purchased and managed a large tea plantation. You were very good at raising tea. In fact, you are considered to be very good at everything you do." This declaration was followed by a minute or two of hemming and hawing.

Another nudge. "Go on."

"There is the rumor . . ."

"Rumor?"

"Conjecture."

"Conjecture?"

Goodenough cleared his throat. "It is whispered in certain elite circles, my lord, that while you were

out in India you did more than simply manage a
tea plantation."

James Gray was astounded. How the devil had
Goodenough found out about that?

"How—?"

His manservant raised his hands, palms facing out,
as if to say *Wait*! "Believe me, Lord Graystone, your
secret is safe with me. I will take it to the grave," he
vowed solemnly.

It was a minute, perhaps two, before James inquired, "Is there anything else?"

It turned out that Goodenough was an absolute
fount of information. He ticked the items off one by
one on his fingers, and when he ran out of fingers
he kept going, all the same. "You are well read. You
are known to be a true horseman. You rarely drink
spirits of any kind. You do not suffer fools gladly.
You are an expert marksman with a pistol and few
would dare to cross swords with you. You have recovered your health and your vigor entirely, if not
your memory. You are single. You have been back
in England for nearly a year and during that entire
time you have remained celibate."

James sputtered, "Good God, man!"

Goodenough conveyed, without the slightest sign
of embarrassment or hint of prudery, and by way of
an explanation, "I did mention to you, my lord, that
I am something of an amateur sleuthhound."

James gave a crack of laughter. "And apparently
a first-rate sleuthhound at that."

"Armchair variety only," Goodenough demurred.

"Perhaps it's time we changed that," James suggested.

His valet blinked owlishly and swallowed. "I beg your pardon, my lord."

"Only if you are willing, of course."

"I am afraid I do not understand," came the admission.

"How is your memory, Goodenough?"

"Excellent."

James nodded his head with satisfaction. "Nothing must ever be written down on paper," he directed. "Paper always leaves a trail that can be traced."

"Like the residue of tobacco."

"Quite so." James continued in the same vein. "Are you adept at disguises?"

His manservant screwed up his face in contemplation. "I think I could be, my lord. I have a certain flair for dramatics."

James was perfectly serious when he advised, "There could also be an element of danger in what we are about to do."

"There is always an element of danger in life, my lord. One could be thrown from a horse, or run down by a carriage, or contract a mysterious and incurable fever, or eat a piece of bad beef, or be set upon by thieves and scoundrels—"

James cut him off. "I get the picture."

Goodenough had gotten the picture as well. He rubbed his hands together in eager anticipation. "When do we start, my lord?"

"Today."

"Where do we start?"

"There are certain personages that I would like to know more about," James informed him. He proceeded to verbally give Goodenough a list of names.

"May I inquire, what kind of information you are seeking?"

"I don't know."

Goodenough comprehended. "Ah, but you will know when you hear it."

"Precisely."

"I won't let you down, my lord."

"I know you won't, Goodenough."

"You know what we amateur sleuthhounds say, my lord?" he ventured.

James had to confess that he did not.

Goodenough smiled for the first time in their acquaintance. It was a subtle and somewhat sly smile. It was quick and clever and slightly predatory in nature. "The game's afoot."

It was a deadly game.

For his life could very well be at risk—again—James deliberated later that same day after he and Goodenough had concluded their talk. Certainly the reputations of others were at stake and possibly even their physical well-being.

In the end James Gray might have his answers. But he would not necessarily recover his memory.

What if he were never to know where he had been and what he had done during those missing months of his life? Would he be able to make peace with himself, calm his inner fears, exorcise his demons?

There was an ancient and rather obscure Sanskrit

saying. *Tat tvam asi:* Thou art that. Loosely translated James Gray knew what it meant. What is . . . is.

He was who he was.

And what would be, would be.

Chapter Eight

Her dream always began and ended the same way.

It began with need, with desire, with a white hot passion, with a man's strong, muscular arms wrapped sensually, protectively around her, his mouth on her mouth, his lips on her lips, and with kisses: kisses that burned, kisses that soothed, kisses that excited, kisses that calmed her fears, kisses that seemed to change the color of the world around her from pale pink to vibrant red to deep, dusky purple.

Her dream began with a resonant male baritone beseeching her, cajoling her, reassuring her, seducing her, and with a pair of extraordinary eyes capturing hers.

It began with a door opening just a crack—somehow she was conscious that it was the gentleman who opened the door—just enough to allow her a glimpse of another world where hopes were fulfilled, visions realized, and longings satisfied. A world where heaven might, indeed, be found right here on earth.

The dream always ended as a nightmare seething with emotion, rife with confusion and misunderstanding, with voices raised in anger, with the threat of violence thick in the air: It could almost be seen, smelled, tasted, touched.

And the nightmare always concluded with the frightening knowledge that he was never very far away.

Tonight Cecile had awakened as she had on so many other nights: heart pounding, pulse racing, lungs gasping for breath, her nightgown plastered to her body, her hair damp and disheveled.

Without bothering to light a candle she threw back the covers, padded across the bedchamber to the dressing table, and picked up a silver hairbrush engraved with her monogram. Her braid had already partially come undone. It took very little to complete the task. Then she yanked the brush through her hair again and again until the muscles in her arm ached with the effort.

Tonight was the night.

Soon she would dress, pull a hooded cape around her head and shoulders—she had wisely decided that a dark color would be better suited to her clandestine activities—and venture forth to meet James Gray in the key garden.

It wasn't as if she had any choice in the matter.

She could trust no one.

She must trust someone.

She required help.

She required his help.

After months of preparation, it was time to start putting her plan into action, and to do that she must have a gentleman like James Gray firmly ensconced on her side.

She must have James Gray. No one else would do.

Cecile put the hairbrush down, and quietly and efficiently went about changing from her nightgown into her outdoor clothing. Since she couldn't manage to tight-lace a corset on her own, she wore none. Since it was essential that she move through Guest House with as little noise and with as few impediments as possible, she also dispensed with the hampering layers of petticoats and the usual assortment of rigid female undergarments and paraphernalia.

It was nearly three o'clock when, key in hand, Cecile slipped out of the grand house in which she was staying and made for the gate of the private garden.

James Gray was waiting for her as he had promised.

"You're here," she whispered a bit breathlessly.

"I'm here," he said, stepping out from behind the concealment of a nearby beech tree.

"Thank you for coming, sir."

"There is no reason to thank me, madam."

There might well be a reason before this night was over, Cecile wanted to say to him. Instead, she suggested, "Shall we walk?"

Graystone offered her his arm. She accepted and placed a gloved hand on the sleeve of his coat.

It was not so cool nor so damp as the first night when they had unexpectedly met in the garden. Once there was some distance between themselves and the wrought-iron gates, Cecile pushed the hood of her cloak back and let it fall to her shoulders.

"Did you have any difficulty getting away from Guest House?" he inquired.

Wraithlike she had slipped from dark hallway to dark hallway, shadow to shadow. "None."

"Are you certain no one saw you leave?"

"I'm certain." She reciprocated. "Did anyone observe you quitting Cork House?"

His answer was as emphatic as her own. "No."

Cecile was curious. It was not, however, idle curiosity. "Is there anyone you can trust?"

James Gray nodded. "My valet, Goodenough." There was a pause. They strolled along the pathway some twenty paces before he said, "And you?"

"My lady-in-waiting, Lady Ann Faraday, but I have tried to keep her ignorant of this business."

"Why?" His inquisitiveness was justified, perhaps, considering the circumstances.

"For her own safety," she stated.

Honesty was always the best policy. In this instance, it must be Cecile's only policy.

Graystone came to a standstill in the middle of the garden path and turned to her. "There is danger?"

"There is grave danger."

He didn't appear in the least surprised by her disclosure. "I thought as much."

It was Cecile's turn to inquire. "Why?"

Tension emanated from the man standing beside her; it was a palpable force. "Gut instincts."

"Do you have keen instincts when it comes to danger?" she asked softly.

The earl's reply was succinct and not particularly modest in nature. "Yes."

"Are they better than keen?"

There was a countable silence.

"Far better," he admitted at last.

Again, no modesty on his part, but Cecile didn't believe that James Gray was bragging or exaggerating his abilities. Indeed, he had seemed reluctant to tell her of them.

She searched his face for a minute. "May I ask, sir, if your expertly honed skills have something, have anything, to do with the years you spent in India?"

His expression was serious. "They have everything to do with my years in India."

She kept probing. She had to. She had to know. "Were you in great danger?"

"Sometimes."

"Was your life in peril?"

Graystone raised a hand and drove his fingers through the hair at his nape. It was a gesture that conveyed his hesitation in speaking of such matters. "At times it was."

"Have you ever been forced . . ." Here Cecile paused and took a sustaining breath before she tried again. "Have you ever been required to fight in self-defense?"

She couldn't bring herself to ask James Gray if he had killed in defense of himself or others.

The man's handsome face grew tight. It took on a gaunt, and almost familiar, appearance in the pale light cast by a sliver of moon that slipped out every now and then from behind the clouds. "I did whatever had to be done, madam."

Then he was her man.

Without further ado, or further conversation, they walked on, reaching the heart of the private garden, which was in the vicinity of the fountain and the ornamental pool with the gazebo tucked in the background. Here, at least, they were assured of being alone. Here there were no prying eyes. No curious stares. No half-hushed whispers.

Cecile removed her brown kid gloves and slipped them into the pocket of her cloak. She leaned forward slightly, reached out with her hand, and allowed the cool water—it spouted from the mouth of a *verde antique* fish—to trickle through her fingers. "I would like to tell you a story, Lord Graystone."

"It is a true story?"

"It is." She shook the water from her fingertips and inquired, "Do you know the history of Saint-Simeon?"

"To a limited degree," he admitted.

"Then please bear with me, sir, while I give a brief account of my country and my family."

"Please proceed, madam."

So Cecile did. "It is generally accepted that Saint-Simeon was an important port as far back as the Romans." She related in an aside: "Indeed, it was from Saint-Simeon that Julius Caesar embarked when he sailed to Greece to fight Pompey."

He was somewhat more familiar, Graystone said to her, with Roman history.

Cecile wisely decided to make mention only of the notable dates and events. "Even before the Romans, the port of Saint-Simeon dated back to the Phoenicians, who presumably constructed it sometime around the sixth century B.C. But it was the Holy Roman Emperor, himself, who conferred Saint-Simeon on a Genoese prince of the house of Girardet in the early fifteenth century. The first prince of Saint-Simeon was Maximilian I, who ascended the throne in 1426. To make a rather long story—" and truthfully an unnecessary story "—into a relatively short one, sir, for the past four hundred fifty years a direct male descendant of the Girardet family has ruled the principality."

The Earl of Graystone said nothing.

Cecile was a little nonplussed.

Without arrogance, and with all due respect, James Gray finally stated the facts. "There have been Graystones in the region known as Devon, one direct male descendant after another, madam, since before the Crusades, since before the Conqueror, indeed, since before there were Holy Roman Emperors."

Cecile understood. "You come from a very proud and a very ancient family, my lord," she acknowledged.

He gave a courteous and excruciatingly polite reply. "I do, Your Serene Highness."

It was a minute, perhaps two, before she said, "Would you grant me a request?"

His bow was stiff, rather formal and consisted primarily of a nod of his head. "Naturally, if it is within my power to do so, Your Serene Highness."

"Here in this lovely garden, may we dispense with titles, with pomp and circumstance, with the notion of proper or improper protocol, with stifling formalities? May we just be two people, sir, as we were that first night? May we be just you and me?"

There was the merest hint of a smile on his face. "Blessed anonymity?"

She smiled back at him briefly. "Blessed anonymity."

"Your request is happily granted, madam."

Cecile picked up her story where she had left off. "Saint-Simeon is a small kingdom, as you know, but the society is steeped in tradition and ceremony much as the society is here in England."

Her companion concurred.

"When a ruling prince of Saint-Simeon dies . . ." Cecile's voice cracked.

Graystone took a step toward her. "Your father?"

She closed her eyes and shuddered. "Both my father and my mother were killed in a horrible accident."

"My deepest sympathies."

Eyes still closed—if she opened them now Cecile feared the tears would flow—she made a movement with her head that approximated a nod of acknowledgment.

James Gray's voice had softened and taken on a quality of concern intermingled with compassion when he said, "When did the accident occur?"

Cecile opened her eyes. "Nearly two years ago." She swallowed and made herself go on. "My elder brother, Alexandre, is next in line of succession. As dictated by law and custom, the official period of mourning for our father, Maximilian V, and our mother was over several months ago. Alexandre will soon reach the age of majority, which in Saint-Simeon is thirty. Therefore, his formal investiture must take place the first week of September."

Graystone listened intently.

"As is also required by law, and as every ruling prince of Saint-Simeon has done before him, Alexandre must take an inviolable oath in the great cathedral before the archbishop, the visiting dignitaries from a dozen countries, and his assembled subjects. To do so, three objects must be present."

Graystone's attention was fixed on her. "What are the three objects?"

"The state crown of Saint-Simeon, representing the crown of thorns most pitiably placed upon the head of our Lord. The golden scepter of Saint-Simeon, the ultimate emblem of authority and sovereignty. And the sacred chalice of Saint-Simeon, said to contain within its elaborately carved outer casement a small fragment of the Holy Grail itself," she said in reverent tones.

"It sounds very solemn."

"It is."

James Gray must have sensed there was more. He waited patiently for her to continue.

"During the ceremony the crown is to be placed on Alexandre's head. The scepter is to be positioned at his right hand. And he is to drink from the sacred chalice."

"And will he?"

Cecile gave her answer in a desperate whisper. "No."

"Why not?"

After all these months of keeping the secret so closely guarded, of never speaking of it, of scarcely allowing herself to think of it, could she say it aloud now?

Gentle pressure was applied. "Is there a problem?"

She nodded.

"Can you say what it is?"

She moved her head again, knowing it was somehow both a yes and a no.

James Gray was obviously making every effort to be patient with her. "Do you wish to tell me?"

"I wish I did not have to, sir," Cecile blurted out. "I must and yet I am afraid."

"What are you afraid of, madam?"

"There are sinister and villainous forces at work here. The moment I confide my secret to you, I fear your life will be in danger."

Graystone folded his lips in an obstinate line. "You have no choice but to tell me."

Tears sprang to her eyes. "I wish it were not so."

"Do not fear for me," he said, jaw tightening. "I have faced death before and made my peace with it."

Still, Cecile hesitated.

"Tell me this," her companion urged, determined, it seemed, to get to the heart of the problem. "Are you in danger?"

Her voice came out small but firm. "Yes."

That apparently settled the matter for James Gray. He was unflinching and uncompromising when he claimed, "I would not have myself safe while you are in danger. I must know."

"Then you shall," Cecile finally agreed. She took

a deep, sustaining breath. "The crown, the scepter, and the sacred chalice of Saint-Simeon are missing."

That confounded Graystone. "Missing?"

She put it as simply and clearly as she knew how. "They have vanished into thin air. They are gone."

"Gone where?"

The worst of it was over now. She had finally confided her secret to someone, to this gentleman. "Gone from Saint-Simeon. Gone from the carefully guarded tower where they had been safely kept under lock and key since the first prince was crowned over four hundred years ago. Gone after all this time."

"When were they taken?"

"Six months ago."

"How were they gotten to?"

"Someone had a duplicate key. And someone managed to bribe the tower guards, who seemed beyond such a traitorous action. Of course, that part is difficult to ascertain since the guards also disappeared that same night," Cecile related to him. "All except for one man, who was left for dead."

"None of this is public knowledge, I presume."

She dug her teeth into her bottom lip. "Only a handful of people are aware of what has happened. My brother, Alexandre, and several of his—and our late father's—closest advisers."

Graystone arched a dark brow in her direction. "And yourself."

"And myself."

"And the mastermind behind the theft, of course. Lackeys rarely think up these schemes on their own." The earl began to pace back and forth in front of her, raising dust and leaves and garden debris beneath his feet in the process. Then he paused, turned, and gave her a sidelong glance. "What will happen if the missing items are not recovered before your brother's investiture?"

"Then Alexandre cannot be crowned."

"What are the consequences if he isn't crowned?"

The consequences were beyond her imagination and her comprehension, although Cecile had been forced to acknowledge their possibility, even their probability, over and over again during the past six months. "He must forfeit his title, his lands, most of his wealth—" she swallowed hard "—and there is a worse consequence."

"What is it?"

"He must forfeit his country."

Lord Graystone frowned, but he wasted no time or energy on lengthy discourse. "Explain."

"If the male heir to the throne cannot be crowned, then it is as if there were no male heir."

"And—?" he urged.

"And if there is no legitimate male heir, then Saint-Simeon will cease to exist."

"Cease to exist?"

Cecile admonished herself to keep calm. "By law and by treaty, the principality of Saint-Simeon would no longer endure as a separate country. It would become part of France."

Graystone's frown deepened. The lines of concentration on his face appeared etched into his flesh. Suddenly he seemed older—and far more formidable—than she could have envisioned. "This is serious business, indeed."

Cecile tried not to sound as though she was without hope, but there was no denying the gravity of the situation in which the Girardets found themselves. "Unless I can recover the crown, the scepter, and the chalice, and return to Saint-Simeon with them within the next few months, all will be lost."

His mouth curved humorlessly. "Does your brother know what you are about?"

"Yes."

"Are you here with his blessing?"

"Alexandre was eventually made to see that there was no other way."

It had taken every last shred of Cecile's persuasive powers to convince her brother that she must be the one—indeed, she was the only one—who could attempt the recovery of the stolen objects.

"No doubt Prince Alexandre was extremely reluctant to put you in the path of danger," James Gray muttered under his breath.

"I was already in danger," she said quietly. That brought his masculine chin up a notch. "That is, nevertheless, a matter to be discussed another time."

He seemed reluctant but willing to accept that, and went on with his inquisition. "Why are you here in England?"

"The guard."

Graystone was very quick. "The one left for dead who wasn't quite dead?"

She nodded. "The man has still not recovered his health, but he was able to tell us what little he remembered overhearing the night the others left him for dead."

"Which was?"

Cecile had committed the words to memory. " 'The master has promised to reward us handsomely once we reach England with the prizes he seeks.' "

"And if the villains failed?"

"The injured guard claimed it was clear that if the thieves were unsuccessful in obtaining the desired 'prizes,' none of them expected to live to tell the tale."

"I doubt if any of them lived to tell the tale, anyway," James Gray pointed out.

Cecile knew her eyes had grown huge in her face. "Do you believe they were all murdered?"

"Dead men can't talk," was his terse reply.

She was suddenly feeling quite warm; almost faint in fact. Her hand went to the closure at her neck. She undid the fastening and allowed the cape to flutter open.

Graystone took a clean linen handkerchief from his pocket, held it under the cool, clear water spouting from the fish's mouth, squeezed out the excess moisture, and offered it to her without a word.

"Thank you," Cecile murmured, pressing the handkerchief to her forehead, to her cheeks—her skin was strangely hot and feverish to the touch—to the hollow at the base of her throat and finally to the underside of her wrists.

James Gray was watching her, staring at her. He caught himself and quickly looked away. It was some time before he said, "You're welcome." It was even longer before he turned and asked her, "What do you require of me, madam?"

"Your help, sir."

"In recovering the missing items." It was a statement of fact, not a question.

"Exactly."

Her companion eyed her speculatively. "Why did you decide to come to me?"

"Because I believe you to be a gentleman, my lord. A gentleman of his word and a gentleman in whom a lady can put her trust." There were butterflies suddenly flitting about in her stomach. "Because you have faced formidable enemies before, and danger, and even death, and this endeavor will not be one for the fainthearted."

Graystone made a loose fist with one hand, raised it to his mouth for a moment, lightly tapped his knuckles against his lower lip, and thought aloud. "Why steal the state crown, the imperial scepter, and the sacred chalice?"

Cecile wasn't certain she had heard him correctly. "Why steal the crown, the scepter, and the chalice?"

Shrewd eyes stared intently into hers. "They can't be sold on the open market."

"That's true."

"Are they heavily encrusted with gemstones?"

Cecile shook her head. "They aren't spectacular like the British Crown Jewels. The gold, itself, and the few embedded precious gems would be worth a fraction of their value if the pieces were disassembled or melted down."

Broad shoulders were raised and lowered. Then,

apparently still thinking aloud, Graystone asked of no one in particular: "Then why steal them at all?"

Cecile hazarded a guess. "Someone doesn't want Alexandre to be crowned the next ruler of Saint-Simeon."

Intelligent, gray eyes were narrowed in speculation. "Who will gain if your brother doesn't ascend the throne?"

"I can't think of anyone," she confessed. "By treaty the principality would become French, but historically France has shown little interest in Saint-Simeon. Our only asset is a port, and France does not need another port. There has never been any particular political movement to make us part of any country."

"I repeat then: Why would anyone want to abscond with the three symbols of Saint-Simeon sovereignty?"

Cecile raised her chin. "I can think of only one reason."

"What is that?"

"Revenge."

Chapter Nine

If you prick us, do we not bleed? If you tickle us, do we not laugh? If you poison us, do we not die? And if you wrong us, shall we not revenge?' "

James recited a quotation from Shakespeare's *The Merchant of Venice*. Act III. Scene I. It was a dramatic passage recalled from his days at Oxford when he had fancied himself something of a thespian. Ironically his skills as an actor had served him far better in India than they had at university.

Cecile of Saint-Simeon gazed up at him with the bluest eyes he had ever beheld and said pensively and a little sadly: "Shall we not revenge if we *believe* you have wronged us?"

A subtle but important difference, James Gathier Gray was willing to concede.

"Warranted or not, revenge is as likely a motive as any in this case," he hazarded. "And perhaps more likely than most." He stopped himself from saying anything more.

The question was, of course, who believed the House of Girardet had so grievously wronged them. Who wanted, coveted, even craved vengeance? Who felt themselves justified in seeking their revenge using means that would, in the end, affect thousands of innocent people as well as those presumed guilty? Who was the villain: the *bête noire*—the black beast?

James had his opinion on the subject, but he wasn't ready to share it with the princess quite yet. He was certain she would relate the remainder of her story when she was good and ready.

Cecile of Saint-Simeon shivered and rubbed her arms as if she had experienced a sudden chill.

"You're cold."

The lady made another movement with her head that was both yes and no.

It was only sensible to suggest that they seek shelter. "Let's move to the gazebo. At least it's partially enclosed and will provide some measure of protection from the night air," he pointed out.

She agreed.

James led the way around the fountain and along the flagstone path toward the small secluded building. On either side of the walk there was a herbaceous border. Beyond the border were rhododendron in full bloom and azaleas and budding roses. The dramatic backdrop of trees in this section of the garden included ash, beech, oak, hornbeam, monkey puzzle, and Wellingtonia.

A twig snapped under James's foot. A small animal, perhaps a brown squirrel, scurried into the nearby brush. The moon slid in and out from behind the clouds.

The night air was cool, but not cold. There was only the slightest hint of a breeze. The distinctive "who, who" of an owl could be heard close by. The creature must be perched on a tree branch overhead. In the distance—it was almost too far away to be discernible—came the melodious sounds of a fiddle being played.

The princess paused and inclined her head to one side. A swath of long hair tumbled around her shoulders and down her back like black silk. She listened intently.

"Do you think it's the same musician we heard the first night we were in the garden?" she finally inquired.

James thought so and said as much as they made their way toward the garden's summerhouse.

The gazebo had been constructed in the 1820s in the style of a classic Greek temple, rather like a miniature Parthenon. All things Greek had been the rage in London during the first quarter of the century as a result of the arrival of the Elgin Marbles.

The magnificent sculpted figures, which had once graced the temple of Athena Parthenos on the Acropolis in Athens, and which had been bought and transported back to England by the British ambassador to Turkey, Thomas Bruce, Seventh Earl of Elgin, were now housed in the British Museum.

Once they reached the mock Grecian temple, James brushed the leaves and debris from the solitary stone bench. Even the bench had been done in the Greek style, he noted, sporting colonnades in place of traditional legs.

Removing his coat, he spread it out for the lady to sit on. It was no sacrifice on his part since he wasn't in the least bit chilled. In fact, he thought the evening rather warm.

Cecile of Saint-Simeon sat down.

James remained standing.

"Please sit," she requested, indicating the place next to her on the bench.

So James sat.

She didn't immediately broach the topic of the theft or the subject of revenge. Instead, his *compagnon de nuit* looked past him, somewhere over his left shoulder, and inquired as to the identity of what was described by her as "an unusual object on a substantial stone pedestal some little distance from us.

"Do you know what it is, sir?"

James turned and glanced in the same general direction. He had made a fairly comprehensive examination of the key garden and its assorted adornments, embellishments, and follies earlier that evening while he was awaiting her arrival.

"As a matter of fact, I do, madam. According to a small bronze plaque at its base, the object in question is a seventeenth-century polyhedron sundial."

That secured her interest.

He went on to explain in greater detail. "Sundials of this type were traditionally found in English gardens from early Tudor times until the late seventeenth century. This particular one not only has a mechanism that tells the time in different latitudes, but there is a moon-dial incorporated into its workings."

"A moon-dial." The word was softly repeated as if it were poetry.

Indeed, James reflected, when Cecile spoke—he said her name silently to himself—it *was* poetry.

She gave a sigh and began to reminisce. "When I was a girl of ten or eleven years my family traveled into the countryside for a holiday." Her voice took on a wistful quality. "I remember there was a picturesque village, a grand and rather imposing hunting lodge surrounded by a verdant forest, a silver river filled with silver fish, and a pristine lake. On one particularly clear night we were standing on the shore, watching the moon rise over the water. The lighted path it made across the lake took my breath away. I asked my mother if there was a word to describe such a beautiful sight."

James was entranced. "Is there?"

She made a subtle movement with her hands. "The word is moon-glade."

"Moon-glade," he echoed.

Cecile of Saint-Simeon inhaled deeply and then slowly exhaled. She seemed reluctant to return to the unpleasant subject of revenge. But it could not be avoided.

As if steeling herself for what lay ahead, she straightened her already perfectly straight back and shoulders, folded her gloveless hands in her lap—fingers tightly interlaced, knuckles white—and cleared her throat. "I suppose we must speak of this business of the theft and the motive behind it."

"I suppose we must."

She cited a French proverb. " '*Le vrai peut quelquefois n'être pas vraisemblable.*' "

James translated for his own benefit. "Truth may sometimes be improbable."

"Or truth is stranger than fiction," she paraphrased. Lips were wetted before she confessed, "I am afraid."

Again?

His brows snapped into a frown. "Of who?"

"Not of who," she said.

His curiosity was aroused. "Of what, then?"

"Your reaction," came the guarded admission. "I am afraid you will think I've lost my mind when I tell you who I suspect of being the thief." The statement was almost immediately modified. "Or, as you have no doubt rightly put it, who I suspect of being the mastermind behind the theft."

"Rest assured, madam, I won't think you have lost your mind," James said to her.

Should he make the whole process less painful for the princess by naming the blackguard himself?

What if he were wrong?

He wasn't wrong.

Nevertheless, James Gray found himself feeling distinctly ill at ease now that he was about to accuse one of her own blood relations of treachery. Indeed, of high treason.

What was, was.

What would be, would be.

He no longer had any choice in the matter. The truth was the truth. It must be faced head on.

Graystone squared his shoulders. "I believe the villain is your uncle, Prince Rodolphe, is it not?"

They were sitting close enough so that he saw the

lady's eyes widen in surprise. He heard the startled intake of air as it rushed into her lungs. She held her breath for a minute, perhaps even longer, before normal, involuntary breathing resumed. He sensed her utter astonishment and her bewilderment.

"How in the world . . . ?"

James wouldn't keep her in suspense. "It was last night at the ball given in your honor. Count Dupre and I were approaching the royal enclosure prior to our waltz. I looked up and saw a tall, dark gentleman standing beside a young woman dressed in white. At the time I didn't know who he was."

"You didn't know who I was, either," she reminded him.

That was true.

James knew his eyes had taken on a hard sheen. "One thing was clear to me, however."

"What was it?"

"The young woman in white—you, as it turned out—either disliked the gentleman intensely . . . or was very much afraid of him." Here James paused and shot a quick sideways glance at her before continuing. "Or both."

"I see."

"So I asked the Count to acquaint me with the man's name," James concluded.

"It was my uncle, Prince Rodolphe."

"It was your uncle, Prince Rodolphe."

Suddenly the princess became agitated. She shot off the bench and began to pace back and forth within the confines of the gazebo, wringing her hands and speaking more to herself than to him:

"Here I was convinced that I had become something of an accomplished actress. I told myself that no one would ever guess my true feelings about my uncle." She stopped and drew the folds of her dark fur-lined cape around her. Her voice was small and very close to a hoarse whisper. "Now it seems that I was fooling only myself."

James hastened to reassure her. "I don't think anyone knows but the two of us."

She resumed her seat beside him. "What, pray tell, makes you say that?"

In this instance, James didn't dare blurt out the whole truth. He couldn't profess that night after night he had dreams about being in bed with a beautiful, young, naked woman. And, despite all evidence to the contrary, he believed her to be that woman. He couldn't say he knew her and yet he didn't know her.

Hell and damnation, it was an awkward situation for a man to find himself in.

So James Gray, Earl of Graystone, fell back on his customary rationale. "Gut instincts."

A momentary smile appeared on the lovely face. "Those finely-honed-in-India instincts of yours?"

"The very ones."

"Then let us hope and pray that you are the only one who wasn't fooled."

He had the same hope and the same prayer.

Cecile of Saint-Simeon lightly ran her fingertips back and forth across the expensive material beneath them on the Grecian-style bench. James swore he could almost feel the caress as if she were stroking his flesh instead of his coat. He suddenly had an incredible—a nearly overwhelming—urge to take this woman in his arms, to crush her against him, and to kiss her.

Graystone was well aware that he hadn't been interested in a female for some time. As his valet had been good enough to point out that morning during their conversation in the study at Cork House: He had been celibate since his return to England . . . and God alone knew how long before that.

He thought only of the woman in his dreams. She occupied his mind waking and sleeping, to the exclusion of anyone and everyone else of her sex.

Or she had until now.

Cecile of Saint-Simeon busied herself for several minutes making minor—and, in his opinion, unnecessary—adjustments to his coat-as-seat-cushion.

The moon slipped behind a thick bank of clouds. The shadows closed around them. The air in the garden was suddenly so still James could hear, or perhaps he only sensed, his own breathing and hers. The night was nearly silent.

"I would like to tell you the rest of my story, if I may," the princess said at last.

"Please do."

And so she did.

"My father was the elder of two sons born some five years apart, and, therefore, he was the heir to the throne of Saint-Simeon. My uncle, Rodolphe Girardet, is the younger son. He has always fervently proclaimed that he would have it no other way." The princess paused and seemed to summon her courage before she went on. "But I don't credit those to be his true feelings in the matter."

"What do you credit his true feelings to be?"

"I think from boyhood Prince Rodolphe deeply resented my father for being the future ruler of our country. I think he was insanely jealous of my father for marrying the woman he wanted to wed himself, although her preference and the deepest desires of her heart were always known." She added in a whisper, "From the time she was a girl, my mother was in love with my father."

"And he was in love with her?"

She swallowed with some difficulty and nodded her head. "It was truly love on both sides."

The question flitted through James's mind: Did he believe in that kind of love?

Tears were hastily, impatiently, brushed from pale cheeks as if this wasn't the time or the place for tears, and the lady knew it only too well. "Furthermore, I'm convinced that Prince Rodolphe's exile from Saint-Simeon wasn't voluntary."

"The world believes it to be so."

"I know."

"What do you believe?"

Blue eyes—had the waters of the Mediterranean Sea ever been quite so blue—were raised to meet his. A perfectly shaped and surprisingly determined chin came up. A sweet voice, surely the voice of an angel, gained strength. "I think my father recognized the threat from within. I believe that in order to save himself and to secure the future for his wife, his children, and his country, he had no choice but to banish his younger brother forever."

Christ, this affair went deeper and contained far more treachery than even James had suspected.

The accusations continued. "Rodolphe Girardet is determined to see that my brother—his own nephew—does not assume the throne. He knows what must be in place for the coronation. He is one of the few people with both the means and the motive to carry out such an outrageous act as stealing the 'prizes.'"

"Is he capable of such revenge?"

Her voice was coldly amused. "Aren't we all?"

James rubbed his hand back and forth along his jawline. "Under extenuating circumstances, perhaps."

There was a mirthless laugh from his companion. "In that case, sir, you think better of the world than I do. We humans are capable of a great many things whatever the circumstances."

This was no pampered and protected princess who had lived in some kind of ivory tower, he realized. Indeed, this was a young woman who had apparently seen her share of the world's ugliness, of its meanness and cruelty.

It was also apparent that Cecile of Saint-Simeon had chosen not to tell him everything. That was her privilege, naturally. Perhaps her full confidence would come another day.

One thing was clear: James Gray must keep his wits about him. Rodolphe Girardet was a man of immense wealth, who possessed a unique social position not in one but two countries, and power that extended beyond even those borders. This was no amateur, no dilettante, that he would be dealing with.

This time the enemy was formidable, indeed.

Sometime during the past few minutes James had come to understand that he intended to help the princess find the missing crown, the scepter, and the sacred chalice. She needed him. He couldn't turn his back on her. Nevertheless, he wanted one or two points clarified.

"May I ask what made you reach the conclusion that your uncle was the culprit?"

It was some time before his question was answered. "I don't like his smile."

That wasn't what James had expected her to say. "I beg your pardon, madam."

"I don't like his smile, sir," she repeated. "I don't like his laugh. I don't like his eyes or the cold-hearted manner in which he watches other human beings as if they were some kind of species lower than himself to be observed under a microscope." Cecile of Saint-Simeon drew herself up to her full height—which was impressive even when she was seated—and declared with feeling, "I do not like him."

That hardly made Girardet a criminal.

This was an exceptionally intelligent young woman, however. She had to know that.

"If he has been in exile then surely you haven't encountered your uncle often," James pointed out.

"Until this past week I hadn't seen him in nearly twenty years," she stated.

"Then when did you form this opinion?"

"I have always held this opinion, as you put it.

My parents warned me from the time I was a child. They told me in the strictest confidence that Rodolphe Girardet was never to be trusted."

"Never is a long time."

"Yes," she said with a sigh, ostensibly of regret. "It is."

There had to be more surely. He didn't trust Girardet—indeed, James Gray trusted few men—but that didn't result in an indictment of wrong-doing.

There was an underlying sense of certainty in her voice. "When I reviewed the facts of the case in a detached and analytical manner, there simply was no other candidate."

"So you settled on your uncle by a process of elimination," James elucidated.

"Exactly." The lady paused and then admitted, "He seemed the only logical choice to me."

"Based on deductive reasoning," he verified.

She nodded her head, sending strands of long black hair brushing along her shoulders with a swish-swish-swish. "And based on my woman's intuition."

Which must be somewhat comparable to his own gut instincts, James reflected.

They were skating on very thin ice, in his judgment, relying, at least for the time being, on her woman's intuition, his gut instincts, and too few facts. But he had worked with less.

"The answer is yes."

The princess perked up. "You'll help me?"

"I'll help you."

She was visibly relieved. "Thank you, sir."

This time it was James who stood and began to stride back and forth across the gazebo, the heels of his boots clicking on the stone-block floor with each step he took.

After a minute or two, he stopped, turned, and announced, "We need a plan."

"I have been mulling over several," Cecile offered. "We must find out where my uncle has stashed the loot."

That drew his brow into an exaggerated arch. Had she been reading the "penny dreadfuls"?

"The loot?"

The princess colored prettily. "The missing items."

"First things first," James admonished. "It's fortunate for us that we travel in the same social circle," he said, thinking aloud. "That will make it easier."

"Make *what* easier?"

"Meeting," he muttered under his breath. "Some rationale will still be required to explain why we meet so frequently."

"Are we to meet frequently?"

"I don't see how it can be avoided." James held up his hands, examined the palms, then lowered his hands. "We must do so without arousing Prince Rodolphe's suspicions. We can't afford to lose the element of surprise."

The lady repeated his words of last night and he repeated hers. "We must be discreet."

"We must be very discreet." James tugged at his shirt collar and cravat. How could a man be expected to think when the flow of blood was practically cut off to his brain? He gave his collar another yank and it came off in his hands. He loosened his cravat and undid several buttons at his neck. Finally comfortable, he advanced: "I'll put my mind to the matter for several days. Then we'll . . ."

"We'll go riding together in Hyde Park on Friday morning," came the suggestion.

"Excellent idea," he complimented her. "Our plans can be finalized at that time."

James felt better now that he had a preliminary course of action in mind. This was familiar territory to him. He knew what would come next. The problem would simmer in his brain for several days until a solution presented itself to him. He had every confidence it would. It always had before.

"I think that is enough discussion for tonight, madam."

"I agree, sir."

He sensed her sudden hesitation. She made no move to bid him good evening or to rise from her seat or to leave the gazebo. It was most peculiar.

Furthermore, Cecile of Saint-Simeon was staring at him as if she couldn't take her eyes off him. "I have one more favor to ask of you."

"What is it?"

"There are certain requests that are awkward . . ." She seemed to be searching for the right word. "That are discomfiting . . . that are difficult for a lady to make of a gentleman."

He presumed there were.

"They can be even more difficult for a princess."

Without a doubt.

"You have spoken several times of what a man may do that a woman may not."

He had.

"At a time like this, I presume it is customary for a gentleman to put his intentions in the form of a request."

James waited for her to get to the point. He assumed she had a point.

"Accordingly, as a lady, I feel I must do the same. I would like to ask you . . ."

Impatience finally took over. "You have only to tell me what it is that you desire, madam, and I will readily comply," James declared.

The princess opened her mouth and took the plunge. "Would you please kiss me, sir?"

Chapter Ten

That voice.

She knew that voice.

That face.

She knew that face.

Those eyes.

She had seen those eyes before, Cecile realized. Those unusual gray eyes that were like no other eyes she had ever beheld. Suddenly she remembered: It was the voice and the face and the eyes of the man in her dream.

Then why wasn't she afraid?

She was afraid, but not in the same way and not for the same reasons as when she awakened in the dead of night, her heart pounding, her throat constricted, her lungs starved for oxygen, her hands clenched into fists, her fingernails digging into her palms, her mind filled—flooded—with dread.

This was a fear that left her breathless with anticipation and a little tremulous from head to toe. This was a fear that made her aware of herself and of this man in a way she didn't recall ever being aware of a man before.

She had asked James Gray to kiss her. Cecile

couldn't imagine why she had made such an outrageous request.

That wasn't true. She knew the reason. It was curiosity, at least in part. She was curious and needful and in want. She wanted to know more about the physical relationship between a man and a woman, between this man and herself. Her mind was inundated with questions, and she believed that James could give her the answers.

She wasn't surprised that the expression on his handsome face was one of puzzlement. No doubt he thought she had taken complete leave of her senses.

Cecile tried to swallow the lump that had formed in her throat. "Have you ever been asked before?"

James's forehead creased into an accordion of frown lines. "Do you mean has a woman ever asked me to kiss her?"

She nodded.

He was succinct. "No."

She became flustered. "But you have kissed a great number of women?"

"I wouldn't say a great number," he replied, his brow smoothing. James Gray apparently adhered to the code that discretion was the better part of valor in personal affairs.

Cecile made another attempt. "I assume that like most gentlemen of a certain age you are experienced?"

Dark brows snapped together again. "A certain age, madam?" he repeated in a slightly sardonic tone.

She hadn't put that at all well, Cecile realized belatedly. "I only meant, sir, that you are no longer a boy."

The Earl of Graystone stood before her, broad shouldered and hard muscled, every inch a man. "That is true."

"And you are experienced?"

"At what?"

Was he deliberately being obtuse, Cecile wondered. "In the ways of the world."

James didn't even blink. "Exactly which world would that be, madam?"

Was the gentleman toying with her? Was this some kind of game he was playing? Was he entertaining himself at her expense? If so, she did not care for his notion of entertainment.

Cecile felt her patience slipping. "Our world, naturally."

"But our world is a very large and diverse world, is it not?" he said pointedly.

She had made a mistake. She should not have asked him. She had done what she rarely—almost never—did: She'd opened her mouth and blurted out her thoughts without first considering the consequences. She had acted on impulse. It had not been a good idea.

Cecile moistened her lips before admitting aloud, "This wasn't a good idea."

The man looming over her quickly countered. "I disagree. I think it's a very good idea."

That caught her off guard. Nevertheless, Cecile managed to collect herself and inform him, "I've changed my mind."

"It's too late," James Gray claimed.

How could it be too late?

She gave a ladylike sniff. "I do not wish to have you kiss me, after all, sir."

He returned her gaze unflinchingly. "You have made a request of me, madam, and I fully intend to comply."

Out it popped. "Why?"

Was that the merest hint of a bemused smile on Graystone's features? "Because I want to."

She breathed in and out. "I don't understand."

"Cecile . . ." Her name came on a soft whisper.

Something inside her crumbled. "James . . ."

He took two steps forward—they weren't even big steps—and ended up standing directly in front of her. His eyes, those elusive colored and yet somehow familiar gray eyes, pinned her to the spot where she sat. "Don't you know that I've wanted to kiss you since we first danced at your ball?"

Cecile was fairly certain she said "no" out loud, but she wasn't altogether sure.

James held out his hand, palm up. It was an invitation. "Would you do me the honor of dancing with me now?"

"There isn't any music," she said in a voice that bore scant resemblance to her own.

As if on cue, somewhere in the distance, but not as distant as it had been earlier that night, the street fiddler began to play his violin. It was a plaintive and melancholy tune. The music paused for a moment and when it commenced again the next song was lilting and joyful and meant to be danced to.

"There. You see," James exclaimed, extending his hand even further toward her.

She could hardly refuse him. She didn't wish to refuse him. She wanted to dance with James Gray. She wanted to be taken into his strong, protective arms and held close to his heart as they swirled around the summerhouse.

Cecile reached out and placed her hand in his. Her fingers were chilled. She should don her brown kid gloves, she supposed. It would be the sensible thing to do. It would be the prudent thing to do. It would be the proper thing to do.

Piffle! She wasn't inclined to do the sensible or the prudent or the proper thing. There was certainly nothing sensible, prudent, or proper, after all, about sneaking out of Guest House at three o'clock for a middle-of-the-night rendezvous. Under the circumstances, why, in heaven's name, would she concern herself with something as trivial as dancing without her kid gloves on?

James drew Cecile to her feet. Her hand was swallowed up by his larger and warmer one, his arm lightly encircled her waist, his body was near to hers.

They waltzed.

It was an entirely different kind of waltz than the one they had shared at the formal ball in her honor. This time there were no spectators, no onlookers, no gawkers staring at them. There would be no gossip, no idle chitchat, no half-hushed whispers. This time they were entirely and blessedly alone.

Due to the close confines of the gazebo, the dance was also far more intimate. There simply wasn't room for James Gray to hold her at arm's length.

And when, at last, the music faded into silence,

James leaned toward her—the pounding of her heart was thunderous in Cecile's ears—and touched his mouth to hers.

His lips were smooth, yet just above his lips, on that lovely little indentation between mouth and nose, and on his chin, was the late-night stubble of a beard. It was slightly abrasive against her skin, but not unpleasantly so.

He tasted of . . .

Cecile wasn't certain what James tasted of. It might be a subtle blend of expensive brandy and fresh peaches and cleansing tooth powder and the fragrant air of the garden.

Or was it the scent of the garden clinging to his clothing, to his hair, even to his flesh that she tasted, savored, inhaled with every breath? Perhaps it was all of these sensations that lingered on her tongue and in her nostrils.

A garden always smelled differently at night than it did during the daytime. On a slightly cool spring night like tonight its aromas were wondrous, heady, sensual, intoxicating. There was a wild, abundant, and inviting lushness to it.

The invitation extended by the garden was to forget everyone and everything outside its boundaries and to become a creature of nature. To be aware of the slightest shift in the wind as it caressed the skin, to feel terra firma underfoot, to take in the myriad scents of fragrant flowers, greening trees, damp, moss-covered bark, last autumn's dried leaves and pine needles transforming into mulch, newly turned earth, to hear the occasional scurrying of a small ani-

mal in the nearby brush or a night bird twittering in
the treetops overhead, to fill one's heart, one's mind,
one's soul with all that was offered.

How could she separate the man from the garden?

For that matter, Cecile mused, how could she separate the man from the night?

James was warm and masculine and utterly delicious. He smelled of the outdoors and clean, faintly
lime-scented soap. His hair was as soft as silk: Cecile
suddenly realized her fingertips were touching the
back of his head where his hair brushed along his
shirt.

To be sure he was tall and broad shouldered and
muscular. But James Gray was more than just a set
of remarkable muscles and a pair of splendid shoulders. He exuded that rare combination of tangible
and intangible strength.

He was a singular man, Cecile realized somewhere
in the back of her mind, preoccupied as she was with
the strange and wondrous delights of his kiss. For
his kiss was singular as well.

Their first kiss was a taste and a touch.

Their second kiss quickly followed on the heels of
the first.

Then there was immediately a third and a fourth,
and very soon Cecile lacked the inclination—or the
presence of mind—to keep count. Of one thing only
she was confident: The reality of James's kiss was far
better than any dream.

How could a man's kiss say so much?

It said she was beautiful and desirable and desired.

It said he liked kissing her, perhaps even loved kissing her. It said that he wanted to go on kissing her.

How could a man's kiss do so much?

She ceased to breathe. She ceased to think. She simply was. She became attuned solely to the senses: What could be heard, what could be smelled, what could be tasted, what could be felt.

Cecile discovered that she hungered for the sound of James's voice, for the distinctive scent that was his alone, for the flavors of his mouth, the textures of his jaw, his cheek, for the way he felt beneath her hands and pressed close against her body, for the way he made her feel.

He made her feel like a woman.

James drew his head back and gazed down into her face. "You are an angel."

Cecile heard herself disagreeing. "No."

He breathed. "Yes."

She stated more emphatically, "No, I'm not an angel. I'm just a woman."

James smiled a slightly bemused and thoroughly masculine smile. "You are a woman, but you could never be *just* a woman. And when I kiss you I feel as though I have died and gone to heaven."

Words.

They could be insincere. Deceitful. Nefarious. Even—especially—seductive.

Words.

Was the intent behind them genuine? Unfeigned? Truthful? Guileless?

Cecile wanted to believe James's words. Did she believe him? Perhaps it wasn't important, or even possible, to know the answer to her question since he was kissing her again and her brain suddenly stopped functioning.

This time was different, however.

This time the kiss they shared was deeper, darker, longer. It made Cecile feel slightly dizzy, definitely breathless, and a bit unsteady on her feet. She realized that her hands were grasping his shirt, that her fingers were clutching at the fine material.

She exhaled his name. "James . . ."

His quicksilver eyes blinked open. "What is it?"

"I can't . . ."

He spoke low. "You can't what?"

"I can't think," she confessed with a small sigh.

"There is no need for you to think." He added, as if concentration wasn't easy, "There is no need for me to think."

"Someone must."

"No one must." James ingeniously diverted her attention. "Kiss me again, my sweet lady, and I will show you what a man can do with his tongue."

Cecile was intrigued, of course. And curious. She'd always been a curious creature. Besides, James's words sent delicious shivers rippling down her back from the nape of her neck to the small indentation at the base of her spine.

She wrapped her arms around his waist, went up on her tiptoes and pressed her lips to his. For a moment or two nothing out of the ordinary occurred. Then she felt the tip of his tongue outlining the contours of her mouth. He was tasting her, luring her, caressing her, seducing her, all with the touch of his tongue.

There was something incredibly intimate about a man parting her lips with his and slipping his tongue inside her mouth. It was something she had not expected.

James did it again.

Then again.

And Cecile was good and truly lost.

Chapter Eleven

The lady was not wearing a corset.

It wasn't the first thing James noticed when he took Cecile in his arms and waltzed with her around the summerhouse, but it was the second or third thing.

When he paused and reflected on the subject, James decided her dishabille made sense. After all, it was the middle of the night. Secrecy had been, and still was, of the utmost importance. Undoubtedly Cecile had dressed without her maid in attendance.

A woman's apparel, if she was a member of a certain social class, was definitely not designed with ease of dressing or independence taken into consideration. In fact, it was assumed that a personal servant would always be on hand to assist a lady with her toilette.

It must be a royal nuisance not to be able to dress—or, for that matter, undress—one's self. Graystone wondered fleetingly why women put up with it.

Ah, well, fashion's loss was his gain. Under normal circumstances there would be several layers of outer- and under-garments, constituting any number of unbreachable barriers, between himself and the shapely Cecile Girardet.

Instead, there were none.

At least none worth mentioning. She was wearing a flowing gown of some flimsy, diaphanous material with a matching chemise beneath it. With his arms under her cloak and encircling her waist, with her body in contact with his from breast to thigh, James was well aware that conventional barriers were absent.

In truth, his shirt and trousers suddenly seemed to fit him like a second skin. He could feel every inch of her pressed against him, from the outline of her breasts to her ribcage and slender waist, to the flare of her hips and firm thighs, to that enticing, slightly rounded mound between her legs.

Bloody hell, the lady had an exquisite figure. In his opinion, she need never wear a corset.

It took every bit of self-control James Gray possessed to keep his hands to himself. He was literally itching to touch her.

It took every ounce of his willpower to resist burying his face between those two soft and perfectly shaped spheres, to not sample her natural allurements—would her nipples taste as sweet and luscious, perhaps a little like ripe strawberries, as his fancy told him they would—to not nibble her through the fabric of her gown.

Egods, James realized, if he didn't concentrate on something else and quick, he would explode.

Kissing.

He would concentrate on kissing the lady the way she deserved to be kissed, the way she wished to be kissed, the way she obviously wanted to be kissed.

So he used his mouth—the serrated edges of his teeth, his lips, and his tongue—not in a studied artifice of a kiss, but with genuine passion and arousal.

Lord, she was sweet.

It had been a very long time since he had held a woman in his arms, kissed a woman with passion at full-throttle, desired a woman as much as he desired Cecile.

James lost track of the time, the place, even the purpose for their clandestine meeting. It slipped his mind where they were . . . hell, *who* they were. All he could think of was filling his nostrils with Cecile's scent, filling his mouth with Cecile's taste, filling his hands with Cecile's bewitching form.

Swearing softly under his breath, James lifted his head and found himself staring down into passion-glazed blue eyes.

The lady blinked several times in rapid succession and said, "What is it?"

The muscles in his thighs tightened. "Maybe this wasn't a good idea, after all."

She clutched at the sleeve of his shirt. "No."

James frowned. "Then you agree?"

Cecile shook her head.

Obviously he wasn't thinking particularly clearly or rationally. "Then you disagree?"

Fine nostrils flared. "It is a good idea."

James almost laughed in the lady's lovely face. "Cecile, how much do you know about men?"

Her voice resonated with bravado. "Enough."

By whose standards? *Enough* was a relative term.

The tables were immediately turned on him. "How much do you know about women?"

"A man never knows enough about women," he stated, flexing his tense shoulders.

"That isn't a suitable answer," she countered.

James gave a short, humorless laugh. "Because there is no suitable answer to your question."

Cecile remained unconvinced. "There must be."

He gave an emphatic shake of his head. "The only question a man should seek the answer to is how much does he know about a particular woman."

It had been Graystone's experience—was there anyone alive who would debate the issue with him?—that knowing women well was one thing; that knowing one woman well . . . well, that was an altogether different and far more difficult piece of business.

A pink tongue was passed over pink lips. "Have you ever been in love?"

An image of the beautiful young woman in his dreams—or was it the image of Cecile—flashed into James's head. "I don't think so," he said at last. Turnabout was only fair play in his book. "Have you ever been in love?"

The lady appeared to ponder the question. "I don't believe so." She went on to make a second inquiry. "Have you ever been engaged or betrothed?"

James was certain this time. "No, I haven't." His fingers shifted at her waist. "And you?"

She stared straight back into his eyes. "No." Then, "You aren't married?"

James paused before replying, "No."

Why did he always hesitate when he was asked that question? The same thing had occurred the night before at the formal ball given in Cecile's honor, when he had been conversing with Silverthorn, his old friend from his days at Oxford.

All of a sudden he realized Cecile was speaking. He caught only the last word: ". . . married."

"I understand you aren't married, either," he stated.

She took a moment, then moved her head from side to side. "I'm not married."

It was the damnedest thing, but James found he could not look away from her mouth. He ended up saying the first thing that occurred to him. "We talk a great deal."

Cecile laughed lightly and a little nervously. "You mean *I* talk a great deal?"

He didn't know what he meant, so he simply smiled at her.

She was serious. "Kiss me again, James."

James kissed her once.

"And again," she urged.

He kissed her again.

"More," she said plainly.

At some point the truth hit James Gray: He wanted Cecile Girardet. But he wanted to do far more than merely kiss her. He wanted to touch her, to caress her, to make love to her.

He wouldn't, of course.

He couldn't.

James had always believed that he was a man in control of himself, physically and mentally. He was promptly proven wrong. For, within a surprisingly short span of time, he went from kissing Cecile to touching Cecile to caressing **Cecile**. His hands trailed along either side of her torso, insinuated their way between their bodies and moved up to cover her breasts.

There was a tiny gasp.

But she did not pull back from him. She did not voice any objections. She simply remained there in his arms, under the tutelage of his hands, quivering and trembling like a thoroughbred racehorse waiting for the Derby to commence, a little anxious, a little eager, impatient for the gates to be opened, wanting nothing more than to take off at a full gallop, but half-afraid to so.

"James . . ." Her tone of voice told him everything he needed to know: Cecile wanted to be touched by him as much as he wanted to touch her.

His hands spanned her ribcage. His fingertips found her breasts. He flicked his thumbs back and forth across her nipples and was rewarded with another gasp, followed by a feminine moan of arousal.

Small beads of perspiration formed on his brow. "Do you like that?" he asked.

She couldn't speak. She simply nodded.

Then he bent over and did what he had only dreamed of doing before: He used the tip of his tongue to lick the spot directly above her right nipple. Then he did the same to the left. Back and forth. Teeth nipping. Lips tugging. Mouth suckling. The front of her gossamer gown was damp when he finally raised his head.

James's voice sounded strangely hoarse even to his own ears when he entreated, "On several occasions you have asked why a woman may not enjoy the same prerogatives as a man. In this situation, I assure you, she can."

With that, Cecile went up on her tiptoes and brought her mouth to his. The angle of incline put her breasts even more fully and forcefully into his hands. She inhaled and exhaled with a warm, honeyed breath that wafted across his face. Then she touched her small, pink, enticing tongue to his lips.

James shuddered.

Christ, one small, slightly intimate caress bestowed on him by this woman and he was covered from the top of his head to the tips of his toes with gooseflesh!

She traced the outline of his mouth, explored the smooth surfaces of his teeth, entangled her tongue with his tongue, pressed her lips to his chin and tasted him, then to his jaw, to his cheek, to the lobe of his ear, to his neck.

He shuddered again.

Cecile drew back and announced a little breathlessly, "Now I understand."

James very much doubted if she did.

She expounded. "When it comes to intimacy of a certain sort . . . this sort . . . there is no difference between male and female, between a man and a woman."

Graystone couldn't help it. He laughed out loud. It felt damned good to laugh, too.

Instantly the color of the lady's cheeks changed

from pale pink to brilliant red. Hastily she began to backtrack. "There is a difference, naturally."

He made a knowing sound. "*A* difference?"

She was flustered. "Well, I presume there are any number of differences."

That wasn't what she had declared only moments before.

James's chest was moving up and down in a semblance of laughter. "I wonder just how many there are."

She hastened to say, "I don't believe we need concern ourselves with the exact number."

James focused his full attention on her. "It could be most enlightening and edifying, perhaps instructive, even revealing, if we were to explore the differences together."

She sniffed. "Now you're teasing me."

"Yes. I am," came the admission.

Without further ado, she abruptly, and successfully, changed the subject. "May I place my hands inside your shirt?"

How could he refuse the lady?

"Of course."

Cecile undid the row of buttons down the front of his linen. Her fingers were long and elegant and cold. When she touched him, James shuddered once again.

"I'm sorry. My hands are cold."

"They are." He might as well tell her the truth. "But that isn't why I shivered."

"It isn't?"

He shook his head. "It's your touch."

She dared to look up at him. "Did I do it incorrectly?"

"There is no correct or incorrect when it comes to these matters. There is only what a man and a woman decide they mutually desire and enjoy."

Once his shirt was open from his neck to his waist, Cecile confessed to him in slightly hushed tones, "I've never actually touched a man's bare chest before."

She reached up and traced a seemingly random pattern back and forth across his skin, stroking him with tentative fingers: sensitized flesh, a smattering of hair, small, nutlike nipples.

James swallowed hard.

With a sense of wonder and bemusement Cecile murmured, "You are beautiful."

Graystone's mind went blank. He couldn't come up with a single response beyond a polite, "Thank you."

Her mouth curved in a benevolent smile. "You're welcome." Then she discovered the thin leather cord he wore about his neck. "May I inquire what this is?"

"It's a leather cord."

"I can see that." She ran her fingertips along its length. "Why do you wear it?"

"I don't know." James was telling her the truth. "I can't remember why I wear it around my neck. I only know I always do."

Cecile's hand fluttered to her own throat and lingered there for a moment. Then she became interested—engrossed was more accurate—in his chest: its strength, its muscles and underlying bone structure, its hardness, the soft, dark hair scattered here and there over its smooth surface, its feel and its taste.

In the end, it was her mouth that did James Gray in. She kissed his chest and took a small bite of his nipple. He heard a groan of sexual arousal and realized, belatedly, that it was his own.

He had allowed this to go too far.

It hadn't gone far enough.

He would like nothing better than to unbutton the bodice of her dress, push her chemise aside and caress her bare breasts. He would clasp her in his hands and gently squeeze her. He would tweak her between thumb and forefinger until she begged for mercy.

Then his hands would find other diversions—there were so very many in her case—and his mouth would take their place. He could almost taste her. He could imagine her nipples protruding against his lips, caught between his teeth, drawn deeply into his mouth.

He had a sudden vision of her lovely body stretched out beneath his, her arms wide open and beckoning as she welcomed him into her embrace. He would sink into her until there was no knowing where he began and she ended.

"Cecile . . ." He groaned his protestation. "We must stop."

She was wide eyed, wild eyed. "Why?"

Dear God in heaven, grant him the strength when he needed it most, James silently intoned. "Because this has gone on too long." And it had gone too far.

"I like kissing you," she said simply.

"I like kissing you."

"I like it very much," she amended.

"As do I."

"It gives me great pleasure," she added.

"It gives me great pleasure as well."

Cecile had no concept of the pleasure she gave him. And he had no intentions of surprising the lady—indeed, shocking the lady—by allowing her to learn just how aroused he was, just how close he had come to the point of no return.

James heaved a sigh. In the hands of this innocent young woman, his once enviable self-control lay in ruins.

He opened his mouth and the words tumbled out. "We can't meet like this again."

She backed up half a step. "I don't understand."

He spelled it out. "We can't meet alone in the garden in the middle of the night."

Her chin came up. "Why not?"

"It's too dangerous for you." If she only knew how dangerous. "You risk too much by coming here."

"There is far more at risk if I do not come."

Graystone was regaining his self-control. The princess had asked for his help and that was all she had asked for. Well, she had asked him to kiss her, but she was obviously naive and inexperienced when it came to such affairs. He must be the one to protect her.

Even if it meant protecting her from himself.

James gathered the fur-trimmed cloak closely around her. It was the first he'd realized she was dressed in black, unlike their last meeting. "You're not the woman in white tonight."

"A dark color seemed better suited to our clandestine activities," she tossed off.

"This is serious business," he warned.

"No one knows that better than I do."

Perhaps not.

James shifted his stance and sought to assure her. "We will find a way, I promise."

"I know." She stood very still. "You once said something similar to me."

He scowled. "Did I?"

"It was while we were dancing at the ball. You said: 'I promise. I will find you.'"

After several moments, he said, "So I did."

"Why did you say those words to me?"

"I suppose because we had arranged to meet somewhere here in the garden and I wanted to reassure you that I'd find you."

"There was no other reason."

The lump on James Gray's head suddenly began to ache. "I recall something about those words, but perhaps I only dreamt them." He reached up and rubbed behind his ear. "Sometimes I feel as though I'm about to remember more."

Cecile stared at him.

"It isn't important right now," James stated.

"I suppose not."

"What is important is for us to recover the crown, the scepter, and the chalice stolen from the tower, and return them to Saint-Simeon in time to guarantee your brother's coronation."

"You're right, of course."

"It's time that we each returned to our beds. Remember, you should go about your official duties for the next several days as if nothing was out of the ordinary."

She nodded.

"Meanwhile, I'll see what can be done about this business."

She added, "Until Friday when we will meet and go riding in Hyde Park."

"Until Friday when we will meet again." The night was growing short. "You must return to Guest House now, Cecile. We can't risk having your absence noticed."

"I wish I did not have to leave you."

"I know."

He also knew she was without artifice, without coquetries, without guile, without pretention. She was not at all what he had expected Her Serene Highness, Cecile of Saint-Simeon, to be. But he must never forget, James Gray reminded himself, that she was a woman first and a princess second.

The words were still echoing in James's head as he bid the lady goodnight at the garden gate and watched as she disappeared inside Guest House.

I promise . . . I will find you.

Had he found her at last?

Chapter Twelve

Blackmail was a beastly business.

But, then, so were betrayal and treachery and treason. One frequently led to another. It certainly had in his case.

It had all begun years ago (sometimes he felt as though he had already lived a dozen lifetimes) with one foolish, indiscreet, and reckless act on his part.

Looking back from his present vantage point, he could clearly see that he had been a rather naive and gullible young man, and even occasionally a rather stupid one. He had taken the bait unsuspectingly, hook, line, and sinker.

That had been his first mistake.

Then he had made a second and more grievous error: He'd assumed that no one would ever find out.

He had repented, naturally. In fact, he could still vividly recall the hard, bone-chilling, stone floor beneath him as he groveled on his knees in the great cathedral, praying for mercy, praying for deliverance from his sins, praying for secrecy.

His prayers had not been answered.

Someone had found out about him.

He had found out.

It had not started with blackmail. The one he now thought of as evil incarnate had been far too clever to take such an unsubtle and direct approach.

No, it had started with friendship. Then there had been a simple request made of him. Just one. He had believed—oh, how strong the necessity for self-deception could become—that the first request would also be the last.

He was wrong.

It was only the beginning. Some months after the first there had been a second request made, and then a year later yet another. Before he could grasp what was actually happening to him, he was embroiled in it right up to his neck.

Often, too often, in the intervening years, he had awakened in the dead of night, his body covered with a fine sheen of perspiration, his chest heaving, his heartbeat a thunderous drumming in his ears, his lungs gasping for air, and with a silent scream on his lips, knowing he had seen in his *aegri somnia*— his sick dream—a noose slowly and inextricably tightening around his neck.

The day had inevitably come when he'd had to face the fact that he was being blackmailed.

Blackmail had led to betrayal. Betrayal had eventually become treachery. Treachery had swiftly—oh, how swiftly and how deadly—become treason.

There had been times over the years when he had played *advocatus diaboli* with himself, arguing that his intolerable and insufferable situation wasn't entirely his fault. After all, he couldn't have seen it coming, could he?

A thousand times, a thousand times a thousand, he had ranted and raged against the fates and called himself a fool.

A small inner voice always reminded him: He had been far more and far worse than a fool.

The French had the consummate expression for it: *âme damnée*, which literally meant damned soul. It suited him to perfection since he had become, since he had long been, the dupe of another and the tool of his treachery.

He had not known to what depths he would be willing to sink to save himself until the ultimatum had been issued: *Do as I ask*—what a small, deceptively simple, profane word *ask* could be, he had learned—*or I will expose you to the world. If you do not obey my commands everyone will know you for what you truly are: weak, contemptible, unnatural, degenerate, corrupt, beyond redemption, rotten to the core, rotten to your very soul.*

He had done as he was commanded.

And from that day forward he had known himself to be an *âme damnée*.

Now and then he still prayed, of course. Why not pray? He made a pretense—hypocrite that he was—of attending church every week, anyway.

Dear God in heaven, and by all of the blessed saints, was there no hope for him? Was there no chance of mercy or redemption or salvation? Could he expect no pity or compassion? Was he beyond all forgiveness? Was he forever doomed?

He was lost.

All was lost.

He could expect no mercy, no forgiveness, no salvation. He had reached a fork in the road many years ago and he had made his choice. There was no going back.

Everything carried a price. In trying to save himself, he had lost all that he held dear. He had forfeited his self-respect and his pride. He had relinquished his good name. He had sacrificed his past, his present, and his future.

It had never been his intention to betray those he loved. Hell was paved with good intentions.

He had served his master well, knowing that if he wished to keep his skin intact, he must do as he was commanded and the consequences be damned.

For whatever the prince wanted, sooner or later the prince got.

Even if it was a man's soul.

Chapter Thirteen

Rudy kept secrets from her.

Rudy *thought* he kept secrets from her, anyway. She was well aware, however, of his clandestine activities, of his nefarious doings, of the games he delighted in playing with other people's lives, of what he called his Chinese boxes: plans within plans within plans.

She, too, had her sources, her spies, and her lackeys. They were every bit as good as the ones Rodolphe Girardet blackmailed into doing his dirty work for him.

Indeed, some of them were the same lackeys.

Moira wasn't quite as dimwitted as she allowed the prince to believe. She had found that it served her far better—it served any woman better—if a man underestimated her.

In truth, the countess considered herself a consummate actress. Acting was one of the numerous skills that she had found it necessary to acquire when her father had sold her to Lord Pale at the tender age of sixteen.

Not that she had been an innocent even then.

First, there had been the burly stable hand at a

nearby farm. She still fondly recalled long, lazy summer afternoons with sunlight streaming between the slats of the barn wall and warm, sweet-smelling hay beneath her backside.

Next it had been the local vicar's son. She had insisted that they sneak behind the church organ during the weekly choir practice. The disparity between the holy place and the unholy act being performed within its confines had appealed to Moira's ribald sense of humor, while the vibrations from the pipe organ had added greatly—and unexpectedly—to her pleasure.

Unfortunately the vicar's boy had been so racked with guilt and remorse that she had lost her patience with him and her interest inside of one month.

Then there had been the tall, blond, handsome man—his name was on the tip of her tongue—who had been passing through the North Country. He had stayed no more than a fortnight, but she had fancied herself in love with him.

The day after her sixteenth birthday Moira Munson had been shipped off to Hoary Manor, the vast and dilapidated country estate of Lord Osgood Pale, her hitherto unseen bridegroom.

At the time Lord Pale had been eighty years old, thrice wed and thrice widowed. He had lacked two of his prominent front teeth—which left him speaking with a slight lisp—rarely changed his linen, and reeked of cooked cabbage and manure.

In addition, the first and only Earl of Pale had seemed to prefer the company of horses to that of men. While the main house, the outbuildings, the tenants' bungalows, and the once renowned formal gardens of Hoary Manor had been allowed to fall into a state of disrepair, extensive renovations had been made to the stables. The livery had been in excellent condition.

As agreed upon in the marriage contract, Moira's family had received a handsome sum of money for her: enough to pay off their debts and guarantee them a comfortable living.

As misfortune would have it, the Munsons were a frivolous lot. Not a single member of the family—with the exception of Moira—had an ounce of common sense or any semblance of a practical head on their shoulders. With their daughter's "dowry" in hand, they had proceeded to live so extravagantly and so far beyond their means that they had found themselves utterly destitute again within the year.

Moira had refused to lift so much as a little finger to help them. Her family had thought her ungrateful.

Lord Pale, at least, had been more than satisfied with his part of the bargain. He had procured for himself another beautiful and virginal bride. And Moira had played the role expected of her to perfection.

She had been appropriately shy and demure on their wedding night, trembling in her bare feet as she stood before her bridegroom, complexion pale, knuckles white, fingers clutching at the modest nightgown that he had insisted she wear.

On cue, the newest Lady Pale had produced sufficient tears, ample virginal shrieks, and enough blood to placate even the most skeptical of doubting Thomases.

Osgood Pale had never known the difference. Not just in the beginning, but throughout the entire ten years Moira had been married to him.

When the depraved old man had become even older and more depraved, he had insisted that a friend visiting his country house be allowed to share in the delights of his countess and wife. That was when Moira had known what she must do.

The arrangements had been made with a London bordello that Lord Pale frequented. The doxie had been an unknowing dupe. For the price of a cheap bottle of whisky she had followed instructions and slipped the powder into her client's drink.

Once the deed had been done, once the hateful old lecher had been dispatched straight to hell—hell was too good for the likes of Lord Osgood Pale, in his widow's opinion—the lady of the night had vanished into the night.

Good riddance to bad rubbish.

Moira had been vastly contented from that day forward. She had ended up with Osgood's assets, Osgood's considerable wealth, and Osgood's country estate. She had even discovered Osgood's family jewels, which she had never been permitted to wear while the miserly earl was alive.

Indeed, when she had unearthed the cache of necklaces and brooches, earrings and tiaras stashed in a chamberpot hidden well beneath Osgood's filthy bed, Moira had plunked herself down on the floor and howled with laughter. There were spectacular diamonds and blood red rubies, deep blue sapphires, South Sea pearls, and vivid green emeralds enough to choke a horse.

Except for the jewelry, she had sold it all off, lock, stock, and barrel, including the deceased earl's stable of prized horses. (The horses were worth a bloody fortune as it turned out.) Then Moira had moved to London, purchased a large and rather ostentatious residence in one of the best parts of town and promptly christened it Pale House.

Pale House was everything that Hoary Manor had never been. It was feminine. It was decorated with an eye to impress, which it did from the moment a visitor stepped inside the front entranceway and beheld the magnificent crystal chandelier in the grand hall. It was spotlessly clean: A small army of housemaids were employed to scrub the place daily from top to bottom.

And it was hers.

No one could—no one would—ever be allowed to take it away from her, Moira reflected as she lifted the brass door knocker on the front of Prince Rodolphe's imposing London mansion.

The butler, a dour-faced gentleman of indistinguishable years, punctually answered the summons. His bow was dignified, his greeting impersonal. "Good afternoon, Lady Pale."

Moira swept past him into the vast entrance hall. "Good afternoon, Rank."

Neither gave any indication of the fact that the countess had not vacated the premises last night until one hour before dawn, although it had been Rank who had handed her up into her carriage. The proprieties must be observed, after all.

Like a sentry on duty, Rank positioned himself at the bottom of the grand staircase. "His Serene Highness is not at home this afternoon, my lady."

An expression of bewilderment appeared on her face. "This is Thursday, is it not?"

"It is, madam."

"Then I have a two o'clock appointment with the prince to attend the Turner exhibit."

"I believe that is Thursday next, Lady Pale."

In a show of vexation, Moira stamped her dainty foot and the tip of her parasol on the marble floor.

On this particular occasion her ensemble consisted of the lavender foulard parasol lined with yellow silk and bordered with lace. Her visiting costume was lavender and yellow silk, also trimmed with rows of lace and satin bows at the sleeves and hemline.

She was wearing a jaunty white chip hat with the turned-up brim filled with a cluster of satin purple roses and a long white ostrich plume posed low at the back. Her hair was done in a Greek coil. Her gloves were white kid. She was a woman all dressed up and apparently with nowhere to go.

Rank discreetly cleared his throat. "This is most regrettable, Lady Pale."

She made a dismissing gesture with her gloved hand. "I suppose it cannot be helped."

Neither Rank's countenance nor his posture altered. "His Serene Highness will be devastated."

They both knew the prince would be nothing of the sort.

"You are undoubtedly right about the date, Rank."
It was Moira's habit to treat servants well; It had
always served her well to do so. "I have never
known you to be wrong."

"Thank you, my lady."

"I must have somehow marked the incorrect
Thursday in my engagement book." She made one
wide sweep of the hallway and turned. "I suppose
the prince is at his club."

"I believe he is, madam."

"There are times I wish ladies were permitted such
privileges, but I suppose it is not to be."

"I suppose not, your ladyship."

Moira gave a well-rehearsed sigh and touched a
hand to the plume on her hat. "Since I am here, I
believe I will take some light refreshment in the
library."

"Of course, Lady Pale."

"Perhaps a pot of coffee and a plate of Henri's
delectable sweets." Prince Rodolphe's chef had been
imported from Paris and specialized in candies and
pastries. She had another thought. "Are there any
fresh berries today?"

"Strawberries, I believe."

"Perhaps a dish of strawberries, then, as well."
Moira was tempted to lick her lips. She hadn't eaten
a bite since a light supper last evening, and she had
no intentions of waiting until the traditional teatime.
"And a small pitcher of cream."

Rank escorted her to the library, opened the oversize double doors and stood politely to one side
while she entered the room.

The library doors were considered a priceless work of art. They were Italian, early sixteenth century, with carved inlaid panels of exotic birds and rare tropical vegetation. The entire surface, from floor to ceiling, was covered in goldleaf.

"It will be a few minutes, madam," the butler said backing toward the hallway.

"There is no hurry, Rank." Moira set her parasol down on a cushioned chair and began to remove her kid gloves. "I will enjoy browsing among His Serene Highness's collection of books."

"I am afraid most of the volumes are in French or Italian," he offered apologetically.

"I read a little French," she said.

A very little.

Except for the latest on Charles Worth's fashions, or royal goings-on, or tidbits of society news, Moira, Lady Pale, rarely read anything even in English.

But this afternoon she was a woman on a mission. There had been no mistake made on her engagement calendar. She had been well aware that the prince would not be at home. Indeed, his absence was a necessary part of her plan. And she had chosen the library with a very particular purpose in mind.

For more than once in the middle of the night Moira had awakened in the prince's bed only to discover that he had mysteriously disappeared. A discreet question asked in the right quarters had given her a partial answer: Rudy did not leave the house.

So where did he go?

And why?

Perhaps the answer was here in the library since it was Rudy's favorite room.

Moira made a cursory examination of the premises, pausing to peruse a portrait of the prince hanging above the fireplace, a marble bust of an ancient Greek or Roman emperor—she always forgot which it was—on a pedestal in the corner, a particularly fine assortment of silver snuff boxes displayed in a glass-topped case by the window, and another case, on the opposite side of the library, which contained several dozen valuable miniatures.

Rudy did fancy his little "collections."

Then Moira stopped in her tracks. There was a recent addition to the library. One she was quite certain she had never seen before. It was a distinctive and singular cabinet with hammered brass hinges, carved ivory pull knobs, and dozens of drawers ranging from the tiny to those no more than medium in size. Even the largest drawer was a meager three or four inches in width.

The cabinet itself was made of dark wood and appeared, from its patina, to be very ancient. The style was ornate and with a suggestion of the Oriental about it. It sat on a low pagoda table between two formal reading chairs.

Moira ran a gloveless hand across the top of the cabinet and was contemplating opening one of the drawers—just for a quick peek inside—when Rank knocked at the library door and entered with the requested tray of refreshments.

Moira did a pirouette on her lavender satin slipper. "This is new, is it not, Rank?"

The butler skillfully maneuvered the large silver tray onto an empty table. "It is, Lady Pale."

"It appears to be very old."

"That is my understanding, madam."

"What is it?"

"I believe His Serene Highness referred to it as some kind of cabinet," he replied.

Moira could see that much for herself. She circled the object under discussion. "Do you know what is in the drawers?"

"I'm afraid I don't, Lady Pale." Rank was discretion personified. "Will there be anything else?"

"I think not." She noticed there were two cups on the silver tray. "Is someone joining me?"

Rank snapped his heels together. "The prince has returned earlier than expected, my lady, and has asked me to inform you that he will be down momentarily."

Moira must not allow her disappointment to show. "Thank you, Rank."

With impeccable timing, Prince Rodolphe entered the library just as his butler was leaving.

"Good afternoon, my dear Countess. I understand there was a misunderstanding concerning our schedules."

Moira wisely decided to downplay the incident. "It was entirely my fault, sir. I had the Turner exhibit jotted down on my social calendar for this Thursday instead of Thursday week." Moira wondered if the prince believed her.

"Ah, I see you have spotted the latest addition to

my collection," the gentleman said with a motion of his hand.

She deliberately instilled a light, teasing tone into her voice. "And which collection, Your Serene Highness, would that be? You have so very many of them."

Rodolphe Girardet touched the ancient wooden box as if he were caressing a woman's flesh. "This is a very rare piece I came into possession of only yesterday."

"What is it?"

"It's called a 'cabinet of curiosities.'"

She leaned toward him. "How intriguing."

"I thought it would be of interest to you," he said in a tone of voice that sent a shudder rippling down Moira's spine.

They were both well aware that she took excessive notice of anything that was out of the ordinary, or unusual, or peculiar. In truth, she had no objection to that which others often deemed bizarre or grotesque or even repulsive.

Moira needed excitement.

Indeed, she craved excitement much as an opium addict craved his drug. She was constantly in search of new sensations, new thrills, new eroticisms.

Rodolphe Girardet was all politeness. "Shall we have our coffee first?"

Moira blinked. "Coffee?"

He strolled across the room to the table. "I see Rank has served coffee and sweets and—" he lifted the lid of the silver salver "—fresh strawberries."

Moira lied. "I am not particularly hungry."

He replaced the silver lid. "Then would you care to inspect my latest acquisition?"

She tried not to appear too eager. "If you would like to show it to me."

The prince reached into his vest pocket, removed a brass key, slipped it into a lock at the base of the cabinet and gave it a twist. They both heard the soft click that followed.

"The cabinet is now unlocked," Girardet stated unnecessarily. He stepped aside. "Would you like to open one of the drawers and see what you find?"

Moira was suddenly nervous. She moistened her lips. "Which drawer should I choose?"

Prince Rodolphe gave a sardonic laugh. "That is for you to decide, Countess. Choosing is half the game."

"Is this a game?"

"Of a sort."

Moira wondered exactly what sort of game it was, for she was acquainted with several of the so-called games that gentlemen enjoyed playing. Osgood had played games, but his "amusements" had never been fun or even pleasant. His had always been painful.

Oh, yes, she had played men's games before, and she had learned much in the process. She didn't trust any man now, and she did not trust this man.

"I'll select the first drawer for you," the prince volunteered, picking one at random. He pulled it open and they both leaned over and peered inside.

"What is it?" she inquired.

Rudy took out the small packet and turned it over in his palm. "The inscription claims that it is a lock of the Emperor Napoleon's hair snipped from his head as he lay dying."

Moira shivered but it wasn't from disgust. "Shall I pick the next drawer?"

"Please do," he urged.

She pulled on one of the carved ivory knobs and quickly recoiled. "It's some kind of insect."

Rodolphe Girardet laughed again. "Don't concern yourself, my dear. It's dead."

"What is it?" Moira almost immediately corrected herself. "What *was* it?"

The prince removed a small handwritten card from the front of the drawer. "This is an example of an African hissing cockroach. The insect is found in Madagascar and is usually three to four inches long and double the thickness of the human thumb." He put the information back and proposed, "Would you like to choose another drawer?"

Moira knew her eyes were glittering. She tugged on another drawer, frowned and removed the small container she had found inside. "Nail parings said to be those of Mary, Queen of Scots."

"What will be next, I wonder," the prince said as he selected one of the larger sliding boxes.

Moira leaned over and quickly straightened, making a face. "What in heaven's name?"

"It appears to be a human finger," he announced.

She read the accompanying card. "A mummified finger said to be one of several severed from a thief's hand who dared to steal from his lord and master. Lourdes, France. 1641."

Rodolphe gave her a long, sideways glance. "That

was considered suitable punishment in those days: If one was caught stealing one lost one's hand."

Her heart was beating a little faster. "Wherever did you find such a chest?"

"Let's just say a certain gentleman knew of my curious nature and of my penchant for collecting. He made me a gift of the cabinet of curiosities."

"He gave it to you?"

"In lieu of payment."

Moira could just imagine what kind of payment. The previous owner had obviously been in debt to the prince—which meant he was being blackmailed by Rudy—and had sought an unusual but mutually satisfactory means of settling his obligation.

"I think one more surprise for this afternoon will suffice, my lady. Why don't you choose the final drawer?"

Moira selected the largest box in the cabinet. When she saw what was inside it, her eyes grew large and round, and she could not prevent the gasp that escaped her lips.

"Ah . . ." Prince Rodolphe exclaimed as he removed the piece of solid glass from its velvet-lined resting place. "Now this is a most intriguing device."

"Is there any card with it?"

He snickered. "I think not, Countess. I believe we both know what it is without a written description."

"It is very large and smooth and elongated," she remarked and swallowed hard.

"Yes, it is," the prince agreed, examining the clear glass appendage from every angle.

Moira couldn't take her eyes off it . . . or the manner in which Rudy was stroking its length with his elegant fingers.

"I believe we will have our coffee later," came the sudden announcement.

Rodolphe Girardet strode to the library doors, made certain they were closed and turned the keys in their double locks. As he turned and advanced across the room toward her, there was a look in his eyes that Lady Pale recognized.

The prince was aroused.

Moira looked quickly from side to side, and shifted her stance. "Rudy, here?"

"Here."

She couldn't quite catch her breath. "Now?"

"Why not now?"

She could not take her eyes from the glass device he grasped in his hand. "It is the middle of the afternoon."

"So it is."

She wetted her lips. "The servants will surely know what we are about."

"The servants are of no consequence."

Moira couldn't deny that she was aroused, titillated, even tingling with sexual excitement at the prospect of what they were about to do.

And, damn him, Rudy knew it as well.

Later that night as she lay in her own bed at Pale House the countess reflected on the events of the day.

Recently she had wondered—feared—that Rudy was beginning to bore her. The episode in the library this afternoon had proved her wrong. At least for the time being the prince could still provide her with the thrills she sought.

She was no man's fool, however. She was not about to become just another object in one of Rodolphe Girardet's collections. For he collected people as surely as he collected objects.

If she should require another source of amusement, Moira, Lady Pale, knew where she could find it. After all, there was always Lord Graystone and the princess.

Yes, if it came to that, they would do nicely.

Chapter Fourteen

This wasn't a ride in the park. It was a bloody parade, James decided, feeling disgruntled with himself, with the circumstances in which they found themselves, and with the world in general.

It wasn't so much the gawkers and curiosity seekers that were troubling him. It was the fact that he had made a promise; a promise he couldn't keep.

What were the exact words he had used to reassure Cecile Girardet the night they had last met in the key garden?

He remembered now. *"I'll put my mind to the matter for several days. Then we'll . . ."*

"We'll go riding together in Hyde Park on Friday morning," she had proposed.

"Our plans can be finalized at that time," he had said with absolute confidence.

James remembered the sense of relief he'd experienced once he had a definite course of action in mind. He even recalled thinking to himself that it was familiar territory, that he knew what would come next. The problem—like all the previous "problems" he had dealt with—would simmer in his brain for several days until a solution presented itself to him. It always had before. He'd had no doubts it would again.

Except this time it hadn't.

It was Friday morning. They were up early and riding along Rotten Row. And he was no closer to a solution than he had been a full three days and three nights ago.

Graystone glanced at the young woman beside him. Cecile presented the perfect picture of what a princess should look like while she enjoyed a supposedly leisurely outing on horseback.

She was wearing a superbly tailored ladies riding suit in black cloth trimmed with a fine linen collar and cuffs. About her throat was a blue gros grain cravat. There was a blue gauze veil wound around the crown of her black beaver hat: The veil picked up the color of her eyes and made them appear even more intensely blue than usual.

Her black riding boots were polished to a sheen. She had the reins clasped in one hand and carried a riding crop in the other, but he noticed that she had yet to use the whip on her mount. She was, of course, riding sidesaddle.

"Is that young personage that foreign princess?" A loud Wagnerian voice sliced through the morning air.

"I believe it is," her companion replied.

James leaned forward slightly in the saddle and made a point of returning the decidedly rude stares of the pair of matrons standing on the sidelines, tongues wagging, voices audible even from a considerable distance.

A lorgnette was raised. "Who, pray tell, is the gentleman with her?" Not even a breath was drawn before another question was posed. "Is he anyone of consequence?"

"I don't think so."

"Is he a foreigner as well?"

"Very likely."

"'Tis a pity." A more than ample bosom rose and fell beneath the weight of a dozen strands of gray pearls. "He is a handsome devil."

James did a slow burn. He felt a muscle in his face start to twitch. "Is it always like this?"

Cecile turned her head and looked briefly in his direction. "Is *what* always like this?"

"People watching every move you make, taking note of every gesture, no matter how inconsequential, every smile, every blessed frown. Strangers attempting to eavesdrop on your private conversations," he related with the full force of his displeasure.

Cecile acknowledged a pair of equestrians passing them on the opposite side of the sandy path. "The Duke and Duchess of Hartcup," she informed him after the couple had ridden by. "We were introduced last evening at a dinner party given by Her Majesty."

The Duke and Duchess of Hartcup were of no interest to James. "You haven't given me a reply."

Cecile drew her delicately marked brows together. "Would you please repeat the question?"

A sardonic smile touched the edges of his mouth. "Is it always like this?"

She looked down at her hands. "Do you mean the unsolicited attention?"

Of course, he meant the unsolicited attention. What else could he mean when every last solitary person in Hyde Park seemed to be observing them? "Yes."

Cecile wet her lips with her tongue and made the admission cautiously. "I'm afraid it is."

His fist tightened on the reins, his thighs flexed around the hired horse's girth, but the animal he was riding took no notice. If it had been Amritsar beneath him, James's tension would have immediately been relayed to his mount.

He remembered to lower his voice. "It is insupportable," he hissed. "How do you bear it?"

Cecile attempted to smile and did not quite succeed. "I have to bear it. I have no choice."

James liked to believe there was always a choice. "What if you did have a choice?"

She drew herself up taller in the saddle. "There have been times when I've wondered what it would be like to *not* be a princess. The public attention is something I have never sought."

"Could you be content without it?"

"Oh, yes, I could be content without all of this," Cecile stated, making a sweep with her eyes that encompassed the bridle path, the duck pond just beyond, the park, and its entire cadre of early-morning visitors. "I could do without any of it." She gave herself a small shake. "Yet I try not to think of such things."

James was puzzled. "Why not?"

"I fear they can never be, and thinking about them

makes me feel dissatisfied and a little sad." Cecile blinked rapidly. "Now smile, Lord Graystone, or everyone will be speculating about what I have said to you that has made you frown so."

James planted a smile on his face.

"You must try harder," she admonished him. "No one will be fooled by that smile."

James showed his teeth. Then he actually laughed at himself. "Not even your two shadows can doubt the jovial tone of our conversation now," he said, with a backward glance over his shoulder at Count Dupre and Lady Ann Faraday, who were riding a discreet distance behind them.

"They are not my shadows. Lady Ann is my dearest friend in the world and my lady-in-waiting. She has been my constant companion for the past five years and goes everywhere I go."

"She wasn't in the garden with you."

"She goes *nearly* everywhere I go, and you know why I came to the garden alone."

He knew. "For peace and solitude."

A delicate nose was raised ever so slightly in the air. "That was the first time."

"And the second time?"

The lady was surprisingly forthright. "I came to meet you. I came to seek your help."

James couldn't resist adding, "And to ask me for a kiss."

Color instantly washed her cheeks. "Please lower your voice, sir, or someone will surely hear you."

"We don't have this problem in Devon."

For a moment Cecile Girardet regarded him with a quizzical expression. "Which problem?"

"Eavesdropping."

A very telling, "Ah . . ."

"We don't have to inspect behind every rock or tree or shrubbery before we dare speak. Why, there are actually places where a man may ride for five miles and more, and never encounter another human being," he said.

She was perceptive. "You sound as if you have done just that, my lord."

"On numerous occasions."

"At night?"

How had she guessed? "Yes, sometimes I ride at night. More often during the daylight hours, of course. I have a first-rate stable of mounts for both men and women to ride. My own horse is a beauty. He's called Amritsar."

"Amritsar," Cecile repeated. "You no doubt named him for the holy city of the Sikhs."

James nodded his head. The lady amazed him. How had she known? "Exactly so."

"You see, I have been reading about your India. And about your Devon."

It wasn't *his* India. And it wasn't exactly *his* Devon.

Cecile added, "Devon sounds remarkable."

"It is."

She gently teased him. "As is your Graystone Abbey, if I remember correctly."

"You do," he concurred. "Devon is a countryside without equal anywhere in the British Isles, and the heart and soul of Devon is Graystone Abbey."

His companion appeared to be genuinely interested. "Is Graystone Abbey secluded?"

"Somewhat."

She paused only briefly before inquiring, "Does the abbey have gardens?"

James suddenly felt the sun full on his face and a smile on his lips. He could hear the subtle difference in his own voice. "It is said that Graystone Abbey has the most splendid grounds in all of England. There are the Old Woods and a pond for swimming and gardens of every size, variety, and description. The rose garden was my sister-in-law's favorite. It is called Milady's Bower."

"Milady's Bower," Cecile repeated in a soft, hushed tone. "What a beautiful name."

They rode on for a minute or two, enjoying the fine spring morning and managing to ignore the inquisitive stares and numerous whispers that were undoubtedly about them.

James found he wanted to tell her more concerning his ancestral home. "Graystone Abbey also has a superb library, a vast collection of paintings and artifacts collected from every corner of the Empire. There is a magnificent medieval chapel on the estate. Indeed, my niece, Alyssa, was married to Miles St. Aldford, Marquess of Cork, in the Lady Chapel last July. We have remnants of one of the oldest turf mazes anywhere, and it's even been bandied about that we have a pair of ghosts, although they haven't been seen since the summer."

Her clear eyes met his as she repeated an earlier

sentiment. "I wish I could visit this Graystone Abbey of yours, my lord."

His gut tightened. "Perhaps once this affair is concluded."

"Perhaps then."

James glanced back over his shoulder again. "Does Count Dupre also accompany you wherever you go?"

Cecile's voice was suddenly businesslike. "Nearly always. The count was first an adviser to my father. When I was old enough to require his expertise and services, he became my personal aide-de-camp. Count Dupre has loyally served the Girardets all of his life. Indeed, I believe we are his life."

"He has no family of his own?"

"None. Only us. Only my brother and myself."

James realized that Count Dupre and Lady Ann had nearly caught up with them on the sandy riding path. He urged his mount along, and Cecile's followed.

"I understand now why you speak of blessed anonymity," he declared. "Are you never left to your own devices and desires?"

"When I sleep."

"Have you slept?"

Cecile breathed in and out. "A little." She glanced in his direction and then quickly fixed her gaze straight ahead. "And you? Have you slept?"

"Some."

She changed the subject adroitly. "I do believe this is the finest weather we've had since I arrived in London a fortnight ago, Lord Graystone."

James recognized that Cecile had developed an instinct for knowing when they might be overheard.

He played along. "Not all of our spring days are foggy and rainy, Your Serene Highness."

"Naturally I am pleased to hear that."

He teased her. "Am I to understand that the weather in Saint-Simeon is perfect?"

"Nearly all of the year," she responded with a polite and very proper smile.

Once the horse and rider had pranced on by them and they were, more or less, alone again, James decided there was no sense in trying to avoid the subject that they had come here to discuss. "About our problem, madam."

"Our problem, sir?"

"Our problem of finding some sort of justification for being together so we may plan the recovery of the missing . . . items." Discretion was nearly always a wise policy.

Cecile reduced it to its simplest form. "We need an excuse to be seen together."

He wouldn't have put it quite so plainly, but that was essentially the situation. "We have a dilemma. We can no longer risk meeting in the key garden. We require a socially acceptable manner of seeing each other often, yet without raising anyone's suspicions in the process."

"Especially my uncle's."

"Especially Prince Rodolphe's." James gave her a sideways glance. "I hope you won't take offense, madam, but it is necessary that I ask you several questions of a personal nature."

Cecile did not appear in the least inclined to be offended. "You may ask me whatever you wish, sir."

James took in a breath. "Is it true that no particular gentleman currently lays claim to your affections?"

"It is true."

That didn't make sense to him. The princess could have her pick of the blue bloods from any number of countries. "But surely you have been courted by princes and dukes and titled noblemen."

"I was."

"Was?"

James was surprised by the hint of bitterness that crept into her voice. "I believe I was considered very marriageable and a good match, as you English say, until my parents died."

"Of course, you've been in mourning." He should have thought of that, James realized.

"The death of my parents was tragically the reason I first put off the suitors for my hand," she stated, leaning forward slightly in the saddle. "Now I have no interest in marrying."

James was dumbfounded. It was a full thirty seconds before he could collect himself. "You never intend to marry?"

She was adamant. "Never."

There was a short, brittle pause. "You have no interest in taking a husband?"

"None whatsoever."

An idea was starting to present itself to James Gray. He did his thinking out loud, but he made certain that Cecile Girardet was the only one who could hear him. "Then we agree that the imperative issue here is how we can search for and recover the missing 'items' without Prince Rodolphe's knowledge."

"That is it in a nutshell."

"I have an idea."

She gave him a sharp glance. "What is it?"

His mind was racing. "Promise to hear me out before you give me your reply."

"I promise."

James plucked off his hat and ran his hands through the hair at his nape.

Cecile smiled.

"What?" he inquired.

"You always do that when you're agitated."

"I am not agitated." Then he thought better of it. "What do I always do when I'm agitated?"

"You comb your fingers through the silky hair at the back of your neck."

He knew his eyes darkened. "Is the hair at the back of my neck silky?"

She looked briefly disconcerted. "Yes."

James cleared his throat. He must not allow his attention to wander. "As I was saying, madam, I have an idea."

"I think we agree that you have an idea. However, you have not told me what it is."

James took in and let out a deep breath before he said, "I couldn't think of anything else, Cecile."

"James—"

"I have lain awake for hours trying to come up with a solution and nothing occurred to me."

"James—"

"Once the pretense has served its purpose, we will find legitimate grounds for you to break it off."

"What are you trying to say?"

He blurted it out. "I will court you, madam."

Cecile was instantly on her guard, he could see. "I beg your pardon, sir."

"I will pretend to court you. I will take you driving in my carriage. I will dance with you at every ball. I will sit beside you at breakfasts, lunches, and dinners. I will stroll with you in the public parks. I will escort you to concerts, to art galleries, to the Charing Cross bookstalls. I will send you flowers and any number of appropriate gifts. In short, I will stick to you like glue."

Her blue eyes grew round as saucers, yet Cecile said not a word.

James rattled on. "This will accomplish two things at once. It will provide us with a reason to be seen together, and it will enable me to keep you out of harm's way."

"Do you believe I am in danger, then?"

"You said so yourself."

"So I did," she acknowledged.

"Do you agree to my plan?"

"Do I have any choice?" she asked, more to herself than of him. Her head came up. "I agree."

James heaved a sigh of relief. "As anxious as we both are, madam, to plunge right into an investigation, we must first put the villain off the scent." He added several words of explanation. "That is a term used in foxhunting."

"How do you propose we put him off the scent?"

He grabbed a quick breath. "For the next two weeks, I will woo you."

"That is all?"

"That is all."

"The Queen would approve."

"How do you know?"

"She is very fond of you and of your family. She told me privately that she considers you to be one of the best men in all of the Empire."

James felt the heat of embarrassment rise to his face. "Her Majesty is too generous."

"I don't believe so. She simply knows a good man when she sees one."

On this occasion he changed the subject. "Once this business has been successfully concluded, you will, of course, return to Saint-Simeon with the missing articles. That will be the ideal time for you to decide to reject my suit."

"You won't mind."

"Not any more than you will."

Cecile made an amendment. "I must insist upon one condition for this partnership of ours, Graystone."

"Yes, madam?"

"The undertaking is my responsibility. It is the future of my country and my countrymen that is at stake. It is my brother's throne at risk. I will have my part in this business. You cannot do the supposedly heroic and manly thing and keep me out of it. That must be understood from the start."

He understood all right . . . which didn't mean that he agreed. "I understand."

"Then I have your word on it."

She had him there.

Reluctantly James said, "You have my word on it."

"When shall you begin your wooing, then?"

"I believe I have already started with this very public display in Hyde Park."

"So you have."

"I propose that we take tea tomorrow afternoon. Perhaps a late supper together on Monday evening."

"I should very much like to visit the bookshops at Charing Cross Road."

"Weather permitting, we will browse the bookstalls on Tuesday." James pondered the logistics problem for a moment. "I believe I must have Goodenough make up a schedule so that we may coordinate the time and place of our engagements."

"An excellent idea," Cecile concurred.

"I would like to escort you around the British Museum one afternoon when time allows. There are some splendid things there I would like to show you."

"I'll look forward to it."

James rubbed his hand back and forth along his chin. "And you might gaze upon me with some favor."

"When?"

"Now."

Cecile gave him a dazzling smile just as the sun came out from behind the clouds again. The day was suddenly bright and fine, the air clean and filled with the scent of flowers.

James found himself smiling back at her.

It seemed that Princess Cecile of Saint-Simeon was a consummate actress. She was already looking upon him as if she were a woman falling in love.

Chapter Fifteen

Naked women without their heads.

That was Cecile's irreverent opinion upon first viewing the famed Elgin Marbles.

She meant no disrespect for the "crown jewels" of the British Museum. Indeed, the collection of classical female figures that had once graced the Parthenon in Athens was magnificent, and they were more than amply draped in their marble robes.

But Cecile had seen enough statues, sculptures, friezes, antiquities of every size, shape, and historical period, artifacts, archaeological wonders, prized works of art, Old Masters, modern masters, castles, palaces, towers, even parks to last her a lifetime.

And through it all, for three entire weeks, James Gray, thirteenth Earl of Graystone, had been a perfect gentleman.

James was attentive, considerate, courteous, thoughtful, and gracious. He was accommodating, amiable, good-natured, gallant, and excruciatingly polite. He had never once tried to kiss her or touch her, other than to offer his arm as they crossed the street, graced the dance floor, or when she was alighting from a carriage.

It was surprising.

It was puzzling.

It was maddening.

The voice of the museum curator droned on: "And this is the Rosetta Stone, Your Serene Highness."

Cecile was all politeness. "Ah, yes, from which the Frenchman, Champollion, succeeded in working out the basic principles for deciphering Egyptian hieroglyphic writing. As a result of his painstaking work over several decades, the long-lost secrets of a vanished civilization were finally revealed."

"I see Her Serene Highness is a student of history," the gentleman complimented her.

"My parents—that is, my late parents—felt it was as important for a lady to be well educated as it was for a gentleman," she informed the little man.

"How singular," the curator sputtered, pushing his spectacles back up his nose.

"Yes, my parents were singular," she agreed.

Cecile noticed there was a dusting of chalk—or perhaps it was simply dirt—on the sleeve of the coat hastily donned when they had been shown into the curator's office. The gray powder was now also smeared across the man's cherublike cheeks.

"I'm certain Her Serene Highness agrees with me. We have taken up enough of your valuable time, sir," James interceded. "We will now happily wander about the museum on our own."

The scholarly gentleman bowed and scraped his way out of the imposing exhibit area whose ceiling soared fifty feet and more above their heads. "Yes.

Of course. Quite. Naturally you may take as long as you like."

Cecile spoke on her own behalf as well as her entourage, which this afternoon included the ever-present Lady Ann and Count Dupre, in addition to James. "You have been too kind, sir."

Then James was drawing her attention to an exhibit case in the next room. "I believe you will enjoy seeing the Portland Vase, Your Serene Highness. It was probably made in Italy around the turn of the first centuries B.C. and A.D."

"It is beautiful," Cecile commented upon examining the blue and white glass vase carved in the cameo technique with traditional mythological scenes. She circled the display. "To think it has survived nearly two millennia."

"It nearly didn't," James told her. "The vase was smashed by a deranged visitor to the museum in 1845. It was restored from more than two hundred pieces."

They walked on some little distance, leaving Ann and the Count to the fabled vase.

"James, it is time we talked," she whispered.

"Somehow I was under the impression that's all we've done for the past three weeks," he muttered.

Cecile cast a meaningful glance at him. "I don't mean that kind of talk."

"Neither do I," he said without the faintest smile. "We must take the next step."

"I agree."

"We must make plans."

"I agree again."

"It is time we acted."

"Exactly."

"Since we seem to be of one mind on the matter, where do you suggest we go from here?"

Already on his way to the next room, James stopped and faced her. "The ancient Roman exhibit."

She was not amused. "You know that's not what I meant."

"I know." He strode along beside her. "Since you haven't up to this point, I think it's time you described in more detail the three missing objects."

Of course. He was right. It was an excellent place to start. "I'll begin with the coronation crown," Cecile said quietly, taking care that her voice did not carry in the cavernous chamber. "It is a circlet of gold. The band is plain metal in the back and rises to a crest in the front. There is a large oblong-shaped pearl set in the center. The pearl is surrounded by diamonds of some little merit, several unfaceted rubies and a number of amethysts and turquoises."

"What is its approximate size?"

She frowned. "It is the approximate size of a human head, of course."

James chuckled under his breath. "I assumed that much. What is its troy weight?"

She formed an O with her mouth. "Fifteen or perhaps sixteen ounces."

He stopped and examined a pair of marble greyhounds found at Monte Cagnolo near Rome, part of a remarkable collection amassed by the eighteenth-century dilettante Charles Townley according to the plaque at the dogs' base.

"So I'm looking for a medium-size crown that could effectively be hidden almost anywhere," James muttered, certainly more to himself than to her.

Cecile shook her head and corrected the gentleman. "*We* are looking for a medium-size crown."

"Quite."

She went on. "The missing scepter is ivory and gold. It is very much like a fancy walking stick, if somewhat longer than the average stick. The top is adorned with a semi-precious jeweled orb, a golden cross and a white ivory dove."

"Distinctive."

"Exceedingly so." Cecile removed a lace-edged linen handkerchief from her black velvet chatelaine pocket and brushed a bit of dust from the sleeve of her dress.

James prompted her to continue. "And the sacred chalice?"

"The sacred chalice is a gold altar cup of eight or nine inches in height," she related. "The base is scalloped along the outer edges. The stem is three-tiered. The cup itself is engraved with the Girardet family coat-of-arms: a dove with a sword clasped in one claw and an olive branch in the other."

"Representing war and peace."

She nodded.

"All of the missing items are unique," James pointed out unnecessarily.

She nodded again.

They passed several exhibit halls without entering. It was another two or three minutes before James remarked to her, "Why must these three objects be present in the cathedral in order for your brother to be crowned?" He made a motion in the air with his hand. "I understand that had always been the tradition in Saint-Simeon, but surely the penalty is too severe in this case."

Cecile tucked the handkerchief away. She would try to explain. "It is believed that if the future ruler of Saint-Simeon cannot guard and protect these three objects, how can he possibly protect and defend his country and its subjects."

James shook his head from side to side. "I understand. And, yet, I don't understand."

"The same can be said for the traditions of many countries," she maintained. "Perhaps that is why they are traditions, whether they be English, Indian, or Saint-Simeon."

"Your point is well taken," he conceded.

"Where do we go from here?" Cecile inquired.

Her companion was preoccupied. "I don't know," came the belated response.

This time Cecile had meant the question literally. "Shall we take the corridor to the left or the one to the right?"

James looked up. Then he glanced around. "Do you prefer to examine additional antiquities from ancient Rome or ancient Egypt?"

In truth, she presumed it was of little consequence to their discussion. But a choice must be made.

Cecile picked one. "Ancient Egypt."

"This way, then."

They paused in front of two black granite seated statues of the pharaoh Amenophis III.

"Can you believe the audacity, the impudence, the effrontery, the absolute gall?" Cecile spat.

James seemed taken aback. "I beg your pardon, madam."

"Look." She pointed to the spot. "Here behind the left heel of the larger statue."

James looked.

There was a name clearly carved into the black granite. Cecile read it aloud. "Belzoni." She could scarcely contain her contempt. "He dared to call himself an archaeologist. The man was a plunderer. Do you know what Belzoni did to earn a living before he went out to Egypt and began to dig around?"

James confessed that he did not.

"He was a strong man at London fairs."

Before she could expound further on the sins of the Italian procurer of antiquities, the museum curator came dashing into the hall, spectacles cockeyed, collar askew, voice quivering as he called out, "Lord Graystone, thank heavens I have found you."

The diminutive gentleman immediately secured James's attention. "Sir, what is it?"

"An accident." He goaded the spectacles onto the bridge of his nose. "There has been an accident."

"Where?"

"Ancient Rome."

"Is anyone hurt?"

"I don't know. I don't know." Chalk-covered hands were clenched and unclenched in turn. "Please hurry, my lord."

James turned to her. "It would be best for you to remain here, Your Serene Highness, until I see what this business is about. I will send Lady Ann and the count along directly."

"I'll wait here." Under the circumstances, it seemed the most judicious course of action.

"You must come now, Lord Graystone," the curator insisted, practically tugging on the earl's sleeve.

James looked back over his shoulder as he reluctantly left her to her own devices in the Egyptian gallery. His parting words were, "I'll return as quickly as I can."

Cecile didn't mind in the least finding herself alone for a few minutes. Solitude had always been a scarce commodity in her life. During the past three weeks, it had been only more so. For she had discovered— she had known it was true from their first meeting— that James Gray was a man of his word. He had vowed to stick to her like glue, and that is exactly what he had done.

James Gray, man of his word.

James Gray, perfect gentleman.

James Gray, passionate lover.

For the hundredth time in the past few weeks Cecile thought of that night in the gazebo. Why had she behaved in such an uncharacteristic manner? How could she have permitted James to take such liberties? Why hadn't she stopped him?

The reason was evident: She had not wanted him to stop. Which meant the man was dangerous. He unleashed something inside her—something sensual, something carnal, something wild and wonderful and free.

And frightening.

She loved the feel of his lips on hers, his hands caressing her body, his mouth on her breasts. Indeed, she would have liked more of his lovemaking, not less.

The truth left Cecile stunned.

What must he think of her?

She knew the answer. James had obviously had his share of regrets and had thought better of the whole business. He had not come near her since that night.

In the future, she would have to be on her guard. She was obviously too easily tempted by what the handsome earl offered. She was too readily *and* too eagerly led astray by him. She wasn't to be trusted when it came to James Gray or his kisses.

Cecile heaved a long-suffering sigh. It was a great pity for she had never met a gentleman more to her liking.

Suddenly she glanced up and perceived that she had not stayed put as James had instructed. She had apparently been daydreaming and wandering. This was a part of the museum where she had never been before.

Where was she?

Cecile peered to the right and then to the left. She was sure she had not passed this way before. Nothing was the least bit familiar to her. She was lost.

Nonsense.

She put her shoulders back and raised her chin a fraction of an inch in the air. She was never lost. She had an excellent sense of direction. She would simply retrace her steps. That must be the way back to the Egyptian Gallery.

It wasn't the way back to anywhere. It was another dead end leading to yet another dead end. She was getting no closer to finding her way out of this rabbit warren of exhibit halls, galleries, and dusty storage rooms filled with massive stone heads (one she recognized as being that of the Buddha), a lifesize bronze horse and suit of armor, the numbered stone blocks of a Greek temple stacked in piles and awaiting reconstruction, than she had been a quarter of an hour ago.

Cecile went perfectly still.

Had she heard something? Were those footsteps behind her? Was someone there?

"James, is that you? Have you been searching for me? You mustn't scold me for not staying put," she called out, and then felt a little foolish for having done so.

There was no reply.

And there was no warning.

Before Cecile could turn around, someone put their hands in the middle of her back and gave her a shove. She fell against the stone wall, hitting her right elbow on a sharp corner. Instantly she broke out in a cold sweat. Pain shot down her arm. She wondered briefly if a bone had been broken.

Before she had the time or opportunity to recover from the first assault, another even more forceful shove landed between her shoulder blades.

The wall in front of her gave way.

It swung open. She stumbled forward into some kind of chamber. Then the opening in the wall immediately closed behind her.

Cecile groped about for a handle, for a lever, for any means to get out. She pushed with her left arm; the right was still throbbing and of little use. She threw the full force of her weight against the wall. It didn't budge.

There was a slightly musty, decayed smell in the air. She tried to ignore the sound of something underfoot skittering across the floor. She brushed away what she assumed was a cobweb.

She finally called out. "Hello!"

Silence greeted her.

She raised her voice. "Hello! Is anyone there? Could you please help me? I'm inside the wall."

Dead silence.

That was when a small feeling of panic began to creep into Cecile's heart and mind. Perhaps there was no way out.

She was trapped in darkness.

There was only darkness.

Chapter Sixteen

Where the devil had she disappeared to?
Why hadn't she stayed put in the Egyptian
Gallery as he had ordered? A bemused smile materialized on James Gray's masculine features. Because a
man did not order a woman—especially a determined and headstrong woman like Cecile Girardet—
to do anything. The lady had a definite mind of
her own.

James retraced his steps from the point where they
had viewed the Portland Vase, through a series of
corridors and exhibit halls to the Egyptian antiquities area.

Cecile was nowhere to be found.

He raised a hand, drove his fingers through the
hair at his nape—what had Cecile called it? Silky?—
and muttered under his breath, "Damn. Damn.
Damn."

Where was she?

He was concerned, but he wasn't about to raise
an alarm that would bring Count Dupre, Lady Ann
Faraday, and every museum official within shouting
distance rushing to the rescue only to discover that
the princess was sitting somewhere enjoying some

quiet moments to herself. Lord knew, the lady had few enough of those in her life.

At a time like this discretion was called for. He would quietly and methodically search for Cecile himself. He would involve the others only if or when he was forced to.

The present situation was entirely his fault, anyway. He was the one who had deserted her and hurried off with the frenetic curator, only to find that the emergency in Ancient Rome had been no more than a toppled statue.

Of course, it had been a statue of some considerable academic and archaeological value, and it now lay on the museum floor, smashed into a thousand irretrievable fragments.

The museum curator had been wiping copious tears from his dust-streaked cheeks when James had excused himself and returned to Cecile . . . or where he had expected to find Cecile.

The skin around Graystone's mouth grew taut. "This is the exact spot where I left her," he growled aloud. "Where would she have gone from here?"

Perhaps the lady had simply had enough of him. After all, they had spent nearly every waking hour of the past three weeks in each other's company. The ruse was working to perfection. The villain appeared to be put off the scent. Indeed, the whole of English society believed that the Earl of Graystone was paying court to Her Serene Highness, Princess Cecile of Saint-Simeon.

Speculation was running rampant.

It was whispered in every drawing room from

Mayfair to Park Lane to Buckingham Palace itself—
James had it on the best authority: his valet and personal sleuthhound, Goodenough—that the official announcement of a betrothal between Lord Graystone
and the princess could surely not be very far away.

James swore softly under his breath.

Maybe he was trying to juggle too many things at
once. If he wasn't careful something was bound to
get dropped and broken. He only hoped it wasn't
the lady's heart . . . or his own.

He had made a mistake. He shouldn't have further
complicated an already complex situation by taking
liberties with the princess that night in the gazebo.
He had known better. He was a man of the world
and she was an innocent. It had been up to him to
keep a potentially explosive situation under control.

His enviable self-control.

What a farce!

In fact, night after night, as he lay awake in his
bed, James had found himself getting hard just recall-
ing the way Cecile had felt under his mouth, beneath
his hands, pressed against his body.

Hell, he was getting hard right now.

It suddenly occurred to Graystone. What if the
lady was aware of his physical reaction to her?
Maybe she had felt his erection and been repulsed
by the very notion of what it signified.

He had much to answer for, James concluded. Cecile had been the blameless victim in all of this. If
any harm should befall her, it would be on his
conscience.

Graystone's heart was suddenly pounding, but his

mind was crystal clear. His senses were razor sharp. His hands were steady. That's the way it had always been in times of danger.

Was there danger?

He wasn't certain. He supposed there was a remote possibility that her sudden disappearance could have something to do with the mission she was on. Either way, he would get to the bottom of this business if it was the last thing he did, James vowed.

And if one hair had been harmed on Cecile's lovely head, he would make someone pay . . . and pay dearly.

James Gray knew what he must do. He must find the princess. He must apologize to her for his lapse of judgment in the gazebo. He must soothe her, perhaps kiss her reassuringly a time or two. Then he must escort the lady back to her entourage. And he must, above all else, be a gentleman about it.

He marched along a stretch of deserted corridor, peering into empty exhibit rooms, galleries filled with artifacts, storage rooms piled high with bits and pieces from every corner of the world.

James opened his mouth. "Your Serene Highness, are you here?"

There was no answer.

Not a sound.

Cutting down another passageway, he inspected the chambers on either side, and came up empty-handed. It was as though the woman had vanished into thin air.

James planted himself in the middle of the last corridor, his feet a good eighteen inches apart, his hands forming fists, and glared into the fading afternoon light.

Where in the hell was she?

He didn't believe for a moment that Cecile Girardet was playing games with him. That wasn't her style. But when another ten minutes had passed and he still had not discovered a trace of the lady, he became genuinely concerned.

His finely honed instincts—those same instincts that he had come to trust and rely on over the years—warned James that the matter might no longer be one of lost and found. It might well have been one of life and death.

A sense of urgency drove him. He turned into a branch of the museum that they had not toured earlier that day. He stopped and cocked his head and listened.

Thunk. Thunk. Thunk.

James listened again, but there was only silence. Had he heard the rhythmic thunking or merely imagined it?

He came upon a large storage area. It was stacked from floor to ceiling. There was a pile of what he judged to be stones from a dismantled Greek temple. A huge head of Buddha rested on its side. There was a hammered mail coat of armor for both horse and rider. And a strange stone wall directly in front of him.

There!

He was rewarded by hearing the thunk, thunk, thunk grow louder. "Cecile? My God, Cecile, is that you?"

There was a faint and muffled cry, "James!"

She was behind the stone wall. There must be a way in. Yet he couldn't detect one, even after careful examination. That usually meant some kind of fulcrum point moved an invisible door.

"Stand back!" he shouted, hoping she could hear him. Then James put his shoulder to the stone and pushed with all his might.

Nothing happened.

He tried again several more times and in several different places, but it was to no avail. Then in sheer frustration, James raised his fist and brought it down on the blasted thing.

The stone wall moved.

There was a very small and very dark chamber concealed behind the stone facade. It was scarcely large enough for one person.

"Cecile."

"James."

"Jesus, Mary, and Joseph!" he exclaimed as the lady collapsed into his arms.

Chapter Seventeen

When Cecile opened her eyes moments later, James was holding on to her for dear life. She was caught up in his embrace, her head resting on his shoulder, her uninjured arm wrapped around his neck.

His eyes were nearly charcoal gray in color. He appeared angry. "How the devil did you end up in there?" He sounded angry.

"Where?"

"In that—" a forceful gesture was made toward the wall behind them "—place."

Cecile reached up with her sore arm and attempted to wipe away the tears she suddenly realized were trickling down her cheeks. "What is that place?"

James withdrew a clean linen handkerchief from his pocket and tenderly dabbed at her face. "Some kind of ancient version of a priest's hole, would be my guess."

Cecile glanced back over his shoulder at the small dark chamber in which she had found herself trapped, and shuddered. She wondered how long she had been confined inside such a narrow space. She had lost all track of time.

James was seeking answers. "Are you ready to tell me what happened?"

Despite her endeavors to appear calm, Cecile's voice came out quivery. "I remember I was . . . day-dreaming." She was not about to confess to the gentleman that he had been the subject of her daydreams. "All of a sudden I realized I had wandered off from the spot where you had left me."

That drew a stern stare. "Go on."

She moistened her lips. "I tried to find my way back, but I could not." She looked up at James with a tremulous smile. "I usually have an unerring sense of direction."

He wasn't exactly furious with her. "Apparently it wasn't unerring this afternoon."

"No, it wasn't," she admitted. "Anyway, I somehow ended up here. I was looking around . . ."

"When you must have bumped against the wall and fallen into the chamber," James finished for her.

"That isn't exactly what occurred."

"Then exactly what did occur?"

She opened her mouth and closed it again.

He waited.

Cecile took a moment to collect her thoughts. She was still feeling surprisingly lightheaded. Was it a result of the incident? Or because James was still holding her in his arms?

"You may put me down now, sir. I am quite capable of standing on my own two feet."

"As you wish, madam."

She steadied herself, dusted her skirts off, and straightened her shoulders.

James pursued his line of inquiry. "You were about to tell me what happened."

"I was exploring the storage area, specifically that wall, when I thought I heard footsteps. I called out your name—you see, I thought you had finally managed to find me—and I was about to turn around when someone pushed me."

Graystone regarded her with a troubled frown. "Someone pushed you?"

Cecile nodded. "He put his hands on my back and gave me a shove. That's when I stumbled against the stone wall. Somehow it opened up and I fell inside. Before I had time to comprehend what was happening, it had closed behind me."

James's tone was fierce. "Then it was no accident."

"It was no accident," she assured him.

The expression on his handsome face was grim. His speech was clipped. "Did you see the culprit's face?"

"No, he was behind me the entire time. There was no opportunity to see anyone."

Dark eyes—the irises were nearly black now—narrowed into slits. "How do you know it was a man?"

Cecile pondered the question. "It was the hand on my back. It seemed too large and too strong to be a woman's."

"Did the knave speak?"

"No. Not a word." Cecile swayed on her feet.

James was suddenly solicitous. "Are you hurt?"

"I hit my elbow against the corner of a stone." She teetered precariously. "I apologize for being such a bother, but I do feel as though I might faint."

James quickly supported her by the arm and led her to a nearby unopened shipping crate. Under the circumstances, it would have to do. There was no other place available to sit down. As she took a seat, Cecile winced.

His mouth curved downward. "Is it your arm?"

"Yes."

"May I be allowed to examine it?"

"Of course."

"I have had some experience with medical matters," Graystone explained as he went down on his haunches beside her. He undid the row of tiny pearl buttons up the sleeve of her dress and pushed the material aside.

"No doubt from your years in India," she remarked, and tried not to grimace as he poked and prodded the region around her elbow.

He glanced up. "There are no broken bones."

"That's a relief."

His touch was gentle. "Although you have no doubt badly bruised your arm."

"Thank goodness."

James frowned.

"Thank goodness it's only a bruise. I need to be healthy."

He arched a quizzical brow.

"So we may actively begin our investigation," she reminded him.

"Ah, yes, our investigation."

Cecile tried to take a deep breath, but the air was unpleasantly warm and stifling in this section of the museum. She wished she were carrying a fan in her reticule.

She focused her attention on James. "Is someone after me?"

His face worked furiously. "I wouldn't say someone is after you. If the scoundrel had meant to do you genuine physical harm, there was ample opportunity."

"Why shove me into that place, then?"

"Perhaps someone was trying to frighten you."

"To what end?"

Graystone rose to his full height—he towered over her—and began to pace the floor in front of her, back and forth, back and forth. "I don't know."

Small beads of perspiration appeared on Cecile's forehead and upper lip. She was suddenly hot. Indeed, she was feeling quite feverish. Her head ached and her stomach was queasy.

"James—"

He stopped pacing and looked down at her. "You're as white as a ghost."

"I feel . . . odd."

"Are you going to faint?"

Cecile never had the chance to answer him. One instant she was sitting upright on the packing crate. The next she simply toppled over into a heap.

The creator of the tight-laced corset had much to answer for, in James Gray's opinion. The cursed thing was a health hazard for every female who was obliged to wear one of the ridiculous contraptions. And all for the sake of so-called fashion.

Bloody ridiculous, that's what it was!

Cecile had swooned before his very eyes, her eyes rolling back into her head. Her complexion was still exceptionally pale. There was a fine sheen of perspiration on the surface of her skin, and her breathing was shallow.

Under the circumstances there was only one sensible course of action for James to follow: He began to undo the row of pearl buttons that ran down the front of the lady's dress.

Underneath the outer garment was some kind of lacy bodice. He unhooked the fastening at the top and hoped that it would at least give Cecile breathing room. Then he looked around for something to fan her with.

The answer was near at hand. Amongst what appeared to be a collection of ceremonial objects stacked in the corner of the storage room was a large, ornate, golden palm frond. Probably very old. Probably Egyptian. Perhaps once used to cool and refresh the person of the pharaoh himself.

James wafted it back and forth across her face and throat.

Cecile gave a low groan and moved slightly. Her eyes slowly opened. She touched the tip of her tongue to her lips. For once James wished that he carried a small flask of spirits on his person. This would have been an opportune moment to administer a medicinal sip of brandy.

"What happened?" Cecile murmured, reaching up to touch her forehead.

"You swooned." He ceased fanning her and offered an explanation. "I believe it was the unfortunate combination of being overwrought—"

The lady instantly cut him off. "I am never overwrought," she corrected.

James felt it only polite to concede the point. He finished his sentence, "—the absence of fresh air in this wing of the museum and the absurd undergarments you ladies feel you must wear."

Cecile's hand fluttered to her bare throat. "My dress is partially undone," she said, trying to sit up.

"Never fear, madam, your modesty is intact," he replied, not altogether in a serious tone.

Her response surprised him. "It was a very sensible thing for you to do, sir. I couldn't seem to get my breath."

"Are you feeling better?"

"A little."

"I wish I could offer you a sip of brandy or a cup of tea or even a glass of water . . ." James looked about. "But there doesn't seem to be anything readily available."

"I will be quite myself in a minute or two," she declared.

As if to prove her point, Cecile Girardet sat up on the shipping crate, smoothed her skirts, patted her hair—tucking in the one errant strand that had dared to come loose from her coiffure—and took a deep, reviving breath.

It was then that James spotted the chain hanging about the lady's neck. Apparently she wore it beneath her garments, for he certainly hadn't noticed it previously.

What captured his interest, however, was not so much the gold chain, as the small circular object dangling from it: It appeared to be a gold ring.

Cecile became aware of his scrutiny. Her hand fluttered to her throat, her fingers closed around the ring. "It was my mother's wedding band," she offered by way of an explanation.

"I didn't mean to intrude," James said, feeling as though that was exactly what he had done.

"You didn't ask."

No, he hadn't asked. But he felt as if he had.

Cecile grew absolutely still. "I had hoped . . . I had wanted . . . I had wished for my parents to be buried wearing their wedding rings, but someone had them removed." Sadness emanated from her. "They were given to me as keepsakes."

James found he did not know what to say.

In scarcely a whisper she said, "*Vous et Nul Autre.*"

His heart thudded. His skin prickled. His throat closed. His voice failed. He suddenly turned cold.

"Do you know what it means?" she inquired.

It seemed like an eternity before James managed to nod his head. "You and No Other."

Cecile trembled and looked up at him. "That is the inscription on the inside of the rings."

His gut clenched. "You wear your mother's ring."

"Yes."

"Where is your father's ring?"

She swallowed and shook her head. "I'm not certain."

"Is it lost?"

Enormous blue eyes gazed into his. "I hope not."

James started to raise his hand to his own throat when they both heard a commotion in the distance, followed by the sound of voices.

"That will in all probability be Count Dupre and Lady Ann," he conjectured. "I was going to send them to you earlier, at the time the curator rushed in and begged for my assistance, but they had decided to go on to the manuscript room."

Cecile panicked. "They mustn't find us like this."

"They mustn't find us like what?"

She corrected herself. "They must not find me sitting here with my dress undone and my chemise showing."

The lady had a point.

She tried to do up her own buttons, but her hands were still shaking badly and the simple task became an impossible one for her.

"I'll do it," James offered, brushing her hands aside. "Can you stand?"

Cecile wobbled to her feet. "Of course."

He bent his legs slightly at the knees—putting him more at eye level with the job to be done—and quickly and efficiently fastened her bodice and did up the front of her dress. Then he turned his attention to the small pearl buttons on her sleeve.

"Voilà!" James took a step back and admired his handiwork. "Other than the fact that you're a bit pale, no one would suspect that you have met any misfortune."

"Thank you, James," she said in a beautiful voice.

"You're welcome, Cecile."

She turned her head in the direction of the approaching voices. "The others will be here momentarily."

"Yes, they will." To his regret, James realized.

"We still have much to discuss."

"And plans to make," he added.

She murmured so quietly that he could barely hear her. "I have missed our walks in the key garden."

So had he. "So have I."

She went on to say more. "It seems it was the only time that we were ever truly alone."

James drew in a long breath and let it out slowly. "It was, but it grew too risky."

She sighed and bit her lip. "I suppose so." Then, "Do you think the roses are in bloom?"

He'd forgotten about the roses. "Perhaps some of the earliest varieties."

Footsteps and voices grew louder, closer.

"Will you promise me something?" Cecile said quickly before the others rejoined them.

He didn't even ask what. "Yes."

"Will you promise to show me the roses in our garden when they are in full bloom?"

James promised.

And he was a man who always kept his promises.

Chapter Eighteen

"Goodenough, your report," James requested of his valet as he was dressing in the privacy of his chambers at Cork House the morning after touring the British Museum.

His manservant held up the coat they had selected for the day's outings: a perfunctory appearance at Graystone's infrequently frequented solicitors and the welcome diversion of luncheon with Lord Silverthorn, his old friend from Oxford.

"Shall I begin with the ladies, my lord?"

James Gray thrust his arms into the sleeves of his jacket, turned in a half circle, and checked his general appearance in the full-length mirror. "By all means, do."

Goodenough commenced. "Lady Ann Faraday has devotedly served Her Serene Highness, Princess Cecile of Saint-Simeon, as lady-in-waiting for the past five years."

This was not news to James. Cecile had informed him of as much herself.

"A different tie, I think," he indicated to his valet, rejecting their first choice.

"Quite so," Goodenough readily agreed. "Perhaps one a little more conservative in style."

"Please carry on with your account," James said once the proper neckwear had been selected.

"Lady Ann suffered the loss of both her parents within a relatively short period of time; apparently due to some mysterious ailment. Naturally she was devastated by their deaths."

James could well understand the young woman's feelings. The same misfortune had befallen his niece, Alyssa, now the Marchioness of Cork. Her father and mother—his elder brother, Thomas, and his sister-in-law, Annemarie—had succumbed to a contagious fever within a few weeks of each other. He, unfortunately, had been out in India at the time of the tragedy.

Goodenough stepped back to survey the sartorial outcome of their efforts. Apparently satisfied with what he saw, he picked up his narrative where he'd left off. "The demise of her parents occurred just after Lady Ann's official debut into society. She was eighteen years old, an only child, and a daughter."

James shook his head. He could almost predict what was coming next.

"Her father's title, his estates, and his income were passed on to a distant male cousin. Except for a modest annual stipend from an inheritance that had traditionally been passed down through the female line and a bit of jewelry from her maternal grandmother, Lady Ann was left out in the cold, so to speak."

James went to the bureau where Goodenough had laid out a clean handkerchief and his leather wallet. Unlike many—perhaps most—gentlemen of his class, he would never again so much as cross the street without a few pounds in his coat pocket. Not after his experiences last summer when he had been utterly destitute.

"What did Lady Ann do then?"

"Rather than agree to a marriage of convenience, she chose to accept an invitation extended by her late parents' friends, Maximilian V and Judith of Saint-Simeon. The Girardets offered her a home, a place of honor within their close-knit society, and hope for the future when the young woman thought there was none to be had."

James got directly to the point. "Is Lady Ann to be trusted?"

"Implicitly. She loves no one in the world more than Princess Cecile." A momentary hesitation gave Goodenough away.

"Unless it would be . . . ?" James prompted as he straightened his necktie.

His manservant became very absorbed in brushing nonexisting lint from the shoulders of James's jacket.

"Are there rumors, Goodenough?"

"No, my lord."

"Innuendoes?"

"Not a single one that I could ascertain."

James slipped his handkerchief and wallet into his pocket. "Then what?"

His valet was reluctant to speak. "It is only speculation on my part, my lord."

"Speculation based on what?"

Goodenough overcame his misgivings. "Gut instincts, if you will pardon the expression."

James couldn't prevent the smile that turned up

the corners of his mouth. "I trust your gut instincts over most men's absolute convictions," he informed the younger man.

His valet was pleased by the compliment: There was the merest suggestion of gratification on his normally stoic features. Goodenough was a fellow who played his cards very close to his chest.

Graystone asked the logical question. "What do your gut instincts tell you about Lady Ann Faraday?"

Out it popped: "I believe she is in love with His Serene Highness, Prince Alexandre."

That pronouncement caught James utterly by surprise. "Cecile's brother?"

"Just so, my lord."

Frowning, James crossed his arms. "She has stayed all these years for the princess and the prince." He dropped his arms to his sides. "Does anyone know?"

"I do not think anyone has the slightest idea besides Lady Ann, of course, and now you, my lord, and myself."

"Excellent piece of work, Goodenough."

"Thank you, my lord."

James sauntered across the bedchamber, unlatched the window, pushed it open wide, and gazed down on the key garden below. The trees were rapidly greening. The garden would presently be in full bloom. Very soon he must keep his promise to show Cecile the roses. "What of the other lady?"

A scowl marred John Goodenough's handsome if still somewhat youthful features. "The former Moira Munson, daughter of a North Country gentleman of no repute, and these past twenty years Lady Pale, wife and then widow of Lord Osgood Pale, is a different kettle of fish altogether, my lord."

No surprises there. "I presumed as much."

"May I speak bluntly?"

"I expect you to."

Goodenough put it in plain, simple, straightforward terms. "The lady is no lady."

"What is she?"

One brow was arched in a knowing fashion. "Lady Pale is many things."

"Such as . . ."

"She is nothing more than a fancy courtesan, my lord. From all accounts, she has had a long and not always illustrious string of lovers from the time she was fourteen."

"Good God."

"Lady Pale is presently mistress to Prince Rodolphe." Seemingly for maximum impact, Goodenough added, "At least on this side of the Channel."

"And on the other side of the Channel?"

"The Comtesse Thérèse Tournaire entertains him."

"Well, well."

"Lady Pale is reputed to be a great beauty, and yet a self-serving and selfish woman."

James reflected on the nature of beauty. The two sometimes went hand-in-hand: exceptional beauty and self-absorption. Cecile was that rarest of women: beautiful on the outside and even more beautiful on the inside.

Goodenough was still talking. "The countess is also something of a paradox."

"Explain."

"Lady Pale is notorious for her greed. It is well known that she expects to benefit financially from her relationship with Prince Rodolphe. Indeed, the prince recently presented her with a diamond necklace that was rumored to have once been in the collection of the dowager Grand Duchess M—"

The conversation James Gray had overheard the evening of the ball in Cecile's honor replayed in his head.

"Do you think they're real, Castle?"

"Damned if I know, Lloyd-Worth, but I understand the fellow has money to burn."

"Girardet is rumored to be a prince of some sort, isn't he? French, I gather."

"None of them seem to have any money."

"Mark my words, this one does."

"The lady is a beauty. Some years younger than Girardet, too. I'll bet she leads him a merry chase."

"Wouldn't mind having her lead me a merry chase just once."

"It would be the death of you, assuming you could meet the lady's price."

"So, you do think they're real."

"They're real all right."

"So the elderly gentleman was right," James muttered under his breath.

"I beg your pardon, my lord."

"It is nothing of import, Goodenough. Just something I overheard about Lady Pale and her famous—or should I say her infamous?—diamond necklace." He brought the subject of their conversation back to its original point. "Why is she a paradox?"

"Because as self-serving as the lady is known to be, she is also kind to her servants. Indeed, to the lower classes, in general."

"Curiouser and curiouser."

"I thought so, my lord."

"A woman of several faces."

"Perhaps more aptly, my lord, two-faced." Goodenough continued. "On the other hand, Lady Pale is a seeker of thrills of every variety, especially those sexual in nature, and she is not overly particular about whom she harms in the process."

Graystone had seen her type before out in India. Beautiful women of a certain ilk. Pampered women. Bored women. Lonely women. Women with too much time on their hands, far too little character and no scruples whatsoever.

James said aloud what they were both thinking. "Lady Pale is not to be trusted. I suspect she is more intelligent than she would like anyone to know, and too clever by half."

"Exactly so, my lord."

"Keep an eye out for that one, Goodenough."

"I will, my lord."

"On to the gentlemen, then."

"Count Dupre is by all accounts exactly as Her Serene Highness described him to you. He has devoted his life to the Girardets: first the father, now the daughter."

"A man of honor."

"A man who has lived an exemplary life according to those who would speak of him at all."

James strolled to the table in the adjoining sitting

room and poured himself a cup of coffee. He lifted the cover of a silver serving dish and discovered fresh strawberries. He popped several into his mouth. It was three or four minutes before he picked up their conversation where they had left off.

Their discussion of Prince Rodolphe took somewhat longer than the others. It concluded with an observation from James. "The man will be a formidable foe, Goodenough."

Graystone was reminded by his companion. "It is two against one now, my lord."

That brought James's head up. He had always acted alone in the past. Working with a partner would be a novel experience for him. "So it is."

His valet snapped to attention. "In fact, I can think of only one man who I consider to be even more formidable than Girardet himself."

"Who might that be?"

"You, my lord."

Graystone crossed the room, briefly placed his hand on the younger man's shoulder and gave it a masculine thump. "Thank you, Goodenough."

Then James began to pace, threading his fingers through the hair at his nape—always a sign that he was agitated according to a certain young woman— and tried to do some serious thinking.

He did not, however, see how a man could accomplish anything of import while he was stuck in town. What James needed was Amritsar beneath him and the familiar countryside of his beloved Devon around him. For it was there, with the wind whipping his horse's mane from side to side—Flick! Whap! Flick!

Whap!—and blowing full force into his face, that Graystone did his best thinking.

Goodenough was very good at any number of things, as he would be the first to admit. This morning James found he particularly appreciated two of his valet's talents: the ability to wait patiently and to keep silent while he did so.

Then James knew what had to be done, and how to go about doing it. Relief flowed through him. "Goodenough, we will require disguises for our next undertaking."

"*We*, my lord?"

"We."

"Am I to assume you mean yourself, my lord, and me?"

James felt in control again. It was a good feeling. It was a great feeling. "That is precisely what I mean."

"May I ask what we will need in the way of disguises?"

"Actually we'll each need two disguises."

"Two?"

"Two separate disguises. Two separate missions."

His valet seemed to have no trouble following Graystone's train of thought. That was another skill James appreciated in the younger man: He didn't have to explain himself at every turn.

"The first venture will require us to masquerade as a wealthy, titled gentleman and his manservant," he stated.

"Surely that requires no disguise, Lord Graystone."

"That is where you are wrong."

Nonplussed, Goodenough blinked. "I don't think that is very likely, my lord."

James suddenly realized he was enjoying himself. "You will be posing as the gentleman, Goodenough, and I will be two places behind you acting as your personal secretary."

The man's mouth dropped open. He snapped it shut. Yet it was still a full thirty seconds before John Goodenough could speak. "That will never do."

"Of course it will do. In fact, it is absolutely necessary for the success of our plan."

"Why?"

"Because I cannot risk being recognized. You must draw all the attention to yourself so that I may fade into the background. I must neither be seen, nor heard, nor remembered."

"Ahhh . . ."

"You, on the other hand, must be unforgettable, impressive—" James made a broad, sweeping motion in the air "—even flamboyant."

Intelligent brown eyes glimmered. "Flamboyant, you say, my lord? That will undoubtedly mean the employment of a foreign accent and grandiose manners."

James detailed the outline of his plan. "In order to pull off our ruse, you will represent yourself as a gentleman of means."

"To what end?"

"A very wealthy foreign nobleman and his manservant are going to pay a visit to the offices of Meeson and Johnson, architects."

"For what purpose?"

"You are going to express an interest in having Mr. Meeson and Mr. Johnson build you the most magnificent palazzo in all of Rome." James tapped his fist against his chin. "Something . . . say . . . on the scale of the mansion they built for Prince Rodolphe here in London nearly a decade ago."

Excitement was clearly apparent in Goodenough's voice. "And our true objective is to . . ."

"Obtain a copy of the architectural drawings for Girardet's house," he said.

Goodenough rubbed his hands together with delight. "The players are in place, and the game's afoot."

James cautioned him. "We have one or two details that must still be seen to." He added as an afterthought, "About the other business I had you look into . . . ?"

"I have located three vessels that fit your stipulations, my lord. As fortune would have it, two of the ships are presently anchored at the West India South."

"They're docked here in London?"

"Yes, my lord."

Graystone's heart thudded in his chest. Perhaps the answers could at last—would at last—be found to this infernal business. "Our second undertaking dictates costumes of an entirely different nature."

"How so, my lord?"

James swaggered across the bedchamber, dragging one leg slightly behind the other, and growled in an unrecognizable accent, "Methinks 'twas time we ran away to sea, laddy."

Goodenough laughed out loud. It was the first time James recalled hearing his valet laugh. "Bravo, my lord. That was splendid, and very convincing."

"We'll have to be convincing where we're headed or it could mean a knife in the back for either or both of us."

"What about Her Serene Highness, my lord?"

"What about her?"

Goodenough consulted the small appointment book that he kept on his person at all times. "According to your schedule, you are to escort Her Serene Highness to a private yacht this afternoon and sail up the Thames to Hampton Court."

"That has been postponed until next week. The princess is taking several days for a well-deserved rest. I believe she is feeling a bit under the weather."

Goodenough turned and looked to the open window. "But the weather is exceptionally fine, my lord."

"Yes, it is."

"I'm fine, Ann," Cecile assured her friend. "It was a silly accident and my elbow was merely bruised."

"I still don't understand how it happened," Lady Ann Faraday admitted as the two of them reposed in a pretty sitting room attached to Cecile's suite.

Ann was curled up in a comfortable overstuffed chintz-covered chair beside her friend—chintz was all the rage this season for milady's boudoir—and Cecile was stretched out on a chaise lounge, her legs covered with a soft woven blanket despite the sunny day.

"I told you before. It was during the brief time Lord Graystone left me to go see what the fuss was all about. The museum curator had come rushing up to him and claimed there was some kind of accident. While they were absent I was poking around in one of the exhibits, and I tripped over something. I can't even recall what. That's when I hit my elbow. It is of no consequence, believe me."

Ann shot her a frown. "If that is truly the case, then why have we cancelled all of your scheduled appointments for today and tomorrow? Why are we sitting in these rooms?"

"For the blessed peace and quiet," Cecile answered truthfully. "I could not endure one more day of it."

"Of what?"

"Eating breakfast, luncheon, and dinner. Taking afternoon tea. Sitting down to midnight suppers. Dancing half the night away at gala balls. Having my toes trounced on by a dozen different gentlemen who all smelled of the same sickening soap. Touring museums and galleries and more museums. Visiting palaces and castles and grand houses. Strolling through parks and gardens and woods. I do not care if I ever see another flower or another tree."

Ann laughed.

It was a delightful sound and one that Cecile was overjoyed to hear. Her dear friend had lost her laugh when Lord and Lady Faraday had died. She had lost it again when Cecile's own father and mother had been involved in their tragic and fatal accident. In truth, neither of them had laughed for a long time.

It was good to hear her dear friend laughing now.

"You're absolutely right," Ann agreed, her brown eyes filled with merriment. "It is a welcome relief to simply sit and read and talk quietly." Then she piped up, "Although it cannot all be quite so tiresome for you as you claim."

"What makes you say that?"

"Lord Graystone."

Cecile put her head back against the small cushion behind her. "He is quite the handsomest man I have ever seen."

"He is handsome."

Cecile glanced over at her companion. "I don't know of another gentleman who is his equal when it comes to good looks and an agile, well-informed mind."

Ann concentrated on the book she held in her hands.

What was it, Cecile wondered. There was something going on here. "Ann, would you please look at me?"

Intelligent, sensitive, deep brown eyes were raised to meet Cecile's. "I am looking at you."

"Is there someone you consider to be more handsome, more attractive, more captivating than the Earl of Graystone?"

The denial came too quickly. "Of course, not."

Cecile's voice softened. "Oh, my dear Ann, in this world there are so few people we can be entirely honest with, so very few people we can love with all our hearts. If there is something you want to tell me, won't you now?"

Ann Faraday closed the book of poetry she had

been reading, folded her hands in her lap, and looked at her friend. "There is one man I consider to be above all others."

"Do you love him?"

"I love him."

"Is there a problem?"

"Yes."

"What is the problem?"

"He can never be for me."

"Why ever not?"

Ann moistened her lips. She started to say something and thought better of it. A moment later came, "Because he is . . ."

Cecile sat up and leaned toward her companion. "He is what, dearest?"

"He is Prince Alexandre."

She was a dunce. She should have guessed. She should have known. The signs had all been there for the past five years and Cecile had simply chosen not to see them. It explained everything. "Oh, my dear Ann."

"You don't mind."

"Of course I don't mind. You are as beloved by me as any sister ever could be."

Ann lowered her eyes and her voice. "Alexandre does not know I exist."

"That isn't true. He simply has a great many things on his mind of late."

"I know."

"He has had to take responsibility for so many things since our parents were killed. And now he must prepare for his coronation. These are heavy burdens, indeed.''

''Indeed.''

''But you may have noticed that he has not shown any marked preference for any other lady.''

''When he marries he will look for a princess.''

''I hope he will be wise enough to look for a woman. A woman he can love for his whole life. A woman of intelligence and charm, education and good breeding. A woman like yourself.''

''Thank you, Cecile.''

''There is nothing for you to thank me for. You mustn't give up hope. Once this business has been taken care of and Alexandre can be crowned, then it will be another matter altogether.''

''What business must be taken care of?''

It was time to tell her friend the whole truth. ''I have something I need to confide to you, Ann. It is the true reason I asked cousin Victoria, Her Majesty, to invite me to London for the season. It is a dangerous situation or I would have told you before. But now, as Lord Graystone and I make our final plans, I feel I must tell you.''

And so she did.

She told Ann everything.

And when she was done, it was very quiet in the pretty, sunny sitting room.

''I'll do whatever I can to help. All you ever have to do is ask me,'' Ann assured her.

''I know, my dear. As a matter of fact, I do have one question I would like to ask you. It may seem like a strange question but I have been wondering for some time." Cecile reached out and took her friend's hand in hers. "Do you know what has happened to my father's wedding ring?"

In the notorious docks district of London two nondescript men entered a boardinghouse that rented out rooms—twelve bob in advance, no questions asked.

One of the pair was rather tall and broad in the shoulders, but that drew meager attention in an area of the city where men, women, and children worked long hours at hard physical labor.

An hour later two salty sailors emerged: unshaven, unkempt, clothing smelling of ale and urine, dirt smeared on their faces and grime embedded under their fingernails and in a ring around their necks. One had teeth yellowed and blackened with rot.

Still, there was something about the two men. The other customers in the pub below moved out of their way, perhaps suspecting that one or both of the seafarers might well be carrying a concealed knife, one as sharp as a razor and could slice open a man's throat with a single swipe of the blade.

The sailors went out into the dark and forbidding London night. No one saw them make their way toward the anchored ship. She was currently called the *Lagos*, but she'd had many names and had sailed from many ports. The *Lagos* was one of several freighters anchored at West India South that had one important fact in common: a captain of Portuguese blood.

The men peered around and then silently slipped up the gangplank, moving like shadows.

No one—certainly not their closest friends, not even their own wives, if they'd had wives—would have recognized John Goodenough and James Gray, Earl of Graystone, that night.

Chapter Nineteen

"We're going to do *what*, my lord?"

James pushed off from his stance leaning against the eighteenth-century Thomas Chippendale lady's writing desk, decorated with Chinese lacquer and delicate landscapes, and, keeping his voice low, repeated, "We're going to break into Prince Rodolphe's mansion."

Cecile gave him a look that spoke volumes. "Have you done this kind of thing before?" She waved the question aside with her hand. "Please don't answer that."

All right, he wouldn't.

"I should not have inquired," she said, tilting her head to one side. "It really is none of my affair." Then she blithely returned to pouring out. "One sugar or two?"

"No sugar," James replied, recognizing the incongruity—the absurdity—of taking tea with a princess, all the while they were planning a burglary.

Of course, they were only going to steal back what was rightfully Cecile's. Well, what rightfully and morally belonged to her brother and to the principality of Saint-Simeon.

"Cream?"

James unbuttoned his coat and stuffed his hand into the pocket of his trousers. This room, this house, this city made him feel like a caged tiger. "No cream."

Cecile glanced up. A small frown formed between her sky-blue eyes. "Tea?"

"I don't drink tea," he said, his voice matter-of-fact.

Cecile replaced his cup on the silver tray. "You owned a tea plantation for fifteen years, and you don't drink tea?"

James shrugged noncommittally, removed his hand from his pocket, reconsidered, and shoved it back. "That's why I don't. It was tea morning, noon, and night in Bhārat," he explained, leaving out the details, a thousand details, of that time and place. "Once I left India I swore I'd never force myself to drink this stuff again."

Momentarily she appeared at a loss. "Shall I ring for coffee?"

"Thank you, no, that won't be necessary."

"Would you like something stronger?"

"Stronger?"

"Perhaps a glass of sherry."

Graystone had no wish to be an ungracious guest. "I rarely drink alcohol. It slows the reflexes and—" he briefly pointed toward his head "—dulls the brain."

Cecile was plainly curious. "What do you drink?"

James had never been one to make public his personal preferences. Indeed, he liked to think that he handled the subject with discretion and aplomb. "Milk. Water. Lemonade."

"Would you care for a glass of lemonade?"

He smiled hard and quick. "If it wouldn't be too much trouble."

A pitcher of fresh lemonade arrived within minutes, served by a maid who dipped and bowed and scraped and exited the sitting room as hastily as possible.

Actually the small parlor was but one of three formal reception areas in this wing of Guest House. It was called the Blue Room and, as one might expect, it was decorated in various shades of blue, from the pale blue silk wallcoverings to bright blue bolsters on the sofa to midnight blue trim on the damask drapes.

Cecile picked up a serving dish and extended it in his direction. "Would you like a sandwich?"

"Yes, I would," he responded with a great deal more enthusiasm than he had shown for her offer of tea.

Frankly James was hungry. He'd missed lunch. He had been poring over the architectural drawings for Girardet's mansion that he and Goodenough had successfully obtained the day before from the offices of Meeson and Johnson, and he had lost track of the hour.

The next thing he knew there had scarcely been enough time to change into fresh linen before presenting himself at the front door of Guest House as prearranged.

James took two of the wafer-thin sandwiches—the damned things were so dainty that each one barely made a decent bite—sat down on the opposite end of the *bleu d'azur* tufted sofa from Cecile, and wondered just how he was going to manage his food, his drink, and the fact that his legs were too long to be accommodated by the space in which he was expected to squeeze them.

After downing two glasses of lemonade and consuming a dozen sandwiches—they nicely filled the void in his stomach—James decided it was time to get down to business.

"Before we start, I feel I must warn you of the very real risk of physical injury that exists in what we're planning to do," he said in preamble.

Cecile sat and sipped her tea.

He glanced at her arm. "By the by, how is your elbow?"

"It is much improved, thank you."

This was tricky, James acknowledged to himself. He had to discourage Cecile from taking an active role in the actual burglary, without seeming to do so.

He cleared his throat. "Skills of a very particular nature will be required if we are to succeed in this scheme."

"I assumed as much."

Surely she could envision the pitfalls. "We will be trespassing on private property. That is highly illegal, not to mention potentially embarrassing if we are caught."

That got her hackles up. "Isn't it also highly illegal to steal the coronation crown, the royal scepter, and the sacred chalice that by his birthright are my brother's?"

Well, of course, it was.

Cecile spoke candidly. "We are both intelligent human beings, sir, so let us be honest with one another. We are talking about stealing into my uncle's residence in the dead of night. That could prove to be extremely dangerous. No matter how well we plan, a dozen different things, a hundred things, could go wrong, and, in the end, we may be lucky to get out with our lives."

So she did understand the dangers involved. "That is why I'm asking you to leave it up to me, madam."

"That isn't possible, sir."

"I don't want you to get hurt, Cecile," he blurted out.

"And I don't want you to get hurt, James," she threw right back at him.

His frustration bubbled to the surface. "But Cecile . . ."

"I told you from the first, I must have my part in this. I must be there every step of the way. We made an agreement, and you gave me your word as a gentleman."

He exhaled on a long sigh. "I know."

She meant every word. "We are in this together, or we are not in this at all."

"You are a stubborn, headstrong young woman, Cecile Girardet," he declared.

"And you are a stubborn, headstrong man, James Gray," she returned in kind. "Now let's discuss our plans for breaking into my uncle Rodolphe's house."

He informed her of the good news. "Goodenough and I were successful in obtaining a copy of the architect's original renderings for Girardet's Park Lane address.''

Her eyes widened appreciably. ''You have a map of the interior of the house?''

James nodded his head. ''Which could prove to be very useful *if* His Serene Highness has, indeed, hidden the stolen objects inside his London residence.''

Cecile seemed confident that was exactly what he had done. ''I can't fathom, having gone to so much trouble to obtain them, that my uncle would allow his 'prizes' out of his sight.''

Neither could James.

''The next step,'' he conveyed to her, ''is for the two of us to memorize where every room is located and where every hallway leads. We must know the position of each window and door, every way in and every way *out*.''

She listened to every syllable he uttered.

James went on. ''We will be making our way through the house at night in the dark, so we need to take that into consideration. If you see anything out of the ordinary as you study the architect's plans, I want you to bring it to my attention.''

''Why?''

He explained the reason. ''I may have missed some seemingly insignificant detail that will help us to discover where the prince has stashed the Saint-Simeon treasure.''

There was a noise outside in the hallway.

James quickly folded the piece of paper and put it back in his coat pocket.

"It's Lady Ann," Cecile told him after listening for a moment. "I have confided everything to her."

He arched a knowing brow.

The color rose sharply in Cecile's face. She stammered, "Well, not everything . . . but nearly everything." James noticed that her hands were trembling ever so slightly. She set her teacup down before adding, "Anyway, she is standing guard outside the sitting room to ensure that we have our privacy."

James took the paper, unfolded it and spread it out on the sofa between them. He pointed to the top and bottom floors of the impressive four-story brick structure. "It's reasonable to exclude certain parts of the house from our search: the kitchens, the larders, and the servants' quarters. We'll concentrate our efforts on the rooms that your uncle uses personally."

"That seems logical to me."

James was still thinking out loud. "I can't imagine that he would conceal stolen property anywhere a servant or a guest might inadvertently come upon it."

Cecile agreed.

He blew out his breath expressively. "That only leaves us with Rodolphe's bedchamber, his dressing room, his study, and three or four other rooms."

She turned to him with a determined air, reached out her hand and patted him reassuringly on the arm. "We'll find a way."

"How can you be so certain?"

The princess was resolute. "I understand what is at stake. I need to believe we will succeed. I cannot allow myself to imagine what will occur if we fail.

And I know we are on the side of what is right and just." Then, with all the hopefulness she could muster, Cecile inquired, "When do we search my uncle's house?"

"Not for several weeks at least."

"Why wait so long?"

"We have a lengthy list of options to consider and plan for. For example, what will you wear?"

Cecile mused, half-aloud, "You're thinking of fashion at a time like this?"

"Not fashion. Pragmatism. We will both wear black from head to toe. I have done this before and I know what is needed for myself. But you will require some kind of female garments that will enable you to move quickly and easily and yet still give you the freedom to run if it should become necessary."

"That's simple." The lady's lovely face brightened. "I'll wear the same thing you're wearing."

James pictured the long, close-fitting pants and shirt he had worn on more than one covert assignment in Bhārat: native garments, dyed to blend in with the color of the night, that had served him exceedingly well. "It just might work," he muttered under his breath.

"What might work?"

"Trousers."

Naturally, Cecile was curious. "You mean like the split skirts that the most daring women are now wearing for cycling?"

James shook his head. "I mean men's pants." His mind was racing. "I can describe what we will require to Goodenough. He will see to it. The man is resourceful, to say the least. Yes, I will leave it to him." He turned and focused on Cecile. "Would you mind standing?"

The princess gracefully rose from the sofa and stood, shoulders back, posture regal.

"Please walk five paces in that direction and then slowly turn in a circle," he instructed.

The lady did as she was requested. "May I ask what this is all about?"

"How tall are you?"

"I am nearly five feet six inches in height," she responded.

"I thought as much." James recalled the night of her formal ball. Even wearing high-heeled satin slippers, the top of Cecile's head had barely reached his chin. "What is your weight?"

"I do not believe that my weight is any concern of yours, sir," the princess stated, looking down her patrician nose at him.

James cleared his throat. "I will simply tell Goodenough that you are shapely but slender." Eight and a half stone was his best guess. He moved on. "May I borrow a pair of your shoes?"

Her jaw dropped in amazement. "For what purpose?"

"You will need the right footwear for this venture. The cobbler must have your precise measurements."

Her mouth formed an O.

"Can you move quietly?"

"I sneaked out of this house twice in the middle of the night *and* returned several hours later, and no one was ever aware of my absence," Cecile Girardet stated, with intense satisfaction.

James couldn't argue with success.

He broached another subject altogether. "While inside the prince's house, we will talk only when it is absolutely necessary and then only in whispers. In order to communicate at other times, we will devise a series of hand signals."

Cecile looked at him challengingly. "What if it is too dark to see each other's hands?"

"Then you must stick to me like glue," James declared, grimly amused.

"I can do that," she said seemingly innocently. "I have learned how these past three weeks from you."

He couldn't help himself. Graystone put his head back and laughed. "You are an amazing woman."

"You are an amazing man."

"You're quick, too."

"As are you."

"I meant quick witted, madam."

Cecile proceeded back to the *bleu d'azur* tufted sofa and sat down. "So did I, sir."

James picked up the conversation. "I am a bit rusty at breaking into a strange house and you have never done so . . ." He looked at her askance. "You haven't, have you?"

"No."

"Then we'll need to practice," he informed her.

The lady had a question for him. "And how do you propose we do that?"

He had the answer ready for her. "We will first break into Cork House."

*   *   *

The game was afoot.

Their costumes had been sewn to specifications, ordered, and paid for by an Indian gentleman who did not speak much English. Nevertheless, he was able to give the East End tailor an adequate description of what he required.

Their footwear was made to order using the sketches provided by a Scotsman who did not bother explaining what he wanted with shoes made of such soft leather. The cobbler assumed it must have something to do with the Scottish jigs he'd heard they danced up north.

The black caps—one a man's, the other a boy's—were easily obtained at a small haberdasher on Dilly Row, as were several pairs of dark socks and two pairs of black gloves. The items were purchased by a nondescript fellow that no one recalled and no one even remembered.

The makeup came from a small theatrical troupe who traveled from village to village, and had never seen the inside of a genuine London theater. They specialized in Shakespearean dramas and were currently performing a somewhat abbreviated version of *Othello*. One evening in Berwick-on-Rye, a well-heeled patron of the arts made a generous donation in exchange for several jars of Othello's tinted melted tallow. No questions asked, no answers given.

The preparations were complete. The stage was set. The players had practiced their roles over and over again, and had committed every detail to memory.

It was time for the dress rehearsal.

*   *   *

Cecile had gone through the precise steps in the precise order a dozen, perhaps two dozen, times before tonight. It was second nature to her now.

She arose from her bed, and, without lighting a candle, slipped into the black pants and shirt and the pair of soft leather slippers. She pinned her hair up on top of her head and tucked the few errant strands under the snug brim of the boy's cap.

She quickly sat down at her dressing table and began to apply the melted tallow to her face. She wiped the excess from her hands and pulled on the black gloves.

The transformation was complete.

Cecile knew their plan by heart.

The goal was to enter Cork House, search four large rooms that corresponded to the four locations they had narrowed their list down to for Rodolphe's mansion, find a cache of fake stolen objects—their whereabouts known only to Goodenough since he had hidden them—and get away with the "treasure."

The doors and windows of Cork House would be locked.

The household knew nothing of their activities.

Everything was identical except for one thing: Goodenough knew they were coming.

But he didn't know when.

Cecile slipped downstairs and, without a sound, let herself out the side door of Guest House and onto the street.

James materialized from the shadows. She had neither seen nor heard him, or, for that matter, even sensed his presence. He had the ability to make himself nearly invisible. Cecile knew it was a skill he had perfected during his fifteen years in India.

They moved quickly, quietly, without speaking, without making a single unnecessary sound.

Tonight James was going to pick the lock on the front door of Cork House. He was very good at picking locks, James had informed her. And he had once spent a very long time in a place with no light. Darkness was his nightmare, but it was also his friend.

It could be their friend.

They moved from shadow to shadow along the tree-lined street. They skirted the length of the substantial, impenetrable fence surrounding the key garden, and made their way to a spot directly across from the front entrance to Cork House.

They moved stealthily. They blended in with the night. They saw no one and no one saw them. There was a dark corner by the front door. Cecile made for it and flattened herself against the building, its stone surface cold against her back.

James went down on his haunches in front of the door. He took a length of wire from his sleeve and inserted it in the lock. He worked swiftly and surely.

Click.

They both held their breaths.

Then James straightened, turned the brass knob, opened the door, and they slipped into the entranceway of Cork House.

As they crept from room to room, searching for the hidden treasure, Cecile realized that the loudest sound was the thumping of her heart. This was no

game. It would never be a game. And next time it
might well be a matter of life and death.

Goodenough had been clever.

James was even more clever. He discovered the
hoard of supposedly stolen goods in the fourth room
they searched. One by one the items were placed in
the cloth bag he had brought for that purpose. Then
they made for the front door.

Cecile's hand shot out to stop him.

There!

James saw it, too. Someone lurking in the darkness.
It might be Goodenough, or a watchman on guard,
or a footman, or even the butler making his final
rounds for the night.

They improvised.

Instead of leaving the way they had entered, they
went further into Cork House. They climbed the back
stairs and made their way along a series of carpeted
halls until they reached a door at the end of the corridor. James turned the knob and, one right after the
other, they slipped into the room. He closed the door
and bolted it behind them.

Cecile heard his sigh of relief.

"We did it!" she whispered triumphantly.

"We did, didn't we?" James said, keeping his voice
low but not whispering.

He must have known exactly where to reach for a
candle for within moments a taper was lit, followed
by the bedside lamp, then another lamp and another.

"Where are we?" Cecile asked.

Somehow she knew the answer before James replied, "This is my bedchamber."

She had never been in a gentleman's bedroom before, Cecile realized as she strutted across the floor—these trousers were quite emancipating when it came to freedom of movement; little wonder men favored them—and took a good look around.

Surely one could tell something of a man's character from his personal surroundings, although seeing James's guest quarters here at Cork House wouldn't be as revealing as, say, his own suite of rooms at Graystone Abbey.

Still, Cecile found it fascinating.

She examined the book on the table beside the bed. No doubt it was the one he was reading.

She read the title aloud: *"The Woman in White."*

"By Wilkie Collins," James contributed.

She went to his bureau next and lightly ran her fingertips over his set of silver brushes—they were engraved with his initials JGG—his leather wallet, a framed photograph of a young woman with a smiling, handsome man beside her. The canals of Venice were clearly visible in the background. "Your niece?"

James nodded. "And her husband. That was taken on their wedding trip last autumn."

"Is she all the family you have?"

James nodded again. "But I'll be a great-uncle, I understand, by next autumn."

Children. She would have liked—loved—to have had children. Now that dream was gone along with the dream of love, of a husband, of a home of her own. Although the details were still vague, she was almost certain that she had been compromised in some way that night a year ago, the night of the

"Incident." She was caught in a situation ripe for scandal. She would not, could not, involve anyone else in her misfortunes.

Cecile sighed. She would never have a wedding trip like James's niece.

"Is this the window you come to when you cannot sleep?" she inquired, pausing by the first in a row of windows that overlooked the key garden.

James's voice was suddenly strained. "Yes."

Cecile opened the window and looked out on the night. The moon was nearly full. The garden was clearly visible. Its scents—there were so very many of them now—wafted up even to the second story of Cork House.

" 'We are near awakening when we dream that we dream,' " she murmured in hushed tones.

She turned and found James watching her. There was something in his eyes, something she had not seen there since the night he had kissed her in the gazebo.

It was desire.

Cecile wished that he would kiss her again. She wished that he would hold her and touch her and caress her.

She was behaving strangely. She was thinking strangely. But these were strange circumstances: to find herself alone with James Gray in his bedchamber in the middle of the night.

Yet, in truth, Cecile could think of no place on earth that she would rather be.

It was so simple.

And yet it was so complex.

It had all started, perhaps, the afternoon that Ann Faraday had confessed to her that she was in love with Alexandre. Perhaps that was the day Cecile had realized she was in love with James Gray.

His expression was guarded. He passed his tongue over his lips. "It's getting late."

She wanted to laugh, but did not dare. Perhaps it was a case of nerves. "It was late when we started."

"It went well."

"Yes, it did."

"So far so good," he remarked.

" 'All's well that ends well,' " Cecile piped up, quoting another cliché.

"We'll leave the bag here." James indicated the fake treasure dumped in the corner. "I'll escort you back through the key garden to Guest House."

Cecile shook her head.

"What is this?" James inquired, imitating her action.

"No."

He frowned. "No?"

"As in I don't want you to escort me back through the key garden to Guest House."

Something flickered behind his quicksilver eyes. "We don't always get what we want."

Cecile laughed softly in the back of her throat. "Do you remember saying that to me the first night we met in the garden?"

He nodded. "I imagined you were a ghost."

"I was no ghost."

"Then I assumed you were the woman in white."

Her eyes went to the leather book beside his bed. "Not that woman in white."

"Then I thought you were a dream," he said softly.

"And you were . . . you are . . . exactly who you have always been."

"And who is that?"

"I'm not sure." Without knowing why, Cecile asked, "Do I know you?"

James frowned and drove his hand through the hair at his nape. "I don't know." He gave his head a shake. "I think you should leave."

Cecile walked toward him, never taking her eyes from his. "I think I should stay."

Chapter Twenty

How to handle a woman.

It was the age-old dilemma every man found himself facing at one time or another, James reflected. He just hadn't expected it to be tonight or the woman to be Princess Cecile.

Not that anyone would have suspected that the slender creature dressed all in black from her head to her toes, a woolen cap pulled low over her eyes, theatrical makeup covering her face, was Her Serene Highness, Princess Cecile of Saint-Simeon. At the moment she looked more like a chimney sweep or a street urchin.

Except, of course, for the close-fitting black pants and the form-hugging shirt that revealed the person underneath was definitely a woman, and one with a lovely and lush figure at that.

What was he going to do with her?

James knew what he would like to do, what he would *love* to do, and that was wash the tint from her skin, strip off the ridiculous outfit she was wearing, tug the cap from her head and, one by one, pluck out the hairpins holding her hair in place. Then he would watch the mass of black, silky stuff tumble down around her bare shoulders.

James sighed. It wouldn't end there, of course. That would only be the beginning. And a gentleman shouldn't start what he couldn't—what he shouldn't—finish.

The trouble was, Cecile was walking straight toward him, and she had insisted that she was staying.

It was strange, but the dark clothes and the dark makeup only served to emphasize her eyes.

She was all eyes.

And he knew those eyes. They were the eyes that looked out at him from his dreams.

James raised his hand and rubbed the lump behind his ear. It was throbbing tonight. It rarely did that.

Cecile was standing directly in front of him, staring at him. She reached up, pulled the cap from his head, and threaded her fingers through his hair.

"It's strange," she murmured, scrutinizing his appearance, "how the tallow covers your skin and makes your eyes seem like the only feature on your face."

"I was thinking the same thing about you," he confessed.

"I have never known another man with gray eyes," Cecile Girardet said to him.

"And I don't think I have ever seen blue eyes quite the extraordinary color of your blue eyes," he told her, his voice deep and his words slowly spaced.

"Except . . ." Cecile prompted.

James gave it about thirty seconds of thought before answering, "Except in my dreams."

She went very still. "Do you dream about me, James Gray?"

"Yes." Should he tell her everything? "You are in my dreams every night."

She caught the tip of her tongue between her teeth. "And you are in mine," came the admission.

He had to disclose the rest to her. "I've been dreaming about you for a long time."

After a pause, the lady inhaled deeply and inquired in a whisper, "How long?"

The old injury behind his ear seemed to pulsate with every beat of his heart. "A year." Graystone reconsidered. "More than a year."

Cecile caught her breath.

James quickly went on to explain, although there was no rational explanation. "I know that sounds peculiar since we have known each other for less than two months."

"That isn't the peculiar part," she said, visibly shaken. "I am almost certain that you have been in my dreams for the past year, as well." Her lips were drawn and white. "It's your eyes. I don't think I could—I ever would—forget your eyes."

His voice was urgent. "I keep envisioning your eyes and your face and your . . ."

"What?"

"And you beneath me on a bed."

"I see you bending over me, kissing me, caressing me," Cecile related, her forehead creasing a moment perplexedly.

James pulled off his gloves and then turned his attention to hers. Next, he removed her woolen cap and tossed it down beside his own. Then he caught hold of her unceremoniously by the hand and urged her toward the adjoining bathroom.

"Come with me, madam."

James sat her down on a cushioned bench in front of the washbasin. He opened the jar of facial cream—Goodenough had guaranteed that the concoction was the best means of removing theatrical makeup—and poured a dollop into his hand. Then he began to gently massage the cream into her skin.

"Close your eyes," he instructed.

He worked the soothing lotion over Cecile's forehead, between the small space separating her eyes, down the bridge of her nose, along her cheeks, her chin, around the shell-like curve of her ears, at the back of her neck, and wherever there was a need.

Then he took a piece of toweling and began to clean off the cream and the tinted tallow. When he was satisfied that he had gotten most of it, James moistened a soft cloth, added some of the slightly lime-scented soap that he preferred and began to wash her face.

"Now you look like yourself," he proclaimed, taking a step back so she could see herself in the mirror.

"Not quite like myself," Cecile contended, standing and removing the pins until her hair finally tumbled down around her shoulders. Then she gave her head a shake.

"I'll be right back." James retrieved the set of engraved silver brushes from the top of his bureau. Then, standing behind her, and with one hairbrush firmly clasped in each hand, he began to work through the glorious and luxuriant mass.

"A man has never brushed my hair before," Cecile confessed in a husky voice.

James not only wanted to brush her hair, he wanted to bury his nose, his mouth, his entire face in it. He wanted to inhale its fragrance, filling his nostrils and his lungs with its distinctive scent, Cecile's scent. He wanted to wrap long, silky strands around his fingers and grasp handfuls of it, tasting it—tasting Cecile—draping dark tresses across his lips, his face, his chest, his groin.

James groaned and closed his eyes.

When he opened them again and looked up he could see their reflections in the gilt-framed mirror. A tall man dressed in black—an odd-looking man at the moment—standing behind a woman all in black. The woman was beautiful, and she was gazing at him with something in her eyes he had not seen there since that night in the gazebo.

It was desire.

James dropped his arms.

"Now it's your turn, sir," Cecile ordered, turning around and pushing on his shoulders until he finally plunked down on the bench she had recently vacated.

An ample quantity of cream was poured into the center of her palm. She dipped her fingers in the small pool of lotion and began to apply it to his face.

James shivered.

She smoothed the lotion over the surface of his skin, massaging every inch of his face, his neck, around his ears, under his chin, even along his nape, pushing the hair aside as she went.

James Gray had never experienced a woman's touch in quite the way this woman was touching him. She was intent—her bottom lip was caught between her front teeth as she worked on him—yet she was gentle and caring.

"Your arms must be getting weary," he suggested as she bent over him.

"Not in the least," Cecile claimed, coming closer to inspect for any spots she may have missed. "You'll have to remove your shirt," she said at last.

"But . . ."

"I can't get to everything that requires washing, otherwise."

"But Cecile . . ."

"I have already seen you without your shirt, for all intents and purposes, on two other occasions, James," she pointed out. "I believe the time for modesty has passed."

Well, when she put it like that. . . .

James stood up and, straddling the cushioned bench, one leg on each side, tugged at his shirttails where they were tucked into his black pants. They finally worked free.

"Sit."

He sat.

"Arms up, please."

James raised his arms.

Cecile reached down, caught the material by its bottom hem and worked the shirt up his torso, over his shoulders and head, and along the entire length of his arms until it came off in her hands. Then she neatly folded the garment and placed it to one side.

Circling behind him, she took another dollop of lotion and massaged it into the skin at the back of his neck, below his earlobes and around to the front of his collarbone. As she worked, James could feel her breasts pressing every now and then against his back.

The woman would be the death of him.

For each time she touched him, each time she rubbed more cream into his flesh, each time she took a clean cloth and wiped away the residue, James could have sworn she was caressing him.

Every nerve ending, every bone, every muscle, every particle of his body was sensitized to her touch.

James Gray acknowledged he had been celibate for a very long time. But he believed if this had been any other woman but Cecile, that would have made no difference.

But it was Cecile.

He could feel his manhood starting to swell, enlarge, grow harder and harder. It pressed painfully against the front of his pants. His only saving grace was the fact he was sitting down.

He snickered silently to himself. Where was his bloody enviable self-control now?

Thank God Cecile seemed oblivious to her effect on him. She dipped a clean cloth into the basin of water and began to wipe away the last traces of makeup. Then she dried his face, rubbed the damp hair at his nape with a towel, came around to the front, tipped up his chin with her fingers and gazed down at her handiwork.

"Now you look like yourself," she said, repeating his words. "Oh, I forgot one thing." She picked up his silver hairbrushes and began to stroke through his hair as he had done with hers.

"A woman has never brushed my hair before," he admitted, echoing her sentiments.

Cecile laughed and called him, "Liar."

James frowned.

She laughed again and speculated, "I imagine that your mother brushed your hair when you were a little boy, and your nursemaid and your nanny."

"If they did, it was so long ago that I can't remember," he claimed, allowing his eyes to close and savoring the joy of being administered to with such infinite tenderness.

Then James felt the soft brush of her lips back and forth across his, the sweet, lingering fragrance of her skin and hair in his nostrils, the pressure of her leg nudging against his thigh, her hand resting on his bare shoulder. And he knew he was lost.

And he realized he was found.

Quicksilver eyes opened and gazed into an endless sea of blue. "Do you know what you're doing?"

"Kissing you," came the slightly breathless admission.

James made another attempt at being a gentleman. "There are a dozen good reasons why you should leave right now," he told her as he held her at arm's length.

"There are more than a dozen good reasons why

I should stay," Cecile countered, inching closer again. "I have been dreaming of your kiss, your touch, your caress. I want the man in my dreams to be the man in my arms."

She was making it even harder for him to be noble. "Are you certain I am that man?"

"Yes," came out strong and true.

What is . . . is.

They were who they were.

And what would be, would be.

He finally saw no reason not to tell her. "I believe you to be the woman in my dreams."

Cecile placed her hands on his shoulders and looked down into his eyes. "Why do we dream the same dream?"

James wasn't certain. " 'I had a dream which was not all a dream,' " he quoted.

She was utterly still, considering.

"Lord Byron."

"That is it, isn't it, James?"

He nodded.

"What we remember wasn't all just a dream." She trembled. "It actually happened."

"I believe it did."

Cecile caught hold of the leather cord James always wore around his neck. It had shifted while she was washing him. A crease formed between her eyes. "What is inside the cord?"

"Inside it?"

She made a motion with her head. "The leather is wrapped around something."

James glanced down at the section she held in her hand. "I don't know."

She was disbelieving. "You've never unraveled the leather to find out?"

He paused and considered, then shook his head slowly. "I remember . . ."

She listened intently. "What do you remember?"

His head was throbbing again. The old wound to his shoulder began to ache as well. "I remember . . ." James paused and allowed the memory to come back without trying to force it to. "I remember that it was very important no one find out something was inside the cord. That's why I braided it the way I did."

"To hide whatever is still inside it?"

Graystone's heart was pounding—*thump-thump, thump-thump*—in his chest. He swore he could almost hear, almost feel, the pounding of Cecile's heart as well.

He raised his eyes to hers. "I think it's time to find out what it is, don't you?"

Her mouth all but disappeared. "Yes."

"There's a pair of small scissors in the drawer behind you." He indicated which one.

Cecile quickly retrieved the scissors. "Do you want me to snip the cord?"

"Yes."

She caught the aged leather between the sharp blades and tried to cut through the cord, but it was to no avail.

James took the pair of small shears from her, found a place along the circle that appeared to be a little worn, and he cut. The effort made a nick in the leather. He put the scissors down, grabbed the frayed strap in his hands, and tore it asunder.

The braided cord started to come apart in his hands.

Tension clung to James's sharply drawn features. It had taken a mere fraction of the time to undo what he now recalled had taken him days—perhaps even weeks—to braid in the dark.

It had been his obsession.

It had been the driving force in life.

It had been his solitary purpose to go on living.

He worked faster. He caught a glimpse of something shiny and he worked faster still. The leather cord fell away, dropping to his feet, and there it was in the palm of his hand.

Cecile was motionless.

"It's a gold ring," James said after a time.

Neither of them seemed to be able to catch their breaths.

Finally Cecile reached out—he noticed that her hand was trembling—then apparently changed her mind, and drew back. "Is there an inscription on the inside?"

James held the ring up to the lamplight, tilted his head to one side, and saw there were words etched into the gold band. "Yes, there is an inscription."

There was a distinct tension in the air.

"What does it say?" she asked.

James read aloud: *"Vous et Nul Autre."*

Chapter Twenty-one

"You and No Other," Cecile translated from the medieval French, her mouth suddenly dry, her hand going to her throat.

James looked up at her from the bench. "Are you wearing your mother's wedding ring?"

"I've worn it on a chain around my neck since the day it was given to me as a keepsake." Her heart beat hard. "I used to wear both of my parents' wedding rings."

He asked the question on both their minds. "Do you think the ring I've been wearing is your father's?"

"I do." Cecile reached beneath the neckline of her shirt and pulled out the chain. The gold chain and the gold ring shimmered brightly against the black backdrop.

James held the golden band that had been concealed within the leather cord in one hand and reached up with the other and grasped the ring dangling from her neck. "They appear to be identical, except mine is larger in size."

"These are my parents' wedding rings," Cecile stated. "I recognize them."

James gave her a long measuring look. "Why am I wearing your father's wedding ring?"

Cecile was intensely aware of his vibrant body pressing against her. "I think I may have given it to you."

He deliberated, his dark brows drawn together. "The woman in my dreams—you—slipped something to me at one point. I realize now it must have been your father's ring."

"I wanted you to have it," she said simply. That much she did remember.

His eyes were dark, smoldering, like the last burning embers on the fire. "Do you think anyone saw you give it to me?"

"Why?"

"I need to know."

Cecile wasn't sure why James needed to know, but apparently he did. "I don't think so." She raised her right hand and rubbed her temple. "It's all such a muddle sometimes . . . as if it were a dream, and yet I know it wasn't entirely."

"It wasn't a dream," James stated. "It happened to you and to me; it happened to us."

"Do you believe we'll ever know why?"

He nodded. "But knowing why isn't as important as simply knowing, as remembering."

Cecile reached out and with her fingertips touched his mouth, there and there. "It is you."

"It is."

Something inside of her wanted to laugh and cry at the same time. She had found him!

Her heart turned. "I wanted you, James."

He trapped her fingers. "I wanted you, Cecile."

"I want you now."

"And I want you."

He unclasped the chain from around her neck, removed the ring that had once been her beloved mother's and slipped the gold wedding band onto her finger.

She took its mate, the ring that had been her father's, and slid it onto his finger.

Then she placed her hand in his.

Cecile understood the significance of what she was about to do. She was going to give herself to this man here, now, tonight. Because she loved him. Because he would be the only man she would ever love. Because whatever the future held for them, they would always have this night.

James rose to his feet, turned down the lamplight and lead her into the adjoining bedchamber. He took her to the open window. He stood behind her while they gazed out on the private garden; their private garden. They inhaled its glorious fragrances. They absorbed its peace and tranquility and serenity. They recalled its inviting lushness, its solitude, its natural beauty.

Then Cecile turned and went into James's arms.

His mouth was on her mouth. His hands clasped her by the waist and brought he up tightly against him. She was aware that his body had changed, that a certain part, a very particular part of him was larger and harder than it had been. It seemed to strain toward her. It pressed against her.

It had been like this once before.

On some instinctive level Cecile knew this was the way it was supposed to be. A man made a place for himself; the woman was that place. They were two separated halves that would join and become one whole.

That was the mystery of it.

That was the glory of it.

She soon had her hands on his bare chest, caressing his skin, tugging at his hair, trailing her fingers over his masculine nipples, feeling his startled reaction as she did so.

James yanked her shirt from the waistline of her pants, and the next thing Cecile realized the garment was pulled over her head and discarded on a pile of clothing collecting on the floor. She stood there in her chemise, aware that the fine lawn and the exquisite lace did little to conceal what was beneath.

James gazed down at her. Cecile recognized the look in his eyes. She knew he could clearly see the outline of her breasts and the hard rose-colored peaks at their centers. His hands came up to cup her, to cover her, to caress her. Then he grasped her nipples between his thumbs and fingers and squeezed.

Cecile heard a low moan of arousal and realized it was her own. "James . . . ?"

"Are you afraid?"

She quickly passed her tongue over her lips and admitted, "Perhaps a little."

He held perfectly still. "If you want me to stop, Cecile, all you have to do is tell me."

"I don't want you to stop."

"Are you certain?"

"I'm certain."

His hands rested lightly on either side of her collarbone. He nudged the chemise off her shoulders and down her arms until it fell to her waist, leaving her bare and exposed.

James seemed bewitched by her. "You're as beautiful as I remember," he said, his voice thick.

She reciprocated, touching his chest. "And you are as magnificent as I remember."

With his index finger he drew an imaginary line from her shoulder, down her back nearly to her waist, around to her ribcage, across her abdomen and up between her breasts. "Your skin is the texture of the finest porcelain."

Cecile quivered with awareness.

He began again, tracing a slow, sensual circle around the outside of her right breast. Then he traced a slightly smaller circle, and then another, and another, each diminishing in size until the last circle encompassed only her nipple. "Your skin is the color of a pale white swan sailing across a tranquil pond at sunrise."

Cecile felt the fine, infinitesimal hairs at her nape stand straight up on end.

He lightly plucked at the tips of her breasts—those so tender and responsive tips—and she felt a delicious shiver all the way down her body to her toes.

He bent his head and the arrowed point of his tongue was on her nipple, flicking back and forth across its sensitive surface, licking her, nipping at her, biting her, creating a need, a desire, a yearning that she did not fully comprehend.

He tugged on her with his lips. He drew her fully, completely, deeply into his mouth, and he suckled her. She could not breathe. She could not think. She could only feel.

Then he transferred his attention to the other breast, and bestowed upon it the same diligence and concentrated care as he had the first. "Your breasts are perfect: the perfect shape, the perfect size, the perfect taste," he praised.

Cecile's knees buckled beneath her. She was quite certain she was going to lose her mind.

His hands were in her hair. His mouth was tasting her hair. His face was buried in her hair. The hair on his chest was soft and it tickled her bare skin. Her breasts were flattened against masculine muscle and hard bone.

James turned her around until she faced the garden again. As she gazed out on the moonlit night, he placed his hands on her. She glanced down and there were his wonderful, strong, long-fingered hands covering her breasts, caressing her breasts, giving her pleasure such as she had never imagined, had never known existed.

Then he stepped away from her.

Cecile waited, cognizant that James was removing his shoes, his pants and the remainder of his clothing. She knew he would soon be as God had made him.

"I don't want you to be frightened by what is to come," he explained to her.

In truth, she was more apprehensive than frightened. "I'll try not to be."

"I want you to turn around now and look upon a

naked man who wants you more than he has ever wanted anyone or anything before in his life. I want you to see what happens to a man's body when the woman he wants, he needs, he desires, is with him. I want you to see me wanting you," James told her.

Cecile turned.

James stood before her in all his natural glory. His body gleamed in the lamplight. His hair was like black silk. His skin was a rich golden-brown. He was all firm flesh and masculine strength. He quite took her breath away.

"Why, you're beautiful!" she exclaimed.

Then there was that part of his body that had undergone great changes. It was suddenly large and hard and *it* protruded toward her. Cecile had the most incredible urge to reach out and touch it, to see what would happen if she did.

She couldn't take her eyes off him. "May I—" she licked her lips "—touch you?"

"If you wish to," came the strained response.

Cecile reached out with her index finger and touched the tip. "You're so soft."

James laughed, yet it was a laugh that contained no merriment.

She repeated the action. "You're so hard." She couldn't stop staring. Indeed, she found herself utterly enthralled. "I have never seen anything like it before. Well, except, perhaps, for a brief moment in my dream, but I do not think that counts, do you?"

James shook his head.

Cecile suddenly understood the depth of her ignorance. "I don't know what I am allowed to do," she confessed.

"On several occasions, madam, you have informed me that a woman should have the same prerogatives as a man," James reminded her.

Cecile stared down at the large swollen rod she now held in her hand. "I do not think that is possible, sir. We are very different: men and women."

"Only in unimportant ways," he remarked. "Well, not unimportant, but only in certain ways, wonderful ways, pleasurable ways."

She squeezed the soft head and uttered an exclamation of surprise when she beheld a drop or two of moisture glistening near a small opening. She wrapped her fingers around its girth and gently squeezed. James sucked in his breath.

Cecile was instantly contrite. "Have I hurt you?"

Tension emanated from James. "No."

She wasn't certain she believed him. "You look as though you are in pain."

He ground his teeth together. "I am, but I am not."

"That isn't logical," she pointed out.

"Sex isn't logical," came in a rush.

Cecile found herself filled with inquisitiveness. "Is that what this is?"

"That is what all of this is," he explained, without explaining anything whatsoever, of course.

Cecile was perplexed. "If this is sex—" she felt very daring and modern; it was the first time she had uttered the word aloud "—then why does a man need a woman?"

James scowled. "I beg your pardon, madam."

She made another attempt. "Why does a man require a woman? He could simply placed his own
hands around himself and accomplish much the
same thing."

James heaved a great sigh. "Well, he could, yet
he couldn't."

"That is no answer."

"I have no other answer at the moment . . ." was
all he managed before she began to touch him again,
caress him, study the length and the breadth of him,
even the nest of soft, black curls that encircled the
base of his manhood.

"May I kiss it?" Cecile finally voiced the question
at the forefront of her mind.

He sucked in air and didn't release it.

She eyed him with a certain amount of apprehen-
sion. "Have I said something I oughtn't?"

James shook his head but didn't speak.

"Have I shocked you?"

He shook his head again.

Her brows rose quizzically. "Why don't you say
something?"

He exhaled. "Yes."

Cecile smiled, little realizing that her smile was
sweet and innocent and beatific. "I understand.
You're saying that I may kiss it." She clapped her
hands together with delight, bent over and pressed
a light kiss on the tip.

It moved.

"It moved," she said, pointing.

"I know," he confirmed.

"May I kiss it again?"

"If you wish."

This time Cecile lingered. This time she licked her lips as she kissed him and received a small taste of his essence, of those glistening drops on the soft, smooth crown.

"This is far more interesting than I had ever imagined it to be," she confessed to the naked man standing before her. "Why, one could even say that it is extremely edifying."

He'd had enough.

He hadn't had nearly enough.

Graystone found himself to be at his wit's end. Well, at the limit of his patience and self-control, anyway. It was time he took command of the situation and the lady.

He reached down and drew Cecile to her feet. "Interesting, madam? Edifying, madam? The relationship between a man and a woman has been called many things over the millennia, but interesting and edifying are not what I expected to hear."

She gave him a look of polite inquiry. "What did you expect to hear, then, sir?"

James unleashed a sardonic smile. "I believe you will know when the time comes."

She appeared mystified. "When what time comes?"

"Trust me, it will be self-explanatory," he told her, before moving on to the next topic he wished to discuss. "If a woman is permitted to enjoy the same prerogatives as a man, does it not follow that a man must be allowed the same privileges as a lady?"

Mediterranean blue eyes blinked several times in rapid succession. "I suppose it does."

"I thought as much," he said smugly.

James went down on his knees in front of her and, one by one, removed her shoes and socks. Then he tugged on the black pants of her costume and the skimpy pair of drawers he discovered underneath, and tossed the whole lot onto the pile of clothing. By the time he was finished, she was completely disrobed.

He rose to his feet, took a full step back and gazed at the young woman in front of him. The moonlight shone in the window behind her, outlining her figure in a soft, white glow. The lamp in the bedchamber was turned down low, yet he could see every curve, every shape, every line of her lovely body.

"You are beautiful," James exclaimed.

She flushed but kept her hands at her sides. "Thank you."

He took half a step toward her. "You're welcome."

Cecile never moved a muscle. Indeed, she appeared to be holding her breath. "You are beautiful as well," came rushing out of her mouth.

James flashed her a smile. "You already mentioned that earlier, but thank you."

She looked briefly disconcerted. "You're welcome."

He took another step toward her. His chest was mere inches from her breasts. Starting at the top of her head, he gently ran his hand down one side of her body and back up the other.

Cecile shivered.

He was totally focused on her. "Do you like my touch?"

She nodded but said not a word. He wasn't altogether certain that she could speak.

The process started all over again. This time James used his mouth instead of his hands, raining a shower of kisses along her forehead, the curve of her cheekbone, that delicate place at the base of her throat, the sensitive spot below her ear, her bare shoulder, her elbow (he took great care in case the skin was still tender), her ribcage, her breast where he lingered—he could not leave her beautiful breasts without a few moment's of special attention—then he moved on to her slender waist, her thigh, her knee, her ankle, even her foot. Then he began the journey anew, returning up the other side.

This time he headed inland and placed his mouth on the soft feminine mound with its sprinkling of dark hair, that sweet, delicious mound that was already damp and swollen.

James touched her with his tongue.

She jerked.

"You didn't hurt me," Cecile hastily volunteered.

"I know," he said, smiling. "If you will just separate your legs a little more, my sweet lady," he urged, placing one hand on each side of her inner thighs.

Cecile did as he requested, parting her feet perhaps five or six inches. It gave him enough room to do what he was hungering and thirsting to do. He flicked her with his tongue, taking first a sip, then a gentle nibble and finally a sensual bite.

She came undone in his hands and under the tutelage of his mouth, crying out his name softly, intensely: "James!"

He could feel her quivering with need, with desire, with unnamed cravings. By the time he returned to take her mouth in a long, drugging kiss, they were both unsteady on their feet.

She reeled. "James, I don't know what's happening to me. I feel so odd . . ."

"I know, my sweet," he murmured reassuringly.

"I don't think . . ."

"There is no need for you to think, Cecile. There is no need for either of us to think. This is a time only to feel."

"But I can't stand up any longer," she burst out with her immediate concern.

James gathered her up in his arms and carried her to the ornately carved Byzantine-style bed that had once belonged ot the Emperor Charlemagne. It was a bed fit for an emperor or an empress . . . or a princess.

He threw back the bedcovers, placed Cecile down on the mattress and stretched out beside her.

"Now you won't have to worry about standing up," he declared as he took her in his embrace and, leaning over her, touched his lips to her mouth, the tip of her breast, her soft, white belly.

"This is how I remember you," she murmured, gazing up at him with eyes that were dark, impassioned blue.

"And this is how I remember you," he replied, parting her thighs, slipping his hand between her long, lovely legs, threading his fingers through the thatch of womanly hair—it had its own texture, its own color—and finding the erotic nub hidden there.

Cecile gasped.

James moistened his hand with her musky essence. Then as he captured her mouth, driving his tongue between her lips, he eased a finger into her.

She arched her back and instinctively raised her hips off the bed. James swallowed her cry of surprised arousal and excitement as his finger was driven deeper and deeper into her body. He slid it in and out, slowly, tenderly, sensing his own body was approaching that inevitable point of no return.

A second finger was inserted alongside the first. She moved against his hand, wordlessly moaning her need, not knowing the words to express what she needed, what she was seeking, her head thrashing back and forth on the pillow.

Then, when the moment was upon her, James could feel her climax as she convulsed around his fingers.

He had intended to wait until her spasms had ceased, but his own body had been too long denied its release. As Cecile shouted out his name, he softly called hers in return and spilled his seed upon the bed beneath them.

It was some time later—he could not have said how much later and, if it had come to that, neither could she—that Cecile opened her eyes and gazed up into his.

Her voice was a raspy whisper. "Is that sex?"

He nodded his head. He shook his head.

A tiny crease formed between her passion-glazed eyes. "I don't understand."

"I know you don't," he murmured, brushing a strand of hair back from her face.

Cecile reached up and traced the outline of his lower lip and then the jut of his chin. "Is there more?"

"There is so much more," James said to her, promising himself that he would not laugh at the lady's question.

"When . . . ?"

"Now."

She sounded almost hopeful. "Will it be like before?"

James exhaled on a long-suffering sigh. How could he explain to her what could never be adequately explained employing mere words? "Yes and no."

Her expression was one of utter innocence. "Will it be two halves joining into one whole?"

Graystone's heart clenched in his chest. Christ, she was so sweet and so trusting. "Something like that."

"Will you touch me again with your hand?"

"In the beginning," he said, slipping his fingers between her legs and discovering that she was still soft and wet and ready for him.

Cecile reached down between their bodies and grasped him in her hand. His penis immediately responded.

"A lady's prerogative, you said," she reminded him.

James's laugh was slightly husky and definitely self-deprecating. "So I did." He might live to regret those words, but not now and not anytime soon, he predicted.

"You have grown impressively large again, my lord," the young woman beside him on the bed observed saucily, seemingly fascinated by the change in his body.

So he had.

"You might wish to think of it as a very large finger," James suggested.

Cecile's eyes widened more than appreciably. "Is that what you do with it?"

James was weary of explaining. In his opinion, the time for explanations was over. It was time—past time—to show the lady exactly what it all meant.

Cecile had never felt like this before.

James was kissing her, urging her lips apart, teasing her with his tongue, delving into her mouth as if he were trying to meld their lips and teeth and tongues into one.

James was touching her, using his strong hands and his bony fingers to steal the very breath from her lungs, the strength from her bones and muscles.

James was caressing her, making her blood sing in her veins, making her body sing with a wild, hot song she had never heard before, making her heart sing within her breast.

She had not known about passion between a man and woman, except for the dreamy memory that visited her at night. But this passion was real. This passion was a fever in the mind. This passion could make a woman forget everything but the way a man made her feel.

James was taking her nipple between his lips and drawing her deeper and deeper into his mouth. Then his handsome and so very dear and familiar face was before her, and his broad shoulders were blocking out everything but him.

He slipped between her legs, and she could feel that part of him pressing against her, pushing against her, prodding her flesh. Quicksilver eyes burned with intensity. And with her name on his lips, he finally plunged into her.

"James!" she cried out.

"Cecile!"

He made love to her with every part of his heart and mind, body and soul, and when he thrust into her for the last time and shouted her name over and over again, seeking his release, finding his satisfaction, Cecile knew a sense of completion and belonging that she had never known before.

Two did become one.

They were, indeed, two halves of the same whole.

James Gray, thirteenth Earl of Graystone awakened and remembered, although he did not yet fully understand.

But he would.

Soon.

It was starting to come back to him: the people and the places, the sights, the sounds and the smells, the myriad sensations, and the feelings, good and bad, happy and sad.

He eagerly took it back into himself, embracing every experience, treasuring every memory, celebrating the victories along with the defeats, for his life had been returned to him.

Cecile.

The reason was Cecile.

James turned his head on the pillow and gazed at the lovely creature sleeping beside him in the massive bed, one arm stretched out along the covers, the other resting on his chest as if she did not want to stray far from his side even in slumber.

Last night this beautiful woman had loved him as he had never been loved before. She had kissed away the hurt in his heart and soul as surely as she had pressed her lips to the scar on his shoulder, tears flowing from her eyes as she remembered how he had received the injury, knowing that she had been the reason.

He would do it all over again if it meant that he could be here in this time, in this place, and with this woman, Graystone told himself. He would do whatever it took to protect what was his: his past, his present, his future.

For now he had a future.

But first he must preserve the reputation of Her Serene Highness, Princess Cecile of Saint-Simeon. He felt certain that Lady Ann would find a way of concealing her friend's absence from Guest House this morning. At least until Cecile could return undetected to her chambers. Goodenough would see to the rest. He was a good man, Goodenough.

James rolled onto his side and stared down at the

sleeping woman. It was still early, he thought, touching his lips to her hand, then to her bare shoulder, then to her mouth.

But it wasn't too early. . . .

Chapter Twenty-two

He was a creature of the night.

He loved the darkness. He always had, even as a child. While the other boys and girls had cowered in fear of the night and had quaked in their shoes at the tales of the terrifying monsters, the devilish fiends from the fiery pits of hell itself, the ogres that chased after children (no child was fast enough to outrun a voracious ogre) and gobbled them up whole, especially those children who dared to misbehave, he had been enraptured by it all.

There was something comforting about the night: its quietude, its privacy, its aloneness.

Rodolphe Girardet preferred being alone.

The night was his favorite part of the day: When everyone else was asleep, that was the time he loved being awake. He often worked late at night. Reading. Thinking. Plotting and planning. Poring over his collections, savoring his latest acquisition, contemplating what his next would be.

During the social frenzy that was known as the London season, there were often dinner parties and fancy dress balls that carried on through the entire evening and into the night, lasting until dawn and often concluding with an early-morning breakfast.

It wasn't that the prince minded engaging in these social functions—indeed, they were de rigueur for a gentleman in his position, but he had no wish to make a steady diet of them.

Still, it never ceased to astonish Girardet the amount of valuable information that could be garnered from a disgruntled or indiscreet spouse, or from an inebriated peer of the realm after a glass or two too many of expensive champagne.

For he was an avid collector of information.

Variety was said, after all, to be the spice of life. Publius had recognized that in the first century B.C. As had Cowper nearly two thousand years later, and, of course, the inimitable yet pathetic Samuel Johnson.

Rodolphe needed variety like most men needed air to breathe. He thrived on it. He craved it. He had to have it. His mind, his body, his limitless appetite for food, drink, women, experiences: They all required daily diversity and stimulation.

There was the very French and the very soignée Comtesse Thérèse Tournaire, naturellement, and the talented Lady Pale, but he required far more stimulus than either of the ladies could provide him with.

There was a brothel down by the London docks, a shabby boardinghouse of sorts tucked away at the tail end of a filthy mews; no more than a tenement really, teeming with the sights and sounds and smells of the city's poorest inhabitants.

There was another house he frequented in the Chinese section of town, and another that specialized in every variation, deviation, and aberration known to man or woman.

A gentleman must have his diversions.

Moira, Lady Pale, was also a creature of the night. Perhaps because she believed that the bright sunlight did not show her complexion to its best advantage.

In truth, most women of a certain age—and Moira was definitely of that age—were flattered by lamplight and chandelier light, candlelight and moonlight. It was the sunlight that was most unkind to them. Its unforgiving glare revealed every blemish, every wrinkle, every gray hair, every imperfection, real or imagined.

Yes, the night could be kind.

The night could also be seductive. The very same lady or gentleman could become quite a different human being once the sun had set and the moon had risen.

Prince Rodolphe had been the honored guest at any number of great country houses during the shooting season when a bell was discreetly rung at dawn so that male and female guests alike could scurry back to their own bedchambers before the ritual of morning tea.

Why, there were even name cards discreetly posted in a brass holder on the door of each bedchamber, so one did not inadvertently return to the wrong room.

There were more things done, said, performed during the dead of night that would never see the light of day.

His Serene Highness, Prince Rodolphe, slipped from his bed, wrapped his silk robe around his nude and at least temporarily satiated body, left the countess deep in slumber—Moira had been quite inexhaustible tonight, mounting him as if she were astride an untamed, unbroken stallion and determined to ride him into a frenzied lather—and made his way downstairs.

He had no need for a candle or a lamp. He had the eyesight of a nocturnal animal. He saw more lucidly in the dark than he did in the daylight.

Rodolphe opened a door and entered a chamber. It was a place he knew well. It was a place in which he spent hours every day. Indeed, it was his favorite place in the entire huge house.

He encircled the room, pausing now and then to touch, to caress a favored object with his sensitive fingertips, recognizing his beloved treasures as much by feel as by sight, for he was a tactile man.

He stood there in the middle of the inky black room and breathed in the night air.

Yes, he was a true creature of the night.

And he loved the darkness.

Chapter Twenty-three

The day is for honest men, the night for thieves.

Tonight he was going to play the thief, James Gray acknowledged, as he leaned back against the seat of the unmarked, undistinguished black brougham.

He raised his walking stick and signaled by tapping twice on the ceiling. "Stop here."

The hired carriage came to a halt. The two black hacks, chosen for their speed and surefootedness, rather than for their beauty—proving that appearances could be deceptive, for no better horses were to be found anywhere in London—immediately obeyed.

James poked his head out between the drawn curtains on the carriage's window. "Wait here," he commanded in a voice that carried to the driver and no further.

"Yes, my lord."

Since it was inadvisable, not to mention indiscreet and potentially dangerous, for James to fetch Cecile in front of Guest House at this late hour of the evening, they had agreed upon an alternate plan. She was to depart by a side entrance and meet him one block away.

Graystone waited.

He did not see or hear anything until there was a light knock—just the merest suggestion of a rap—on the carriage door.

"James?" came her recognizable whisper.

"Yes."

He quickly turned the handle and opened the door. The slender figure in black—as a matter of fact, it was the same head-to-toe black costume that Cecile had worn for their practice break-in into Cork House—slipped into the brougham.

James was about to latch the door behind her when another female form followed Cecile into the carriage and plopped down on the seat beside her.

"What the devil?" exclaimed Graystone.

Three people—two inside the carriage and one atop—simultaneously whispered: "Shhh!"

"It is Lady Ann," Cecile explained. "She has insisted upon coming along."

James sank his teeth into his tongue. He was sorely tempted to employ language that a gentleman did not use in front of females, let alone in the presence of ladies. "Has she, indeed?"

The fair-haired young woman, wrapped in a dark brown, hooded cloak, stated determinedly, "I will not allow the princess to go about tonight on her own."

"The princess is not on her own, madam," James informed Cecile's lady-in-waiting. "She will be with me."

"And with me," came the assurance of another masculine voice as a head of chestnut hair appeared from above and poked through the carriage window.

The expression on Lady Ann Faraday's pretty face was transformed into a frown. "Who, may I inquire, is that person?"

"I am Goodenough."

James offered a somewhat more comprehensive explanation. "He is my man, Goodenough."

Cecile saw fit to contribute under her breath, "They say the more the merrier."

"Not in this case," James corrected her. "The more people who are involved in this business, the greater the odds are that something will go wrong; and the greater the chance that we will be discovered."

Cecile reached across the carriage and patted his knee reassuringly. "Nothing will go wrong, James."

He was not reassured.

Neither, apparently, was Lady Ann Faraday. "There was an 'incident' about a year ago, my lord. At the time I was persuaded to let Her Serene Highness go off on her own one night. I have regretted that decision every minute of every hour of every day since. I could not live with myself if I allowed anything similar to happen again to my dearest friend in all the world."

"Ann, that's enough," came a belated admonition from Cecile.

"It is true, and we both know it. It was a disaster that night, Lord Graystone, as you well know," the blonde claimed with a pointed look in James's direction.

"I'm not certain I comprehend your meaning, Lady Ann," he admitted. In truth, he didn't have a clue.

"But I do know this is neither the time nor the place to clear up such matters."

"It can wait," Cecile interjected.

James relented. He had little choice. Time was of the essence. "Since you are here, Lady Ann, you may stay. But you must promise not to leave the confines of this carriage under any circumstances. Is that understood?"

"It is, my lord."

"You are to remain at your post as well, Good-enough," came his next order.

"Yes, my lord," came the muted response.

"The two of you must stay put no matter what you think or assume is happening inside Prince Rodolphe's residence. I will personally guarantee the princess's safety. That is and always will be my utmost concern. I don't want to have to worry about the two of you as well."

"What of you, James?" Cecile spoke up.

"I can look after myself. I have before under far more treacherous circumstances, believe me." He spoke to his valet-cum-carriage-driver for the evening. "Goodenough, you are to stop around the corner from our destination. Her Serene Highness and I will proceed the rest of the way on foot." He tapped the ceiling again with his walking stick. "Now let us be off."

When they reached the designated street, James gave his final instructions before he and Cecile slipped from the carriage. "We will return within two hours."

Then they immediately disappeared from the sight of the pair waiting with the brougham.

James and Cecile moved swiftly.

They moved silently.

They moved from shadow to shadow without being seen or detected. It was almost as if they had become shadows themselves.

James only hoped that his information was accurate: Girardet was at a dinner being given in his honor tonight. The dinner party would be followed by a few hands of cards, according to his sources. Indeed, more than a few hands, for it seemed that His Serene Highness was very fond of playing cards and even more fond of winning—which he did on a regular basis.

In fact, it was well known that Rodolphe Girardet had no need to cheat at cards because he was the best player among his friends and acquaintances. They often played just to keep him happy, knowing all the while they would lose.

There would be servants present in the prince's house tonight, of course. That was to be expected. But, with the possible exception of his valet and the butler, Rank, they should all be abed.

During the planning stages James had selected a door at the side of the impressive four-story mansion. The lock was an easy variety to pick, and the entrance would provide them with the shortest route from the hallway to the prince's suite.

Their strategy was a simple one: He and Cecile would begin their search with her uncle's bedchamber and dressing room. If they came up empty-handed, they would move downstairs to his personal study and the library.

The lock was quickly picked. They made their way into the house. They paused near the entranceway and listened. No alarm had been raised. No unusual sounds were audible.

James gave Cecile a sign with his hand, indicating this was the way up the back staircase—the servants' staircase. Indeed, he could see the layout of the entire house clearly in his head.

In their soft leather shoes the two of them climbed the steps, maneuvered along the second-floor passageway, and slipped into the prince's bedchamber with no more noise than that made by a scurrying mouse.

The moon was full and shone in the row of windows that faced the boulevard, illuminating the bedroom as brightly as a dozen candles would have.

The prince certainly knew how to live like a king, James reflected, as he and Cecile went straight to work. The chamber was opulent: silk wallcoverings, ornate gilded mirrors, elaborate furnishings, including a huge canopy bed draped in gold brocade that must have come straight out of a French chateau.

Their search was methodical and thorough.

The procedures had been mutually agreed upon in advance. Nothing must appear to have been moved or touched. No one must ever know they had been in the house.

Common sense must prevail, as well. The missing crown, scepter, and chalice were not small items. It was also likely that they had been stashed in a common hiding place. For this had been no ordinary robbery. And Rodolphe Girardet's motive had been no ordinary motive. He was a man who would enjoy, perhaps even insist upon, taking out his "prizes" and gloating over his possession of them in private, what he would regard as his ultimate triumph.

James took the bedroom. Cecile took the dressing room. At the end of their allotted thirty minutes in this section of the house, they had discovered nothing beyond the fact that Girardet was a fastidious gentleman with an enormous wardrobe.

It was time to move downstairs.

James put his mouth to Cecile's ear and whispered, "The study is next."

She nodded and followed him out of the bedchamber. They flattened their backs against the wall and moved along the corridor until they reached the grand staircase. They made it to the study without incident.

The study turned out to be spacious and masculine. It contained an oversize mahogany desk and an equally oversize leather chair that sat behind it. There was a black horsehair sofa, an assortment of tables and chairs, a cabinet filled with exotic and expensive liquors, and a welcome absence of bibelots.

At one point Cecile bumped the edge of the liquor cabinet with her shoulder and there was a faint tinkling of glass.

James could almost hear her gasp behind the hand that flew to cover her mouth.

They both froze in place.

They waited five minutes. Then five more. James

crept to the study door and opened it a crack. There was no sign of a lamp suddenly being lit. There was no indication of any movement. Thank God, it appeared that no one had heard them.

Within another quarter hour, James was satisfied that the missing objects weren't in Girardet's study. But, for the first time since this business had started, he was also beginning to have doubts.

What if Prince Rodolphe had not hidden the stolen items here in his house?

What if the prince wasn't the thief, or even the mastermind behind the theft?

Just because Rodolphe Girardet was devious, just because Cecile neither liked nor trusted the man (neither did James, for that matter), just because her late parents had warned the princess about her uncle since childhood, it did not necessarily follow that he had stolen the crown, the scepter, and the chalice.

Surely there were a handful of other men—and women, too, for that matter—who might have a reason or a motive of their own to steal the princely treasure of Saint-Simeon.

This was no time for doubts.

James gave the signal. They reconnoitered at the study door. Cecile put her face close to his. Her breath wafted across his skin, stirring the tiny hairs at his nape, causing him to shiver, making him suddenly aware of her as a woman, as the woman he had made love to again and again in his bed only three nights before.

It seemed like a lifetime ago.

His body began to stir in response.

Hell and damnation, Graystone, James swore at himself. There was more important business at work here tonight. This was no time to think of sex.

Cecile whispered, "What if it isn't here?"

James tapped down his own doubts. He turned, placed a reassuring hand on her shoulder and moved his lips against her ear. "It will be. Don't lose heart. We'll go across to the library."

The library was purported to be one of Rodolphe Girardet's favorite rooms, according to the saucy housemaid who had chatted and flirted with the dustman cleaning out the coal-burning fireplaces one afternoon several weeks before. (Goodenough had later claimed that it had taken two full days to get the coal dust out of his nostrils.)

The heavy velvet drapes in the library were drawn against the moonlight. They would be forced to use the candles they had brought with them.

James struck a match.

They each took a lighted taper—James went in one direction with his and Cecile headed in the opposite—as they made a cursory examination of the room.

They met back where they had started from.

Cecile dropped her voice to a scarcely audible level. "There must be thousands of books here."

"Girardet is a collector."

She pointed out one particular table on the opposite side of the library. "He has excellent taste. That display case appears to contain priceless miniatures. In fact, there are even ones of my parents, Alexandre, and myself."

James felt her shudder.

"I wonder what that is," Cecile whispered, indicating a wooden cabinet with numerous drawers of varying sizes. She quietly tugged on one of the ivory handles. Nothing happened. Then she tried a second drawer. Again, it wouldn't budge.

James spotted the keyhole at the bottom of the unusual cabinet. "It's locked."

"It's too small, anyway," she murmured low.

He understood her meaning. Regardless of the cabinet's actual contents, the objects they were searching for wouldn't fit into any of its drawers.

They searched the library quickly and efficiently. Not an easy task when the room was filled with so many strange articles, when it consisted of so many nooks and crannies.

Standing in the center of the room, James did a slow, full 360-degree turn. Maybe the missing crown, scepter, and chalice just weren't here. Maybe he had overlooked a vital clue that would give him the answer he obviously didn't possess. Maybe he was wasting his time. Maybe he needed to start from the beginning and reconsider the problem from an entirely different perspective.

Then James noticed that Cecile was holding her candle up to one of the bookcases and appeared to be studying the volumes along a particular wall.

He came up beside her.

The titles were all in French, Italian, or Latin. One section was devoted to the subject of history. Not just ordinary history, either. The entire bookcase was filled with tomes on royal history, the rise and fall of princes, kings, and emperors. One volume in particular caught Graystone's eye; he couldn't have said why.

James softly read aloud the words embossed on the leather spine. *"Aut Caesar Aut Nullus."*

Translating from the Latin, Cecile murmured, "Either a Caesar or a Nobody."

He was getting that feeling in his gut again, James recognized. That strange yet familiar feeling; the one that forewarned him, the one that he had learned to listen to over the years.

He put his face directly in line with Cecile's: "It's here."

"The treasure?"

He nodded his head.

"Why?"

He pointed to his midsection.

"Ah, those famous gut instincts of yours again."

He nodded curtly.

"Where?"

He shook his head.

They held their candles high and began a more thorough examination of the room. Cecile was about to move the book in front of her—indeed, it was almost as if a brilliant idea had occurred to her—when they heard a noise.

Voices.

Footsteps.

Someone was in the main entrance hall just outside the library door. They quickly doused their candles.

James instilled urgency into his voice. "Hide!"

Cecile quickly looked around.

"Behind the drapes," he hissed.

They dashed for cover, pulling the heavy brocade material around them. Then they stood utterly still.

The library door opened and the voice of Prince Rodolphe could be heard saying, "You may lock up for the night and go on to bed now, Rank. I will be spending some time here in the library."

"Yes, Your Serene Highness," came the reply.

One set of footsteps receded. They could detect the sound of the library door closing.

Then there was silence.

James could discern the soft, familiar movements of someone moving quietly about an often-frequented room. Candelabra were lit in several locations. With a quick glance to either side of them, he made sure there were no signs of their presence behind the heavy draperies.

What the dickens was Girardet doing back so early, anyway? The prince wasn't supposed to have returned home for at least several more hours.

But he had.

And Graystone had more pressing matters on his mind. Like not being discovered. Like keeping Cecile safe until he could find a way out of this bloody fine mess.

If worse came to worse, he wasn't unprepared. He had seen no reason to alarm the princess, however, by telling her that he had a rather sharp and deadly blade slipped into his pantleg. He had also failed to mention the pistol that was secured behind his back in the waistband of his black pants.

Graystone always liked a little extra insurance when dealing with this kind of business.

Through the slightest opening in the drapes, James watched his opponent. After lighting the fire and then a cigar, and pouring himself what appeared to be a snifter of brandy, Girardet moved to the bookcase where he and Cecile had been only moments before.

The prince pushed on something—or perhaps he pulled; James couldn't see for certain—and then stepped back as a whole section of the bookcase swung open.

James didn't move a muscle.

Cecile swallowed the sound of astonishment that he'd sensed was on the tip of her tongue.

A hidden door.

Why hadn't he thought of the possibility? Then James recalled the expression on Cecile's face in that instant before they had heard Girardet in the hallway. She had thought of it. Perhaps because of that day in the British Museum when she'd inadvertently fallen, or been shoved, against the invisible door.

The lady had been about to discover another secret room!

Candelabra in one hand, a glass of brandy and a cigar in the other, Girardet stepped around the corner of the bookcase and disappeared. Within several minutes there seemed to be more light pouring from the secret chamber.

What to do now?

James had to think and think fast.

They had no choice but to go ahead with their

plans. They couldn't risk trying to break into Girardet's house a second time. It was now or never.

And it was time to find out what was in Rodolphe Girardet's hidden room?

James held a finger to his lips, signifying to Cecile that silence was of the utmost importance. He held out his hand and indicated further that she was to remain where she was.

She shook her head vehemently.

He glared at her.

She glared right back at him.

There was no time to argue and there was certainly no time to reason with the lady. She was stubborn and headstrong and she would, in the end, do what she bloody well wanted to, anyway.

James reached behind him and retrieved the pistol from its position at his back.

Cecile's eyes enlarged.

Parting the brocade drapes with one hand, James slipped out from behind them and made his way across the library. He reached the bookcase and peered around the corner.

Girardet was seated in the center of the small secret chamber, smoking his cigar, sipping his cognac and staring at the rare collection of three items arranged on a table before him. Then he put his handsome head back and laughed with self-satisfaction.

That's when James became aware that Cecile was beside him. Not only was she standing at his side, but she was grasping a pistol in her hand.

I, myself, am an expert marksman.

The words from that first night in the key garden

echoed in his head. And somehow James knew that she intended to march straight into the beast's lair.

"Mine," the prince proclaimed with a sense of smugness and superiority. "All mine."

Cecile stepped around James and into the lion's den. "I'm afraid not, Uncle."

Chapter Twenty-four

Cecile had known the instant he had entered the house. She had sensed his evil presence even before she had heard his voice in the hallway, or his footsteps on the marble floor, or his brief conversation with the butler.

She had known it was Rodolphe Girardet, formerly of the tiny and idyllic kingdom by the Mediterranean Sea; the beautiful principality of Saint-Simeon.

Her Serene Highness, Princess Cecile of Saint-Simeon, looked down upon the man she despised above all other human beings. Indeed, she realized, he was the only human being that she actually did despise. Her hand was steady on her pistol.

"I see you are seated upon your throne," she observed with all the disdain she could muster.

Rodolphe Girardet was sitting in an elaborate chair of gilded wood, embellished with scrollwork and intricate carvings. The cushions on the seat and the back of the chair were embroidered in the manner of medieval tapestries with scenes of wimpled ladies, armored knights, and turreted castles. There was even an ornate crown, stitched with thread of gold and silver and inlaid with precious gemstones, interwoven into a crested headrest.

"It is a chair fit for a king . . . or a prince, don't you agree?" The question was rhetorical. He turned his head toward the intruders, his expression and demeanor utterly calm.

"Where did you steal *it* from?" she demanded, meaning the priceless chair.

"Tsk. Tsk. I'm sure your parents taught you far better manners than that, young lady." The prince didn't bother waiting for a response. "As a matter of fact, since you have inquired, this throne was once among the countless possessions of Louis Seizième, himself."

"Louis the Sixteenth was convicted of treason against his people and his country, and was condemned to die on the guillotine. They chopped off his head. Or had you forgotten?"

Girardet ignored her comment, took another sip of his cognac, and held it momentarily on his tongue. "Who can these intruders be who feel free to break into a gentleman's private residence, apparently in order to lecture him on ancient history?"

"Not so ancient history," Cecile reminded him.

Her uncle made a nonchalant gesture with the manicured hand holding his cigar. "I must confess I cannot quite fathom the manner of your dress. Could it be that you are garbed as thieves in the night?"

Cecile's anger, long buried but never forgotten, boiled to the surface. "You are the thief, sir."

"And who are you, madam?"

She knew full well that her uncle recognized her. He was playing games with her. He was always playing games.

Drawing herself up to her full and proud and considerable height, she proclaimed, "I am Her Serene Highness, Princess Cecile of Saint-Simeon."

"You do not look like a princess to me."

"And you, sir, do not look, act, behave or in any other way resemble a prince." Cecile was just warming up to her subject. "You are a pathetic man." She stopped herself. "No, you are a pathetic *creature* who sits in this small, secret, private hole in the dead of night gloating over the symbols of Saint-Simeon's sovereignty. A sovereignty that you could never begin to know or understand, and you will certainly never have."

Rodolphe Girardet took another sip of his cognac and another puff on his expensive cigar. He tipped his chin up ever so slightly and blew the aromatic smoke into the air.

"I'm surprised you haven't crowned yourself," Cecile added, glancing at the altar before him.

It was covered with a fine royal purple cloth and upon its surface, carefully arranged, were the coronation crown, the royal scepter, and the sacred chalice of Saint-Simeon.

"It is enough that I possess the symbols of Saint-Simeon's sovereignty," her uncle said at last, "and that Alexandre never will."

"He will now," Cecile stated unequivocally.

"You are mistaken if you believe that I will allow you and this henchman of yours to take my prizes from me." Girardet smiled at her, and it was a condescending, even a pitiable smile. "By the way, my dear Cecile, I have seen you looking prettier. This costume—" he made a general, circular motion in the air with the hand clasping his cigar "—does nothing to flatter you."

"It makes me invisible."

Dark, malevolent eyes glittered in the confines of the smoke-hazed chamber. "*I* can see you," her uncle hissed like a snake. "I have always been able to see you."

Cecile would not allow him to see her fear. She would not allow him to sense her fear, for she knew that he could. "You didn't know I was in the library when you entered it a few minutes ago. You didn't see me then, Uncle."

Girardet's face changed slightly in both expression and color. It was the first chink in his otherwise seemingly impenetrable armor. "That was a small error."

"On your part." Cecile struck again with her verbal rapier. "You are not invincible. You make mistakes, dear Uncle."

"I see you have made one, as well, dear Niece." The prince tried to divert her attention by shifting his attention to the man at her side. "I presume the accomplice with you is the ever-present suitor for your hand, the Earl of Graystone."

James answered for himself. "Girardet."

The prince nodded his head ever so slightly. "Graystone." He sniffed. "I suppose you imagine yourself a worthy opponent."

"You said it, not me."

Prince Rodolphe indicated the stolen objects on the

table in the center of the small, secret chamber. "Is that what this melodramatic scene is all about?"

James answered succinctly. "Yes."

"So you are here to help my niece return the coronation crown, the royal scepter, and the sacred chalice to Saint-Simeon so Alexandre may be crowned the next ruler of that insignificant speck of land with its pathetic little villages, its goats, and its goat-herders."

Cecile noticed that James remained standing outside the doorway without actually entering the room concealed behind the bookcase. She also realized that his pistol had vanished.

"If those are your true feelings, I wonder that you bothered to steal them at all," James ventured. "After all, Girardet, you already live like a king on both sides of the Channel."

"Yes, I do," the man repeated, obviously immensely pleased with himself.

James arched one brow in a knowing fashion. "But that is the whole point, is it not?"

The prince frowned. "What is the whole point?"

Graystone delivered the coup d'état to her uncle's ego. "You live *like* a king, but you are not a king."

"You never will be a king," Cecile added.

Girardet sprang to his feet, thrust the still-lit cigar to the rare and expensive carpet underfoot and ground it out with the heel of his elegant shoe, set down his cognac, and declared, his voice dripping with venom, "If I cannot have the throne, then no one shall have it."

"That isn't true," Cecile contradicted him. "Prince

Alexandre will soon assume his rightful place on the throne. He will be the next ruling prince of Saint-Simeon."

An ugly sneer emerged on the once-handsome features. "That will never come about. Alexandre's doom and the doom of Saint-Simeon is but the third and final stage of my stratagem, and it will succeed as surely as the other two already have." Girardet seemed to forget their presence for a moment. He rubbed his hands together. "The entire plan is coming to fruition just as I had conceived it."

"You are lying," Cecile dared to announce to his face.

The gentleman smiled at her, and it was a smile that sent ice cold shards plunging straight into her heart. " 'What is a lie, 'tis but the truth in masquerade?' I believe it was Lord Byron who penned that," the prince mentioned, regaining control of himself. "You see, my dear Cecile," he began, looking from her to James and back again. "You were also part of my grand scheme."

Cecile suddenly felt quite ill.

Girardet focused on James Gray. "I assume your intentions when it comes to my niece are honorable."

"The most honorable."

"Then you intend to have her as your wife."

"I do."

Prince Rodolphe seemed immensely pleased by the prospect. "I see that you are in love with her, and that sweet Cecile is in love with you." He made a small clicking sound with his tongue as if to say "what a pity." "It would have been a love match."

"Our feelings for each other are none of your bloody business," James informed the man.

The prince circled the throne twice and came to a halt behind it. He leaned forward slightly, rested his elbows on the back, shook his head, and proclaimed, "It is my sad duty to inform you, Graystone, that you cannot marry my niece."

James gave the other man a stony stare. "I don't need your permission."

Girardet threw up his hands and shrugged his shoulders. "That is true. But that is also not the reason you can't marry her."

Cecile did not wish for this conversation to continue. No good could come of it. She held her pistol a little higher in the air and ordered, "Stop now, Uncle, or I shall shoot."

"You aren't capable of shooting me," Girardet said in a seductive tone, taking a step toward her.

"She may not be, but I most assuredly am," James said, holding his hand over Cecile's for a moment and aiming her pistol at the prince's heart. "You will now explain."

"Please, James, let it be."

"Have no fear, Cecile."

"That is sweet," the prince said. "You are so protective of her, my dear Graystone. I wonder if you will feel quite as protective once you learn the truth."

Quicksilver eyes narrowed. "How would you know the truth, Girardet?"

"Because I arranged the whole course of events, naturally. I have been planning my revenge since my elder brother, dear Max, kicked me out of my own country twenty years ago. My revenge is upon the entire house of Girardet, down to the last man, woman, and child."

"You are a bastard."

"I know." Girardet didn't appear to be in the least offended by the other gentleman's description of him. In fact, he seemed delighted by it. "For reasons of my own choosing, I won't tell you the first part of my Grand Scheme, but the second was the ruination of Cecile, and the third is the destruction of Alexandre."

James was holding utterly still beside her. "What do you mean the ruination of Cecile?"

Prince Rodolphe turned first to her. "I'm sure you remember, my dear, how you were once courted by every eligible prince, duke, nobleman, even a minor king or two from every corner of Europe."

Of course, she remembered.

"Then your beloved parents were accidentally killed, and you went into mourning, as was only appropriate. But the official period of mourning has been over for some time now and yet you haven't entertained a single offer of marriage." Girardet tapped his chin with a soft, white hand. "I wonder why."

"What I choose to do or not to do, and why is none of your business, sir," she stated adamantly.

Blue eyes so very unlike her own lit up. Her uncle went on as if she hadn't spoken. "I will tell you why. Because one night, not long after your mother and father's tragic demise, a special powder was slipped into the drink you were given at bedtime. You were awake and aware, but impotent to fight its effects. Do you remember being taken from the palace to a ship anchored in the harbor?''

She remembered.

His cruelty knew no bounds, no decency. ''Do you recall finding yourself stripped of every last article of clothing and thrust into bed with a naked man, a stranger, a common seaman with no past, with no future, not even a real name?''

Cecile felt tears scalding the back of her eyes, yet she vowed she would not allow this monster to see her cry.

The prince was immensely pleased with himself. ''I arranged the entire incident, of course. It was all part of my grand scheme: making certain that Cecile could never make an advantageous match on the marriage market, that she was blemished, spoiled, sullied—'' he relished the words, rolled them around on his tongue, savored the taste of them ''—ruined.''

Cecile was suddenly afraid that the man beside her might attack her uncle and do himself harm. She could feel the anger emanating from him as if it were a tangible force.

Girardet regarded James. ''So, as you see, you cannot have her, Graystone.''

''I can,'' he stated.

''You can't.''

''She is not blemished, spoiled, sullied, or ruined in my eyes,'' he stated adamantly.

''Oh, it isn't the shame of 'soiled goods' that prevents a marriage between the two of you.'' The prince was positively chomping at the bit to deliver the pièce de résistance. He delivered the final blow. "It is because Cecile is already married."

Cecile's legs turned to quince jelly, but she still managed to stand her ground.

Nothing could have prevented Rodolphe Girardet from finishing his story now. "The couple were discovered *in flagrante delicto*, as it were. There was nothing else to be done, but the captain of the ship must perform the ceremony then and there. I have the certificate of marriage, of course." The gentleman was chortling loudly. Indeed, he was nearly choking on his own laughter. "My niece, the last princess of Saint-Simeon, is the wife of a poor, pathetic, penniless vagrant named Gathier who has neither been seen nor heard from since. Society tends to be unforgiving about these things, Lord Graystone. You cannot live in sin with her. And you cannot marry her. That would be bigamy."

"It would not be bigamy," James Gray declared, immovable.

"A woman cannot have two husbands," the prince pointed out, still laughing at his own clever machinations.

"A man, on the other hand, is apparently permitted to have two mistresses," expressed an exasperated female voice from inside the library door.

They all turned.

"You have sent me on a bloody fool's errand, Rudy," Moira, Lady Pale, announced as she swept across the book-lined room and came to a halt behind the trio.

"Call for help, Moira," the prince ordered. "Can't you see that I am being robbed? Raise the alarm."

"I don't have to if I don't want to," the countess snapped at him. "I'm not the one standing there caught with his pants down, in a manner of speaking, and with a pistol pointed at his heart." She whisked the ermine-lined cape from around her bare shoulders—her gown, what little there was of it, was bronze-colored satin—and tossed it across a nearby chair. "I repeat, I do not like being made a fool of, Rudy. I went to the gentleman's house as you suggested. I sneaked into his bed and I waited. But he did not come."

There was silence.

Then Moira put her head back and laughed at her own unintentional witticism. "He did not come."

"Of course, he didn't come, you stupid woman. He wasn't at home. Graystone is standing there directly in front of you."

Moira took a step closer and peered into James Gray's darkened features. "I believe I prefer you without the makeup, my lord. You were much more handsome when I saw you at the ball in Her Serene Highness's honor." Then she disregarded him and glared once more at the prince. "Thanks to your brilliant scheme, Rudy, I nearly ended up bedding some lowly footman."

His retort was stinging. "I'm certain it wouldn't have been the first time, my dear countess."

Apparently Lady Pale did not care for his insinuation. "Do you think that no one knows of your own diversions, Your Serene Lowness? Do you honestly

believe that the ramshackle boardinghouse down by
the docks is a secret?"

"Shut up, Moira!"

"Or the house on Chou Lai Street?"

Rodolphe Girardet's complexion was reddening.
"I'm warning you."

She threw it right back in the prince's face. "Moira
knows all about your dirty little secrets."

"And I know all about your secrets," Girardet re-
taliated. "I know it was you, for example, who arranged the accident my niece had at the British
Museum."

That brought a gasp of surprise from Cecile.

"I only intended to frighten her." Lady Pale turned
to the princess. "It was supposed to be a *plaisanterie*,
a little joke. I didn't mean for you to get hurt. The
tough got carried away with the job he was hired to
do." The countess looked the younger woman over
from head to toe. "By the way, I like you much better
this way."

Cecile caught herself before she said thank you.

Moira turned to the prince. "I didn't mean any
harm. I've never really harmed anyone."

Rodolphe Girardet snorted in disbelief. "Never
really harmed anyone? What do you call murder?"

Lady Pale paled. She tried bravado, but it wasn't
altogether convincing. "I'm sure I have no idea what
you're talking about, Your Serene Highness."

"Don't try to play the innocent. That act wore thin
years ago, my dear. I have proof that you slipped
arsenic to the doxie who made certain that Lord Pale
drank it down like a good boy. You, madam, are

guilty of murdering your own husband." He added as a nice finishing touch, "An offense for which you could hang."

"Do you have any notion of what it was like to be sixteen years old and sold off in marriage to a filthy old man of eighty?" Moira shuddered and, as if taken by a sudden chill, wrapped her arms tightly around herself. "At least if I did have Osgood killed, it was to protect myself. It was in self-defense. What's your excuse, Rudy?"

"We won't speak of this anymore tonight," he said, quickly trying to change the subject.

Her beautiful head shot up. "Why not speak of it? I thought we were letting all the cats out of the bag tonight. I heard you inform Lord Graystone that he can't marry his beloved Cecile because she's already the wife of some common seaman. And now we all know that you were the mastermind behind the theft of those . . . objects." Moira pointed at the coronation crown, the scepter, and the chalice on the table. "So, why not tell them everything?"

"Shut up, you stupid cow, or I'll see to it that you end up with a rope around your neck," he roared in a rage.

Lady Pale did not appear intimidated by the threat. "And I have proof that could put you on the gallows, Rudy," she declared with all the apparent hatred in her soul. The woman turned to Cecile. "It was no accident, you know."

Cecile found her voice. "What was no accident?"

"Any of this," Moira said with a gesture that seemed to encompass the four of them, the library, the huge mansion, London, and the world beyond. "I have valuable information."

"I will see to it that you are paid for your information," Cecile said with disdain.

"Don't get uppity on me, princess. Not all of us were raised with a silver spoon in our mouths. I've had to work for everything and anything I have, and I've worked hard."

"I promise to reward you handsomely, Lady Pale. I always keep my promises."

Amber eyes narrowed to catlike slits. "I believe you do, Your Serene Highness. All right, here it is. It was no accident. It was all part of Rudy's revenge."

He lunged for his mistress and stumbled over the Louis Seizième chair. "Moira!"

"Rudy!" she mimicked his outrage.

"You have served your purpose, now shut your mouth," he commanded.

The countess looked down her pretty nose at the man and laughed in a most self-delighted and unladylike manner. "I believe you have it wrong, Your Serene Highness. You have served your purpose."

"You bitch . . ." he sputtered.

"Now, now, Rudy, such language," the beautiful woman scolded him, wagging her finger back and forth. "By the by, I have always known that you detested the nickname Rudy. It's the only reason I insisted upon calling you by it."

The rage burned brightly in the prince's piercing blue eyes.

The former Moira Munson continued with her explanation. "I have my own network of spies. They're very good at what they do, which is to gather and sell information. I now know that it was all planned and executed in the name of Rudy's revenge: your abduction and forced marriage, the theft of the crown, the scepter, and the chalice to prevent your brother from assuming the throne, and the death of your parents, of course."

Cecile felt her knees start to give way. Her hand, the one grasping the pistol, began to shake. For the first time tonight, she felt truly afraid. "I think you had better explain what you mean by that last remark, Lady Pale."

Moira pointed her finger at Prince Rodolphe. "He arranged for the accident. He had their carriage sabotaged. He even stood there and watched as it plunged into the river and they were drowned. It was your dear uncle who murdered your parents."

James saw Cecile's hand begin to shake. He knew her strength and her legs were about to give way and she was very likely to faint, hitting her head on the sharp corner of the bookcase.

He had a dilemma. Go for his own pistol, tucked into the back of his waist, and let Cecile fall. Or grab her and take a chance that Girardet might get to her pistol first.

Graystone made his choice.

By the time he had Cecile safely in his arms, it was Moira, Lady Pale, who had taken possession of the pistol.

"Step out into the library, all of you, where I can keep an eye on you," the countess ordered.

"Now, Moira, my dear . . ." Girardet cajoled.

"Especially you," she snapped at the prince. "I want you to be a good boy, Rudy, and fetch me the files I know you must have on me and dear old Osgood."

The gentleman snickered.

Moira pointed the deadly weapon straight at his heart. "I am an excellent shot, Your Serene Highness, and I don't mind killing a snake like you any more than I did that snake Osgood Pale."

No one in the room doubted that the countess meant every word she said.

Rodolphe Girardet unlocked a cabinet beside a delicate display case filled with silver snuff boxes. He reached inside and withdrew a thick leather folder, then a second and a third.

Moira urged him toward the fireplace. "Now, burn every last piece of evidence."

He was given no choice. One by one, Rodolphe Girardet fed each letter, each billet-doux, each scrap of paper, each written testimony, each paid-for-cash proof into the flames until they were all consumed and nothing more than ashes.

"Ashes to ashes," Lady Pale murmured to herself as she watched the fire devour her past sins. Then she turned to the prince. "Now we're even. In future you will leave me alone because I still possess the proof that you were responsible for the deaths of Maximilian V and Judith of Saint-Simeon. That will be my personal insurance policy."

"You are not half as stupid as I had thought," Rodolphe Girardet admitted to the woman.

"And you are not half as intelligent as *you* thought," she said and laughed again. The countess gazed around the room. "I suppose the question is where do we go from here? What, in heaven's name, am I going to do with you?"

"What you will do, Lady Pale," commanded a masculine voice from the doorway behind her, "is back up very slowly and give me the pistol in your hand."

James realized that Cecile's eyes were finally opening. She pushed herself up into a sitting position and exclaimed: "Count Dupre, it's you. Thank God, you're here!"

His Serene Highness, Prince Rodolphe, formerly of Saint-Simeon and more recently of Paris and London, leaned against the valuable and antique fireplace mantel and said, with a laugh that never reached his icy blue eyes, "Yes, thank God, you're here, Dupre. You're just in time for the fun and games."

James could feel the fight temporarily go out of Cecile's slender body. She looked up at her aide-de-camp, her wise counselor and valued adviser, at her friend, and she rasped, *"Et tu Brute?"*

Chapter Twenty-five

Damned if he did.

Damned if he didn't.

There wasn't going to be any easy way out of this one, Graystone acknowledged to himself. But since when was that any different from the other twenty, thirty, even forty times he had found himself in a similar situation?

With one exception this time.

Cecile.

There had been other people he had cared about, fought to protect, risked his own life to save: friends, *bhai-bund*, coworkers, his drivers, his *ghariwans*, but never the woman he loved.

That was when the truth hit James Gray right between the eyes. He was in love with Cecile Girardet, and he had never told her so. He had never actually said the words to her. And if he didn't think fast, if he wasn't very clever and very careful, if he didn't manage to get them both safely out of this messy situation, he might never have the chance to tell her.

First things first.

First, he had to assess his advantages and his disadvantages, his friends and his foes. They weren't necessarily one and the same, either, a valuable lesson that he had learned the hard way on several occasions in Bhārat. A foe could sometimes be an advantage, just as a friend could be a liability.

To his advantage, he was the youngest, the strongest, and the most heavily armed gentleman present in the library. He also had the element of surprise on his side: No one, other than Cecile, knew he was carrying a weapon.

To his disadvantage, he was outnumbered by Prince Rodolphe and Count Dupre two to one.

Moira, Lady Pale, was unlikely to come to the aid of either Girardet or the count. That could be to his advantage. Unfortunately, it was also highly unlikely that the countess would side with him. The lady was a survivor. She would blow whichever way the wind happened to be blowing at the moment.

It was a definite advantage that Cecile was a fighter and she was on his side, but she'd been dealt a couple of harsh blows tonight, and he wasn't certain how quickly she would recover.

James decided to watch, wait, and listen: Patience could ofttimes be a virtue just when a man was feeling the most impatient. Then, when the time was right, he would make his move.

Cecile brushed herself off and got to her feet. She stood there, her slender shoulders back and her dignity intact, in spite of the fact she was dressed in theatrical makeup and strange garb, in spite of the fact there was a pistol pointed at her by a man she had considered a loyal friend, in spite of the fact that she had just learned the truth about her parents' fatal accident.

"Did you know?" she asked Count Dupre.

"Did I know what, Your Serene Highness?" he responded, his own composure suffering.

"Naturally he knew," piped up Rodolphe Girardet from his position by the antique fireplace. "Dupre has been involved in this business from the beginning." The handsome prince made a perfunctory movement with his pale white hand. "Let me think for a moment. When did it all start, Edmond?"

Count Dupre interrupted the other man unceremoniously. "I would like to explain to Her Serene Highness myself."

"Explain what?" came an arrogant snort. "Explain that you betrayed her trust and Alexandre's? Explain that you deceived Maximilian and Judith, as well? Explain that you are a traitor to the Girardet family and to your own country? You sold them out one by one, Edmond, and there is nothing you can ever do to change that."

Cecile's eyes grew huge in her face. They were brimming with tears as she stared disbelievingly at the gentleman she had known from her childhood. "Why?"

Count Edmond Dupre shamefully summed it up in one word. "Blackmail."

Stunned, Cecile repeated the word. "Blackmail?"

He nodded his small head with its thinning hair. "Prince Rodolphe has been blackmailing me for some time."

"For some time," hooted Girardet as he thumped

the palm of his hand several times on the mantel-piece, sending a pair of valuable seventeenth-century porcelain figurines rattling against each other. "You call twenty years *some time*?"

"All that time?" Cecile said despairingly as if moving her lips was difficult.

The count managed a nod.

It seemed she still could not fully grasp the implication of what he was confessing to her. "How could you?" Cecile spread her arms. "We loved and trusted you. Why didn't you tell us?"

"It was because I loved you, all of you, that I couldn't risk your finding out," Dupre admitted. He shrugged his shoulders, sending the gold-fringed epaulets swinging from side to side. "It was a simple request at first. Nothing important. Nothing vital. Just a small, seemingly insignificant question with an insignificant answer." He heaved a heavy sigh. "Then it was another request and then another, and it grew into what it has become before I realized what I'd done." The count snapped his heels together and made a formal apology. "I extend my deepest regrets to you, Your Serene Highness."

"I don't think an apology, however heartfelt, quite makes up for the fact that you contributed to her parents' death and the situation in which she now finds herself," the prince smirked. He turned to his niece. "Don't you even want to know what I have been holding over dear Edmond's head all these years?"

Cecile shook her head and said in a small, yet firm voice, "I don't want to know. If the count ever wishes to confide in me that is up to him." With piercing blue eyes, she pinned her uncle to the spot where he stood. "But it is not for you to divulge, sir. You will, at least, behave like a Girardet when it comes to this."

"Thank you, Your Serene Highness," the count mumbled gratefully, with the remnants of his self-respect gathered about him like a tattered coat.

James knew the opportunity would never be any better than it was at this moment. Girardet had relaxed his stance, thinking himself in complete control of the situation.

Dupre held the weapon, but he was preoccupied with the damning truth being revealed about himself.

Lady Pale was keeping quiet as a church mouse, Graystone observed. The woman was obviously smart enough to know when to keep her mouth shut.

And Cecile . . . Cecile was the wild card in all of this. She was upset, yet she appeared surprisingly calm. James wondered if she realized that he still had his pistol.

He had to act before Girardet decided to take the weapon from the count. He didn't believe that Edmond Dupre could bring himself to shoot the young woman he had looked after her whole life, whatever the circumstances.

The prince, on the other hand, probably wouldn't hesitate to shoot each and every one of them, and that included his mistress—she was no doubt his former mistress now—and his own henchman, not to mention Cecile and himself.

It was now or never.

"As long as confessions seem to be the order of the day—or should I say the order of the night—I have one to make myself," James proclaimed.

His announcement seemed to catch everyone in the library off-guard. It was almost as if they had forgotten he was in the room.

"They say confession is good for the soul," the prince said. "But I've never held that opinion myself. Still, if it will make you feel any better, Graystone."

James turned, took two steps in Dupre's direction and stared down into the man's pallid face. "I bear the permanent mark of your walking stick on my back, sir."

The count cringed, but the pistol remained steady in his hand. "I am afraid I don't understand, my lord."

"I'm sure you don't. But you will. Suffice to say that you once raised that walking stick and brought it down across my shoulder, driving me to my knees."

"But I would remember," the little man claimed, scowling. "I don't remember."

Next, James turned his attention on the prince, moving ever so slightly closer to Dupre as he did so. "I was down by the docks several weeks ago. The West India South, as a matter of fact. While I was there I had a most enlightening conversation with the captain of a ship called the *Lagos*."

There was no reaction from Girardet; he continued to lounge against the fireplace mantel. But Dupre was getting something of a wild look in his eyes.

James went on. "Naturally, it was a bit difficult for us to have a dialogue since the captain spoke only

Portuguese and a smattering of Italian, and I speak only a few words of each."

"Your story is beginning to bore me, Lord Graystone."

"It won't be much longer, Your Serene Highness, I promise. And I always keep my promises. I think you will find it fascinating before it's all said and done."

James noticed that Cecile had begun to take note of what he was saying. She knew something was going to happen. He could see it in her eyes . . . those incredible eyes of hers, those eyes that he would never forget as long as he lived.

"Anyway, as I was saying, I was chatting with the Portuguese sea captain, and lo and behold, the man recognized me."

That got the prince's regard. "He recognized you?"

James nodded and nonchalantly took another half step toward Dupre. "It seems the captain remembered me." He turned and glared at the count. "Which is more than I can say for you, monsieur."

"Go on," Cecile urged.

"In turn, I told the captain that although I didn't recall his face, I did remember his voice." In an aside, Graystone explained, "He has a very deep and sonorous baritone. Anyway, we both agreed that this was a remarkable coincidence." James snapped his fingers together. "Then the captain remembered why he remembered me."

The prince was enthralled. "What was the reason?"

"Well, for one thing he recollected that I had worked as a sailor on his ship for several months after his crew had found me floating, half-dead, on a piece of a shipwreck in the middle of the Indian Ocean. Then he also managed to recall that after a certain 'altercation,' he had me thrown in the ship's brig."

It was Girardet who inquired, "What would an English aristocrat be doing in the brig of a Portuguese ship?"

"An excellent question, don't you all agree?"

They all nodded their heads.

"At the time the captain didn't know who I was. It seems that even *I* didn't know my own identity. I was suffering from a form of amnesia. The simple truth was I was regarded as the least important member of the ship's crew. I had no papers, no identification, no friends, and no family. I was a nobody and, therefore, I was expendable. So I was chosen for a particular mission."

James moved a little closer to Dupre, turned, and looked the man straight in the face. "Look into my eyes, Count, and tell me that you don't recognize me."

Count Edmond Dupre stared into eyes that could be the color of fog, eyes that could quickly change to quicksilver, eyes the color of heather on the hill just after the rain, and he let out with a distraught cry: "It cannot be you!"

"Yet it is!"

That was the instant when James leaped. He grabbed the pistol from the count's grasp and wrestled him to the ground. He was stronger and faster and younger. It all happened so quickly that before anyone could react, Graystone was back on his feet and facing them, this time with Cecile's pistol clasped in his hand and a ferocious smile on his handsome face.

"Move, Dupre, where I can keep an eye on you."

"You won't get far with one pistol," the prince pointed out with a perfidious smile.

"I think I will," James stated, pulling an even larger and more lethal weapon from the back of his pants. "Cecile, quickly get behind me."

Cecile immediately moved behind him.

There was a feral grin on Graystone's features as he finished his story. "It took a long time for the pieces to all fall into place. But I remember now. I was shipwrecked on my way home from India to claim the titles and lands that were mine after my elder brother died. The *Lagos* took me aboard, but I didn't know who I was . . . or even where I was going. I worked like a slave for a small amount of food and passage across the ocean. And when the ship anchored in Saint-Simeon, I found myself in a unique position one night. For I awoke to discover myself in bed with an angel." James Gray laughed lightly and shook his head. "I thought I had died and gone to heaven."

"What in the bloody hell are you talking about, Graystone?"

"Your plan for revenge has failed, Girardet. Prince Alexandre will be the next ruler of Saint-Simeon, and he will rule wisely and well. Princess Cecile of Saint-Simeon is far from ruined. Indeed, her situation is just the opposite."

"What do you mean?"

James realized that he was enjoying himself. "As the French say: *à bon chat, bon rat.*"

"What does 'to a good cat, a good rat,' have to do with this?" the gentleman demanded to know.

"Tit for tat, Girardet. Despite all your schemes and stratagems, Cecile will have one husband and only one husband. Do you recall the name on the marriage certificate you claim to have in your possession?"

"Of course I do. The man wrote his name as Gathier."

James bestowed a smile of pure pleasure upon the prince. "Then let me tell you my full name. I am James Gathier Gray, thirteenth Earl of Graystone."

"Gathier?"

"Yes."

"You were the sailor?"

"I was the sailor you made sure Cecile was wedded to that night."

"But . . . how?"

"By the grace of God and the determination of a woman."

Rodolphe Girardet put his head back and bellowed with frustration and rage. "We will see who wins in the end, Graystone."

"This is the end, Girardet."

"I think not, my nemesis." And with that, Girardet made a lunge for Lady Pale, clutching her in front of him, using her as a human shield. "The earl is too much of a gentleman to shoot even the likes of you, my dear Moira, in order to get to me."

Then the prince slipped behind a fold of heavy

drapes, gave the countess a shove that sent her reeling, and seemed to vanish.

By the time James rushed across the library, Rodolphe Girardet had disappeared through a large open window.

It was at that exact moment that Goodenough and Lady Ann Faraday—with the butler, Rank, in tow—burst into the room.

"The prince will have a headstart on us, Lord Graystone, but I know where he is headed and I will lead you straight to him," Count Dupre was vowing less than ten minutes later. "We will require a carriage and several swift horses."

"I happen to have those directly outside, sir," Goodenough volunteered. "I know you ordered us to stay put, my lord, but there was so much coming and going from this house that Lady Ann and I decided we must disobey your instructions."

"It is of no consequence, Goodenough."

"I will drive the carriage, then, my lord."

James shook his head. "You must stay here with Lady Ann and guard the treasure of Saint-Simeon and the princess. Count Dupre and I will go after Girardet."

Cecile stepped up. "No."

Not again!

"I am coming with you, James. It will waste valuable time if we stand here and argue about it."

"We must hurry, then, Your Serene Highness," urged the Count. "The prince keeps a small yacht anchored on the River Thames. That will be where he is headed. It was to be his escape route if he should ever have to leave London in a hurry. I heard him speak of it several times."

"If no one minds," spoke up Moira, Lady Pale, "I will collect my things and be on my way."

No one seemed to mind.

The countess stopped at the door of the library and glanced back for a moment. "You can count on Rank. He is an excellent man, but like so many of us, he was being blackmailed by the prince through no fault of his own."

"Thank you, Lady Pale," the butler said with a respectful bow before she closed the door behind her.

"Goodenough, you're in charge until we return."

"Yes, my lord." Perfectly polished shoes clicked as John Goodenough snapped his heels together.

It was a night that she would never forget, Cecile of Saint-Simeon realized as she stood on the London docks wrapped in Lady Ann's cloak and gazed out over the River Thames at the scene unfolding before her horrified eyes.

They had reached the water's edge just as her uncle's yacht had been pulling away from its moorings. As she and James stood on shore, Count Edmond Dupre had raced—indeed, as if with the last of his breath, his strength, his determination, even his heart—and leapt onto the deck of the boat. Then he had turned and saluted her.

They would never know, Cecile supposed, if the two men saw the ship bearing down upon them in the dark—surely they had seen its warning lights—but it quickly and neatly cut the yacht in two.

"I don't believe he ever learned to swim," Cecile said sadly.

"Who can't swim?" James asked.

"The count. Nor my uncle, for that matter. Neither of them can swim." She added, "None of the Girardets can swim."

James said after some little time, "The river has claimed its own. It claimed Count Dupre and it claimed the prince. Perhaps there is justice, after all. Girardet has met the same fate that he decreed for his own brother."

Cecile sighed, and she felt the hatred and the revenge wash out to sea with the tide.

"Perhaps the count saw this as the gentleman's way out, a last chance to redeem himself."

"In my eyes?"

James shook his head. "Not even in his own eyes. But perhaps in God's."

" 'Vengeance is mine; I will repay, saith the lord,' " Cecile murmured into the night. "Romans 12:19."

"*Tat tuam asi*," James quoted. Then he translated for her. "What is is."

James was who he was.

She was who she was.

And what would be . . . would be.

Chapter Twenty-six

She had accomplished everything that she had come to London for nearly three months ago, Cecile realized as she unlocked the gate to the key garden and entered its sanctuary one last time.

She had recovered the coronation crown, the royal scepter, and the sacred chalice, and she would be returning home with the three imperial objects before Alexandre's investiture, thereby securing her beloved brother's rightful place upon the throne of Saint-Simeon, as well as the future of her country and its citizens.

She had sought the answers to her own questions. She now knew everything. Her mind was at peace.

Through the natural course of events and, perhaps, because of the infinite wisdom and mercy of God, justice had been meted out to its fullest measure.

She said a quick and silent prayer for the tortured soul of one Edmond Dupre. Some day, one day, Cecile told herself, she would also find it in her heart to pray for Rodolphe Girardet . . . but not quite yet.

That only left James.

What was she to do about James?

He was her husband, and yet he was not her husband. She was his wife, and yet not his wife. They were married, but by no choice or through no decision of their own at the time. Surely such a marriage could not be valid in the eyes of the law, or the church, or even God.

Yet, she was in love with James Gray, and she loved him. He was surely the best man she had ever known; in his heart, in his mind, in his soul. He was everything a woman could want in a man, in a mate, in a husband.

Cecile reached the ornamental fountain in the center of the key garden and leaned over to dip her fingers in the cool waters of the pool. Small fish—they were no more than tiny slivers of silver and gold and bronze—came darting to the surface to nibble on her fingertips.

She heard herself laughing softly, and she realized that some of the happiest moments of her life, the moments of unequaled joy, of greatest freedom, of truest serenity and contentment, of genuine passion and the desires of a woman's heart had taken place in this sanctuary, in this private garden with James.

This was the place she would carry in her heart always. It would give her joy when she needed joy. It would provide her with solace on those days when she sorrowed for what might have been and was not to be. It would give her memories to cherish when she was lonely, until many years hence, perhaps, when her heart would beat for the last time and she would think of James in that final moment.

* * *

James found her by a thicket of rosebushes that were in full bloom, their branches and stalks weighted down with pale pinks, bright and joyful reds, pure whites with a mere hint of blush along their fringe: colors that rivaled Cecile's perfect complexion on this perfect and sun-filled spring day in London.

"Oh, to be in England now that April's there!"

Browning had chosen his words wisely and well. And he, James Gray, had not missed April in England this year. He had made himself that promise in the dark, dank hold of a ship's dungeon, and he had kept that promise.

He had not missed April, nor the spring, nor life returning to every corner of this glorious garden, nor the greening trees, nor the roses in bloom, nor the azaleas or rhododendron.

Most of all, he had witnessed the miracle of hope restored and life being renewed, as his own life had been given new hope and renewal by this woman.

As he quietly moved along the garden path—Cecile must have heard him and yet she gave no sign of it—she bent over to inhale the roses and their sweet, unforgettable fragrance.

The words came from Graystone almost unconsciously:

"Go, lovely rose!
Tell her that wastes her time and me
That now she knows,
When I resemble her to thee,
How sweet and fair she seems to be."

Cecile lifted her head and glanced up at James. She straightened and said: "Oh, the pretty words and poetry do drip so easily from your tongue, sir."

Graystone frowned and begged to differ with the lady. "If they do, madam, then it is not unlike my ability upon the ballroom floor that first night we danced."

She frowned as if trying to remember.

He explained. "It was not my talent at waltzing; it was you."

"And the pretty words?"

"It is not my gift for quoting poetry; again it is you, Cecile. It is you, and only you. For, believe me, no other woman has ever had reason to think me talented in either dance or speech."

Waving his explanations aside, she observed, "The garden is in full bloom."

"It is, indeed."

"You promised to show me the roses when they were at their peak," she said.

"And here I am to keep my promise," he pointed out.

Cecile paused and looked up at him. "Is that why you have come? I thought it was, perhaps, to say good-bye."

"Good-bye?"

"I am leaving soon," she stated.

"Leaving?"

"I am returning to Saint-Simeon with the coronation crown, the scepter, and the chalice."

"Returning to Saint-Simeon?"

Cecile made an exasperated sound. "Why do you repeat every word I say?"

"Because . . ." His mind was blank.

"Because . . . ?"

"Because I didn't know. I didn't realize. I didn't think." James realized that he wasn't expressing himself at all well. He drew himself up to his full and considerable height in front of Cecile and declared, "You can't leave."

"Why not?"

"Because I said so."

"That is no reason," she said, laughing at him.

"You can't leave." Graystone stood his ground firmly. "You are my wife."

"Through no fault or desire of yours, sir, as we both well know. We were both the victims of my uncle's nefarious plot. He is now dead and his proof can die along with him. You are free."

Graystone's mind went blank again. It was several minutes and several paces further along the path before he caught up with the lady and said, "Free to do what?"

Her answer was blithe, even offhanded. "Free to be whatever it is you want to be. Free to go wherever you want to go. Free to do whatever it is you wish to do. Free to marry. Free to remain single. Free to simply be free, sir."

James realized that his heart was pounding so loudly—indeed, it was thunderous—in his chest that she must surely hear it as clearly and distinctly as he did. "Then you have set me free to go through the rest of my life as a lonely man."

Cecile stopped dead in her tracks.

"For I will be a man without the woman he loves at his side. I will be a man who never knows the joy of having children of his own or grandchildren. I will be a man condemned to a solitary existence. Is that the freedom you would wish for the man you love?"

"I am afraid," she admitted at last.

He had to know. "Afraid of what?"

Blue eyes, eyes the color of the sky on this cloudless day, stared into his. "My fear is that you somehow feel obliged to marry me because we . . ."

"Because we made love to each other?" he finished for her.

Cecile Girardet nodded her head. "I am a proud woman, James Gray. I would rather live the rest of my days alone than marry out of obligation and duty."

"That is not my fear," James quickly confessed to her. "I fear being alone."

"Alone?"

He immediately corrected himself. "No, it is not being alone that I fear. It is being without you. It is having you with me only in my dreams. I could not bear that anymore . . . to live only in my dreams because that is the only place you are with me, my love."

"Oh, James . . ."

"Don't you understand even yet, Cecile? In finding you, my love, I have found myself."

Tears appeared in her eyes.

"Marry me all over again. I promise I will give you freedom such as you have never imagined. I will give the moon and the stars and all that is in the firmament. I will give you your very own kingdom by the sea . . . for that is what Devon and my beloved Graystone Abbey will be: your kingdom, your home, your haven. It will be our world away from the world. It will be the world we create for ourselves."

"This is the way my dream was meant to end," Cecile confided to him. "I just did not know it until this moment." She went up on her tiptoes and pressed her mouth to his and whispered, "You are the man of my dreams come to life."

And James Gray realized that he had, indeed, at last awakened and remembered, and he did understand.

He whispered into the ear of the woman he loved above all others, even himself, "Come with me, my beloved Cecile, and 'grow old along with me. The best is yet to be.' "

Epilogue

Julian Franklin Guest, Earl of Stanhope, was sitting on the verandah of a Tuscan villa, a glass of slightly warm, heavily aromatic red wine at his elbow and the post, recently arrived from England, stacked on a three-tiered table beside him.

He put his head back for a moment and allowed the sunlight, filtering down between the branches of an olive tree, to bath his face. Then he inhaled the sweet, distinctive fragrance of the vining flowers cascading over a nearby garden wall: splashes of bright red and deep purple and dazzling pink against textured terracotta.

He raised his head from the back of the lounging chair—there was a small, embroidered pillow tucked behind his neck and several more at his feet—and, eyes squinted against the bright Italian sun, gazed off toward the horizon.

In the distance were the green hills of Tuscany, and somewhat nearer, avenues of tall, distinctive cypress trees, and just below the villa, in the valley, ripening vineyards.

Julian took a sip of his wine and leisurely, even lazily, gathered up the stack of mail. Amongst the usual assortment of business dispatches and personal correspondence was a letter from his younger sister, Elizabeth, Lady Wicke.

He picked up a fruit knife from a plate of lush, ripe peaches at his elbow, and slit open the envelope— a clipping fell onto his lap. He began to read his sister's letter.

He chuckled once or twice, as he always did when he read Elizabeth's letters, and found himself smiling at the antics of his nephew, Jack, age two.

It was, however, the last paragraph of the letter that was of particular interest to Julian:

> I would not put it past you, dear brother, known as you are for your stratagems and machinations, to have somehow arranged it all. Why else, pray tell, should the princess, your houseguest in London for the season, and Lord Graystone find themselves quite literally in one another's backyard?
>
> But as the bard, himself, William Shakespeare, penned long ago: "all's well that ends well," and it has all ended very well, indeed.
>
> Your loving sister,
> Elizabeth

Julian Franklin Guest picked up the newspaper article that had fluttered to his lap and perused the details. It was an announcement of royal affairs and doings in the *Times*, dated August 1879. Of particular interest was a notice at the end.

James Gray, thirteenth Earl of Graystone, and Cecile of Saint-Simeon, now Lady Graystone, renewed their wedding vows recently before the Archbishop and the assemblage in the Lady Chapel, Graystone Abbey, Devon.

In attendance for the occasion were Her Majesty, the Queen; Their Royal Highnesses, the Prince and Princess of Wales; Their Graces, the Duke and Duchess of Deakin; as well as the Marquess and Marchioness of Cork (niece to Lord Graystone), and the Duke's younger brother, Viscount Wicke and Lady Wicke.

Lord and Lady Graystone will now journey to the bride's former home for the official investiture of her brother, His Serene Highness, Alexandre, the next ruling prince of Saint-Simeon.

Author's Note

Historically Saint-Simeon is very loosely—and I emphasize *very loosely*—based on the principality of Monaco. For example, it was from the port of Monaco that Julius Caesar embarked when he sailed to Greece to fight Pompey. And it was Monaco that the Holy Roman Emperor, Otto I, conferred on a Genoese prince in the tenth century.

In all other ways, Saint-Simeon, the tiny and idyllic kingdom by the sea, is of my own creation.

I have never thought that being a princess is all it's cracked up to be. What most women respond to, I believe, is the idea of being treated like a princess. So it was perfectly understandable to me why Cecile of Saint-Simeon would have no trouble at all trading in her title and her crown for the man she loved, for the beautiful Devon countryside and for the magnificent country estate known as Graystone Abbey.

Furthermore, Percy Shelley may have been correct when he wrote nearly two centuries ago, "Hell is a city much like London," but modern London is one of my favorite places in the whole world.

Indeed, if there is heaven on earth, perhaps it is a particular little street not far from the Tate Gallery (I will not tell you where exactly, you must discover it for yourself), lined on both sides with shade trees and pristine white houses with their windowboxes overspilling with bright flowers. At the end of the street, discreetly tucked between a row of high hedges and nearly indiscernible, is a wrought-iron gate leading to a glorious garden.

And, yes, it requires a key to enter.